THE
COTTAGE
D.C. CUMMINGS

Published in 2021 by Provoco Publishing who own the publishing rights.

ISBN: 978-1-8383742-2-8

Cover Design and Artwork - © Provoco Publishing
Logo Design - © MJC at Provoco Publishing

Photographs reproduced under license by kind permission of Jane Murray

Edited by Hache. L. Jones

I would also like to thank several people, who taught me that talent, like true love, is something you must believe in.

Gary Charles
Graeme Parker
Carol Kettley

The following people, for being instrumental in my life, and for making my world a better place.

Florence May Hughes
Frances Richards
Neil Carson
Martyn Carson
Andrew Murray

'True love is like ghosts, which everyone talks about,
But which few have ever seen.'

Francois De La Rochefocauld

DEDICATION

For Sandra May Richards, my mum, with love.

PROLOGUE

He was growing restless, like a tempestuous breeze, gathering momentum, swirling around like a dervish. Dust bunnies scurried out of his way as he prowled the quiet, desolate cottage. He listened down the years and heard the laughter of yesterday ringing in his eager ears. Long forgotten feelings reached across the decades, love spanning time.

His heavy sigh sent the shadows spinning out of control amongst his loneliness and he swiped ineffectually at the cobwebs in the corners, disturbing the spiders who shared his home with him. He roamed through the cottage, an air of lonely petulance following him.

He needed her! Where was she? What was taking so long? He groaned, and pain filled the stone walls like lies fill a hungry heart, eager to believe what it is being fed.

VERONICA

ONE

Closing the door with a loud bang, he scurried out of the house onto the stone flagged pathway as fast as his slippery loafer shoes would allow. He leapt up the three crooked, stone steps to the roadway, trying to get away from the place as fast as he could. He never liked doing viewings on this spooky neglected old cottage, he was well aware of the myths and legends surrounding it. It had been on his estate agency's books for a couple of years now and even at a knockdown price, no offers had been forthcoming. Until today; and he'd had to physically push his fist in his mouth to prevent himself from shouting in triumph, when the woman, on her second viewing, told him she'd pay the asking price and move in as quickly as possible.

Now, he moved as quickly, eager to get away from the place. In his haste, he dropped the keys to his company car. He broke into a cold sweat as he fished them out of the gulley, so strong was his urge to flee this unpleasant little terrace. He struggled into his car, turned the keys in the ignition then heard the engine purr into life as he gave a sigh of relief and accelerated away at considerable speed.

Inside the cottage, all became quiet again as the car's engines faded into the distance. A sigh of relief flittered through the stone walls; cobwebs stirred and then settled down in quiet, dark corners again; timber beams creaked and settled into the still, dark quietness. They had gone, and he was alone again.

***

Weeks later, Vera Matthews sat in the waiting room of her solicitor's office, wondering for the umpteenth time why he was taking so long?

Gerry always made an appointment for a specific time, and then left her waiting in the reception area, drinking vile instant coffee, and smiling at an uneasy looking receptionist. Three quarters of an hour was a record even for Gerry, and she had a deadline to meet. She was just about to stand up and tell the receptionist that Gerry could go and bugger off, she would put off signing the contracts for the cottage she was buying until another day, when her old friend could be more punctual. As she was preparing to take her leave, the telephone on the receptionist's desk shrilled loudly enough to make both Vera and the receptionist jump. Heaving an audible 'thank heavens', the receptionist looked up and told Vera to go through, Mr Maitland would see her now.

Gerry's desk was littered with papers, deeds, plans and most importantly, the Contract for her cottage. She skimmed over the standard terms and conditions, happy that she was buying the Freehold with Full Title Guarantee as she scribbled her rather flamboyant signature across the bottom of the sheet of paper that, along with her two hundred thousand pounds, would transfer ownership of the cottage from the Estate of Henry Winterton (Deceased) to herself.

'Nearly signed as Honey L'Amore!' Vera grinned to Gerry, handing the papers back to him.

He looked startled. 'Good Lord! Can't have that Vee, old girl.' He checked that her signature did, in fact, say Veronica Matthews and satisfied that it did, he looked up and smiled at her.

'Well done! By the end of the week, '*Enchantment Cottage*' will be yours!'

Vera smiled. 'There's nothing very enchanting about it, Gerry, at the moment. It's a bit of a tip, rather old fashioned, dirty and a bit spooky looking, to be honest. The odious young estate agent called it *Creepy Cottage* several times!'

They shared a laugh at the estate agents' expense and then Gerry took Vera out to have a quick glass of champagne in the local trendy wine bar across the road, to celebrate her forthcoming house ownership. He grinned to himself as he noticed how out of place Vera looked, with her rather drab long brown skirt, and mustard yellow sweater both of which, he knew, hid a stunningly desirable and very sexy body. Her long, wavy blonde hair, so perfect for grabbing handfuls of whilst in the throes of passion, was plaited and coiled at the nape of her neck. She wore no makeup; her rounded metal framed spectacles hid her mesmerizing green eyes. No-one took any notice of her, when greeting Gerry, not even the two people he'd noticed reading Honey L'Amore erotic novels. Well, how would they know that this nondescript and unsuitably dressed woman he was sitting with was, in fact, the author of the words they were so avidly imbibing, and that given the right circumstances, Vera Matthews magically transformed into the sultry, and very sexy Honey L'Amore, bestselling erotic novelist.

Vera was tired of the wine bar, with its trendy décor and even trendier clientele. She had the beginnings of a new story taking shape in her head. She wanted to get back home to begin working on it. Draining her glass, she nodded to Gerry that she'd had enough, and left. She hailed a passing cab to take her home, a rented flat which smelt of curry from the Indian take away below it. How she longed for the peace and tranquility of a cottage in the country!

***

Trudy McAlister knew what she wanted. He was tall, over six foot, she surmised. He had dark hair, silver temples, and a smile which melted her heart like warm chocolate sauce drizzled over banoffee pie. Banoffee pie, however, with or without sauce didn't wet her knickers with desire, like the hunk she had spotted at the bar was doing right now! She'd just argued with her soon to be *ex*-boyfriend, given that she'd poured the contents of his pint of lager over his head and told him to sling his cheating arse! Which he promptly did. Trudy was still angry, but she knew that being angry made for some great sex, and the object of her desire would hopefully be a willing candidate. She confidently walked up to a vacant bar stool near her prey; gracefully seated herself in one fluid movement designed to reveal as much stocking topped thigh as possible and ordered a whisky. She smiled at the man and he nodded.

In that moment, they both knew they were going to end up in bed together. He knew he would soon be running his hand up her curvaceous body and have her long legs wrapped around him. Trudy knew that she would be ripping off his shirt, running her hands down his toned torso to the buckle of his belt, which she'd undo, unzip him, and release his hardening desire so that she could drop down on her knees and taste him for the first time.

He would grab her shiny brunette hair, the colour of conkers, and hold her head in place so that he could thrust his engorged cock into her willing, red-lipped mouth. He knew she would be good. He knew that she'd understand how to take the full length of him in her mouth, and suck hard, then release him, licking all the way up his shaft to the tip. He grew hard, just thinking about the things to come.

***

Vera gave a frustrated moan and shut her laptop with a thud. The trouble with writing bloody erotica was that she turned herself on in the process of turning her characters on. She could feel her breasts heaving, her own nipples hardening just like Trudy's were under Donovan's touch - that would be his name – Donovan! Almost reluctantly, Vera slipped a hand into her cotton panties and knew that she would feel a moist slick in between her legs. How long it had been since she had had sex? She sighed again, not willing to think of the answer. Instead, she brought herself to a swift, unsatisfactory orgasm with her fingers, then headed for the shower, thinking of Trudy and Donovan. How much more intense their orgasms would be, in her book.

Once in the shower, Vera in her mind's eye, mapped out a rough plot for Trudy and Donovan. Honey L'Amore's readers knew Trudy McAlister was a private dick – True Mac, as she was affectionately known. She was already onto Donovan, having been called in to investigate him by his Company, who suspected him of embezzlement and fraud. Vera hadn't yet decided how bad Donovan was going to be, but she knew in this novel, Trudy was going to have difficulty separating her work life from her love life. Rinsing soap out of her golden hair, Vera sighed again – she must stop sighing! – and wished she was as lucky in love as her heroine. She also wished that she was going out that evening because of a love interest, and not because she had a promotional appearance in one of the city's numerous Swingers Clubs. Tonight's booking meant that, once out of the shower, Vera had to begin the transformation into Honey L'Amore - famous risqué author and '*The Woman Every Man Wants to Fuck.*'

The transformation didn't take long. As her agent, Mortimer Blake kept telling her, when the raw material is *that* good, she didn't have much to do. She applied makeup, dried her hair, and slipped into a revealing designer outfit. Adding these little touches, like a great portrait artist, turned her into a walking work of art. Within half an hour, she was calling Mortimer to remind him to collect her.

'I'm in the car, on my way to you, Miss L'Amore,' he growled, lasciviously, down the telephone.

Vera hated drawing attention to herself, but when she was Honey, she got attention overload. Dressed tonight in a shimmery gold mini dress which just skimmed her bottom, high gold stiletto sandals, a black stole and black bag were slung over her fake tanned shoulder and her mane of golden hair tumbled down over the other. Her green eyes were emphasized by long fake eye-lashes; her cheeks glowed, the highlighter she used showing off her high cheekbones and perfect kitten like face. Hearing the car horn hoot impatiently, Vera sashayed to the door, curvaceous hips undulating tantalizingly; her bosom bouncing jauntily as she walked quickly across the street and eased herself into the waiting car.

Mortimer grinned like a Cheshire cat. God, he enjoyed these promotional evenings that he spent with the goddess like woman which Vera became. If only she was "Honey L'Amore" in real life, and not the dowdy Veronica Matthews. He could really go for her then, instead of using her as a convenience as and when the two of them needed each other.

'Stop staring at me like that, Mortimer, and let's get this thing over and done with!' Vera snapped, catching her companion's lecherous eyes skimming her ample breasts. God, how she longed for her cottage, she thought, as Mortimer's Bentley roared her into the city where she had no desire to be, pretending to be the person that everyone thought she was.

TWO

Harry stepped back from the row of newly built stone cottages, hands on hips, and gave a smirk of silent satisfaction. At last, the cottages were now ready to be occupied by the mill workers who would rent them off him and be closer to their work, on the other side of the river. This would improve productivity for him and the lives of the mill workers, some of whom had to travel miles to get to work and back, over fields and dirt tracks. They were often tired, and late when they arrived. Having them live opposite would be good for them, and for the estate.

He turned his back on the stone terraces, still doing quick calculations in his head as to how many families each cottage could house – they were two bedroomed, with two rooms downstairs and a basement. Three families could easily be accommodated, each family having a floor of their own, which meant homes for some twenty-seven of his workers. The tenth cottage, slightly bigger than the rest, he had decided would be his. An escape from the big house, from his family, from normality and from convention. Harry did not like convention, because it kept him from doing what he wanted to do, and Harry liked to do as he pleased. What pleased him right now was Isabella and now he had just the thing to please her, too.

***

Isabella was, at that precise moment, sitting in Winterton Hall, the 'Big House' as it was known locally, being the Winterton family's country seat. Isabella was taking tea with Harry's mother and sisters and she was bored. The daughter of a local landowner and wife to another, Isabella had little regard for talk of the group of businessmen, who had joined forces and finances with Harry and his father to buy several cotton and textile mills in the area. The conversation being bandied back and forth did little to interest her despite her father's wealth coming from it. She cared not about the great switch from the agricultural occupations of their various males, who were investing heavily in the new *'Industrial Revolution'* by buying or building mills on land once used for arable farming and grazing land.

'Of course, we were convinced to do this because of Henry,' Lady Winterton, Harry's mother, was saying now. She was a stiff, staunchly conservative woman who neither approved nor disapproved of her eldest son, but generally agreed with him where business was concerned. Both she and Henry – she did not call him by the nickname he had adopted – had excellent commercial brains and used them well.

At Harry's name, Isabella perked up and felt a strange frisson in her belly and down below, between her legs, which made her cheeks redden in shame. Married at eighteen, Isabella had gone to the marital bed a naive virgin and because her husband, Thomas, preferred the attention of various mistresses who knew what they were doing, unions between herself and her husband were, thankfully, rare, and rarely satisfying for Isabella. However, Harry in the same room as Isabella could produce feelings within Isabella's anatomy that being in the marital bed with her husband could not. She blushed again at the thought of sharing a bed with Harry Winterton and turned her mind back to the conversation to stop herself thinking of it.

Harry's mother did little to stop Isabella's train of thought, however, as she continued to extol the virtues of Harry's recent foray into mill ownership. Apparently, Harry had persuaded his father, Lord Winterton and two of his business associates, to buy the mill that sat neatly on the bank of the River Irving, which ran conveniently through their little village. Thus, the river would be a convenient source of waterpower for the production of textiles and cotton, using the latest technology. The days of the grand families' incomes coming solely from agriculture were disappearing!

At the thought of being in Harry Winterton's bed, Isabella stood up with a rustle of her peacock blue overskirts and excused herself, saying that she felt rather hot, and would take a stroll around the grounds to cool down. In actual fact, the feeling between Isabella's legs was becoming rather uncomfortable and she was feeling sensations down there that were becoming rather difficult to disguise.

She swept out of the drawing room, not giving Lady Winterton the chance to object, or to call for a maid to accompany her, which was a good thing, given that the first person she ran into as she rounded the corner towards the riverbank and the open countryside, bordered by a gravel pathway suitable for walking, was Harry Winterton, the cause of her very pleasant discomfort.

Harry, having divested himself of his horse, had been striding unseeingly deep in thought since his visit to the cottages across the bridge and almost cannoned into Isabella, turning the blind corner, and heading in the opposite direction. Reaching out a hand to hold Isabella upright, he smiled at her discomfort and something else was in those beautiful, dark blue eyes. Harry recognized sheer unadulterated longing when he saw it, and he gripped her elbow tightly as if in answer of her unspoken lust for him. He smiled again as she tried desperately to regain control of herself. She was a picture; her breasts, pert and satisfyingly large, heaved in the tightness of her frilled chemise, her cheeks displayed a rosy glow and her eyes – well, those eyes – they belied the innocence of her expression.

'My apologies, Lady Harmer. I trust that you are not injured in any way?' Harry's words were solicitous, his look over her body back up towards her pretty face and not quite so innocent eyes, was not.

Isabella managed to return Harry's gaze with a steady one of her own.

'I am quite alright, Lord Winterton, although it is no thanks to you, given that you nearly knocked me off my feet when you came around the corner so quickly. I feel quite faint.' Isabella said as she lifted a hand to her brow, feigning dizziness. She knew she made a pretty picture, and that Harry liked pretty things.

'I should escort you back indoors, Lady Harmer, and have you attended to!' Harry's lips twitched into a smile; he knew well enough that Isabella had no intention of going back inside.

She shook her head, and her curls flew flatteringly around her heart shaped face. With that beautiful fox coloured hair, she looked a little like a vixen, thought Harry, feeling the stirring in his loins becoming uncomfortable.

'I am quite alright,' she repeated again, 'although perhaps some company would be nice?'

Harry bowed his head and offered her the crook of his arm, which she took happily, her heart beating more quickly, and that feeling between her legs producing a wetness she'd never experienced before. It both puzzled her and excited her at the same time.

They walked together in silence for a while, entering a secluded courtyard at the back of the house, which bordered rough woodland. Stone seats provided the perfect excuse for Isabella to feel faint again, and for Harry to have to sit down beside her until she felt well enough to continue their stroll.

'Should I call for someone?' Harry suggested. 'You look rather flushed.'

He lifted his hand to her brow, which did feel warm; he trailed the hand down her soft cheek, her chin, her neck, till the hand was resting on her chemise, and her heaving breasts.

Isabella gazed at him, with desire apparent all over her face. She made no move to remove Harry's hand, now cupping her right breast lightly. He'd moved closer to her.

'This is inappropriate,' he whispered, his other hand taking hold of hers, as his warm lips touched hers in a light, gossamer kiss.

'Very much so, Lord Winterton. If only it were not so public. Despite us being within a courtyard, I fear someone may see, or appear through the doorway at any moment and catch us *in flagrante!*'

Harry smiled again, thinking of his cottage and of having Isabella truly *in flagrante* within its walls.

'I should not have kissed you. It was very inappropriate of me. Let me escort you back to your companions. I fear if we stay here, I would be even more inappropriate, Lady Harmer.'

'As you wish.' Isabella replied, feeling the wetness trickle slowly down her inner thighs, knowing full well what they both wished would soon be granted.

THREE

She was here, at last! He stared excitedly out of the window and watched intently as the removal men carried in furniture and crates. There was an air of anticipation about the place; he hadn't felt that for so long. He hung about in the shadows, not wishing to hinder the general hubbub around him. He wished he could help, but he wouldn't know where everything was to go. Instead, he contented himself with imagining a future that included being loved again, after his heart had been locked away within these stone walls for so many years.

Throughout the day, he only caught intermittent glances of her; she kept coming in, racing around the cottage, disturbing spiders who scurried away worriedly; she created a whirlwind of wonderous activity; a vortex of anticipation that sucked him in and held him enthralled. He drifted silently amongst the crates, the packing cases, the general hubris of inhabitation. Occasionally, his wanderings would create their own little dust storm, like a whisper; but in general, he remained unseen. Watching, waiting.

***

By eight o'clock that sweet, September evening, Vera was exhausted with the sheer effort of the move and all that it had entailed; but she was pleased that the effort had brought about relative order into the two rooms she'd prioritised – the office and the bedroom.

She wandered through to the office. It wasn't really a room, as such, more a passageway with a staircase up to the bedrooms and bathroom, and a perilously steep staircase down to the basement kitchen. It was, however, just large enough for her bureau, where she did most of her writing; and a small cream sofa where she planned to sit, overlooking the river at the rear of the house, listening to the rush of the water and reading when she had the time. She smiled to herself as she contemplated lazy Sunday mornings, accompanied by nothing more than a bacon and egg sandwich, a pot of good coffee and any other novel in the world besides one written by bloody Honey L'Amore! A vague breeze touched her bare upper arms and she shivered, she looked around, wondering if she'd left the front door open.

Walking back into the living room, to check, she opened the door anyway, and climbed up the three uneven and worn stone steps – worn with the footsteps of time, she thought. Standing on the top step, she surveyed her new surroundings with some satisfaction. The cottage was not overlooked, straight ahead of it was the fork in the road which led up a steep hill to some of the oldest cottages on this side of the river, which ran directly behind the cottage. She could see what must have been a farmhouse at one time, standing on the crest of the hill surrounded by trees. The road forked to the left, out of sight, so she shifted her gaze to her left – another hill. This, her removal men had discovered, was a dead end which led to a wooden kissing gate that gave access to the only main road into the village. She would walk up there to the top one day and check out the view of the surrounding countryside. Treetops rose graciously above rolling hills, leading you from Lancashire into Yorkshire. How troubled this area must have been during the Wars of the Roses, she imagined, with hostilities rising and neighbour set against neighbour. Sweeping her eyes down the hill, to the right, there were two rows of higgledy piggledy terraced cottages, their fascia's old, time scarred with twists and turns and gnarled old stones out of place. Beyond the cottages, there was a dead end; to the right, the road continued to the bridge which had once been swept away during winter floods after the river had burst its banks. To the left, the road became cobbles again and there was a single-track lane leading to the railway station where the steam trains called periodically. She smiled at the oldness and the peacefulness of it all and knew she would be happy here.

Still smiling as she returned indoors, she admired the solid stone wall and fireplace with its thick oak beam mantle, the inglenook – not quite big enough to sit in, but perhaps a fire basket, and some candles could. She looked at the low beams on the ceiling – a close inspection had revealed that they were not original, but they did create an air of old-fashioned charm. Shivering again as another breeze brushed against her, creating goosebumps on bare flesh, she rummaged in a small box labelled 'bathroom' and found what she wanted. Sponge, soap, bubble bath and loofah. Time to check out the antiquated plumbing system and have a bath.

The bathroom was draughty, she thought, glancing up at the window again as that breath of cold air caressed her. She frowned, and decided to invest in a new, double panel radiator for this room.

A reluctant groan emanated from the brass taps as she turned them on fully, and watched the water almost begrudgingly flow from their lips. Swirling in some bubble bath, and then throwing a towel over the radiator, she started to undress. Leggings peeled off her long, shapely legs, panties pulled down revealing her shaven pussy and a slightly protruding tummy which she kept meaning to do something about; top pulled off and flung on top of the small pile of clothes on the bathroom floor. She unclipped her bra, releasing gorgeous, full breasts with large pale brown nipples which hardened in the slightly chill air, despite the steamy heat which was rising from the bath. Again, she felt that breeze wrapping itself around her naked body like a vine.

Hastily, she jumped into the inviting hot water, and slipped her tired and aching body under the froth of bubbles, tipping her head back on the roll neck of the bath. A hand gently caressed her cheek. A cold hand. She sat bolt upright, startled; the hairs on her neck standing on end – hackles risen, like a dog on alert. She peered around into the now steamy atmosphere. What the hell was she looking for? She was here alone, and she knew it! Get a grip, Vera, she told herself, letting out an audible sigh of relief as she slipped back under the foam again.

The easing enfolding of the water against tired limbs lulled her into a half awake, half asleep state. She might have dozed, she wasn't sure. She sighed again, giving herself up to the gentle, yet insistent stroking of her clitoris. Tiny bolts of pleasure shot through her tired body, as the heat gathered in between her legs. The stroking became harder, much more direct and she could feel her clitoris bud harden beneath the firmness of the movement of the fingers. Cold fingers, on her very hot sex. She groaned this time, as her legs spread a little further apart. The fingers moved slightly, circular motions, opening the lips of her pussy. They probed and eased themselves inside her. She gasped, pushed towards the sensation and undulated her hips slightly in perfect synchronicity with the pushing and probing and parting. The fingers worked slowly, making her swell, making her pussy contract against the movements. He felt her excitement and he knew he matched it with his own as he felt long forgotten tremors of desire lick through his body as he pushed two, then three fingers inside her hot, slick wetness. He could feel her gathering; riding his movements – he wished it was his cock inside her, but a roll top bath was not big enough for the two of them, and he was too far gone in his ardour to want to stop to undress. His fingers drilled into her relentlessly as she rose; climbed higher. She gasped again, her pussy gripping the demanding fingers, her body beginning to shake with the excitement of orgasm. Oh, God!

With a terrified and confused start, she sat up in the bath gasping, and trembling. She looked around the bathroom, peering through the steam; breasts heaving, breath coming in short gasps. She couldn't focus until her orgasm has subsided fully. She collapsed against the side of the bath; the side panel was cold against her hard nipples. A frenzy of sexual bliss, excitement, retreat and terror overtook her, and she raised her eyes, watchful, expectant; looking for the owner of the cold hand, with the fingers that made her feel fiery.

Everywhere was still. The cottage seemed to sigh with peace and satisfaction. The room was empty, as her rational thought process told her it should be. All she could see was hazy shapes of steam, evaporating in the cooling heat of the bathroom. All she could hear was the occasional drip, drip from the cold tap, which needed a washer, and the relentless sound of the flow of the river at the back of the cottage. There was no-one else there. Only her. Or was there?

She had felt it, it was real. She was sure it was. The touch of the hand against her cheek. Then, the caressing of her now throbbing clitoris, the fingers insistent and knowledgeable; the parting of her pussy, the pushing, the penetrating. She had felt it.

The bathwater sluiced reluctantly away from her warm body as she rose from the bath, stepping out onto an old threadbare bathmat, left behind from the previous occupants. She grabbed her fluffy, cream bath sheet and wrapped its warmth around her, padding into the front bedroom to find pyjamas.

Her bedroom was her haven. He followed her in and was surprised at how orderly the room was, given the chaos of the kitchen, the living room and the spare bedroom – all littered with crates, cases, books, crumpled packing paper and discarded newspaper which had held precious ornaments and mementos during the move. He rustled some paper now, and she looked around sharply as the pages of a newspaper fluttered to the floor. He moved away, caught her frown as she saw the movement and he stole to the dark corner, by the door.

Vera, drying herself off now, looked around and was satisfied with the womanly decadence and order. Here were expensive damask silk coverlets, Egyptian cotton sheets, small hillocks and valleys of soft, plump pillows and cushions. At the foot of the brass bedstead was an ottoman, piled high with colourful towels; the bedside tables housed lamps which threw soft, pinky gold hues across the room; the wardrobes had been built and were now full of Vera's clothes; the marble topped washstand held antique bottles; perfume, jewelry boxes and trinkets; make up bags and toiletries. Vera liked her bedroom and her office orderly. She needed the bedroom to calm her after a day in her office, writing. There was no television or radio in the bedroom, just the blissful silence of the night.

Dressed in fluffy, check pyjamas, Vera trudged wearily back downstairs to the basement kitchen, for a much needed mug of tea. Leaving the teabag inside because she had no idea where any spoons were, she returned to the peaceful bliss of her bedroom. She opened the window revelling in the silence. No car engines, no rowdy takeaway customers shouting the odds. Having left the noisy, intrusive city behind, the quiet calm of a country night was her reward. Somewhere in the distance, an owl hooted.

Tired now, she looked around the orderliness of the room – that far corner could do with a lamp, she thought, noting how full of shadows it was – it needed brightening up. But not right now, she thought, as she switched off the bedside lamp and gave herself up to the darkness and sleep.

***

It was warm in bed. He'd not been so warm for so long. The coverlet was light yet rewardingly comforting against his cold, stiff frame. He lay down, stretched out and let out a sigh of contentment, which floated around the sleeping form next to him like a breath of cold, night air from the open window.

Vera shivered beneath the duvet and pulled it further over her. She coughed, and then resettled into sleep. He couldn't stand it any longer. He had to touch her. He reached out a tentative hand, and when it didn't waken her, he allowed it to rest on the delicious curve of her breast, which he could see, having escaped the pyjama top she'd insisted on wearing. He was thankful that she had discarded the bottoms before she had climbed, scented and weary, into bed.

He turned to her now, a small rush in the bedcovers as his body laid down on top of hers. She sighed and groaned an almost inaudible sigh of pleasure as his weight settled about her, spreading her legs wider to allow him access to her most secret places. His long fingers sought and found eager nipples, hardening under his touch as he caressed the pale brown areolas; not touching the nipple bud itself, but delighting in watching it contract and harden with the suggestion his fingers made. He kissed each hardened bud, before making his way down her stomach.

His kisses traced a frost patterned pathway to her mound of Venus, where he would travel down the other edge to reach the folds of her womanhood. At last. At last, his mouth could taste her. She arched her back, and sighed sleepily, legs opening slightly wider, invitingly. His lips kissed her pussy, and he felt warm wetness spill forth as his tongue delicately traced the contours of her labia. Moving upwards in small, unhurried movements, he lapped slowly at the tip of her clitoris, standing to attention now, unfolding like a flower greets the sunshine that makes it grow. He swirled his tongue in sweeping circular motions around the hard, hot hub of her and he felt her undulate beneath his eager mouth. Pushing her sex towards him, he obliged and gathered her bud in his mouth and sucked slowly, gently, feeling her swell, feeling her need grow.

She was neither asleep nor awake now. All she was conscious of were the delicious sensations she could feel between her spread legs. Her hands grasped the head between her legs, pushed the face down, burrowed him into her so that he could take more of her into his mouth and lap her to abandoned pleasure. She arched her back wantonly, and he moved upwards again, mounting her as her legs wrapped around his torso. He traced her wet clitoris with the tip of his cock, then pulled the engorged, thick shaft downwards towards her open pussy.

She gasped as he entered her slowly, oh, maddeningly slowly – she wanted him to force her apart, to rip her apart with his eager thrusts, but he held her captive that while longer. Slowly, he inched his way inside her. She was tight and hot and wet, her arousal growing now. He felt her push a hand between them, as her eager, desperate fingers sought to rub her hard clit while he thrust. In. Out. In. Out. Her legs tightened around him, her fingers pleasured herself and his release came in a blinding whiteness of desire as he thrust hard and deep inside her. Her head back, her back bent over in abandoned delight, he drove himself into her as hard as he could, gathering his pleasure in her moans of delight. She rose to meet him, and their release was simultaneous and glorious. It had been so long. The wetness she felt on her cheeks were his tears.

FOUR

Isabella shifted, raised a sleepy hand to her face and brushed away stray lock of dark hair which had escaped from her nighttime ringlets. The cottage was quiet, only a distant cockerel could be heard; otherwise, the tiny stone house sat in utter silence and Isabella knew Harry had gone.

Unused to fending for herself, she sat up and rested the weight of her naked body onto her elbow, and then slowly, very slowly, the memories of the previous night returned to her – their meeting in the courtyard seemed so long ago now; now that she knew him. Now that she was here, she was able to enjoy the delicious sensations which Harry drew out from her body until she was a delicious, quivering mess beneath him, and he took her again and again.

She smiled, letting the delicious feeling of Harry kissing her, Harry undressing her, Harry pushing her back onto the tiny bed, in the tiny stone cottage he was so delighted with, and he delighted her with his tongue in places that she had never thought would be touched by another's hand, let alone a tongue. Her smile grew larger as she recalled the feeling of his lips kissing the tiny bud above her pussy, a bud which unfolded with every kiss, every touch of his mouth until he had taken it all and had sucked on it, causing her to arch her back and gasp out loud as she grabbed his hair – unable to contain the feeling of rising and falling, wanting him to carry on, wanting him to stop. Never before had she been made to feel like this, and she found herself responding in ways she'd never have imagined before – touching him *there*! Feeling the hardness of his shaft as he pushed open her sex and thrust again and again into the warm wetness of her.

She found she was touching herself – seeking out that tiny bud, which was growing hard beneath her fingers. Isabella delighted in the sensations she could produce within her own being. She had never known that this was even possible. Beneath the thin, rough blanket, she spread her legs and allowed the pleasure to build, her fingers seeking and exploring as her clitoris grew wet and hard, and her pussy contracted as she finally, almost gratefully, sank two of her fingers inside her own self.

Gasping aloud, she lay with her fingers still inside herself, until her breathing became normal again, and the sensation of unadulterated joy and pleasure left her.

Embarrassed now, she drew the blanket around her, as her juices flowed between her thighs and her shame overcame her.

***

Vera awoke to the sound of a distant cockerel, crowing; and then silence. Perfect, wonderful, uncluttered silence, the antidote to what she knew had been a restless first night in her new home. She raised herself upright in bed and glanced at the crumpled, damp bedclothes. Smiling, she thought the messy bed reminded her of nights of passion, long ago. Then the smile faded on her lips, as she became aware of a soreness, an aching between her legs, and the smell. It was the smell of sex. In her bedroom. Where only she was. Or was she? Alone? Some instinct made her glance over to the far corner of the room, near the door – the one that she was definitely going to buy a lamp for today, as she noted the restless shadows, shapeshifting silently.

Reaching for the bedside lamp, she switched it on to relieve herself of sitting alone in the inky, early morning light. The warm glow relaxed her, and she sighed with relief, then shook her head at her stupidity.

'You've had a bloody sexy dream, Vera, you silly cow!'

Laughing as she said this aloud to herself, she flung her legs over the side of the bed. Her breath caught, her words died on her tongue as she sat on the edge of the bed and stared at the dried semen on her thighs.

No! NO! NO! Her brain screamed. This wasn't right. This wasn't real. It couldn't be real. She was alone. She touched her thighs, she slipped her hand in between her legs, fingered her pussy, raised her hand to her nose and smelt sex again.

A breeze, a fluttering of cold air scurried across the room, across the bed and momentarily she could have sworn she felt an arm rest gently around her shoulders. She fidgeted. The feeling disappeared, but her mind raced. What the hell had happened last night? Had she been raped? A hot panic seared through her body – was he still here, her rapist? Her ears strained to hear for an intruder, but only the silence met her senses.

She was still tense when she pulled on her discarded pyjama bottoms and wrapped a dressing gown around her tight body. She crept slowly and as silently as she could down the stairs, afraid, alert, but there was no-one there. Satisfied, she shrugged. Perhaps she was over-wrought with the move.

Standing in her office, she could hear the ever-present rush of the river below, as it flowed relentlessly past the cottage on its way to the countryside beyond. There was no other sound. She stared at the brooding darkness of the kitchen stairwell and decided to check the living room, just to err on the side of caution.

All was still, except for the fretful shadows, which jumped around the edge of her vision, casting odd shapes across the walls. Her eyes swept around, took in the boxes, the furniture dumped in the middle of the wooden floor, the bare oak mantle awaiting decoration. The solidity of the stone wall gave her comfort, somehow. It was a fortress, a castle. Her haven. Impenetrable. She shook her head and gave a low laugh into the quiet darkness, mocking herself for her stupidity. There was no intruder, no rapist. She was a bloody writer with an overactive imagination, for Gods' sake!

Smiling to herself in the dark, and no longer afraid, she went purposefully down to the kitchen, snapping on the electric light at the foot of the stairs - she'd get an electrician in later and have a second switch installed at the top of the stairs, so she wasn't walking down the fairly steep wooden staircase in the dark. She pottered around, picking her way through the debris of her move, hunted down teaspoons, and made herself a large mug of tea which she took back upstairs to her office.

With the river hurrying by below, she watched the milky dawn light push its way across the dark velvet sky and felt calm and peaceful enough to write.

***

He was awake; awake in a delicious aftermath of love, of physical contact which had felt so real, so comforting, damnit – so arousing. He was sure that somehow, he could still smell the scented body lotion she had generously rubbed into her skin last night, after her bath. His senses, dulled of purpose for so long, were now flooded with desire and longing for her.

Moving silently, unseen, through the cottage, not wishing to disturb her in her fevered writing, he drifted amongst the packing cases, occasionally dislodging a paper, some shiny wrapping material. He wandered through the boxes, fingering her belongings, familiarizing himself with everything that she owned, trying to get to know her through the touch of an ornament, the memorizing of the words of a poem, intricately carved into a piece of wood. He cast eager eyes over papers bearing her name, books, cushions, vases – all the things that she liked, that she was going to use to make this stone shell into a home.

***

Home! At last. Vera threw her case down and abandoned it in the lobby. Walking through into the living room, she sank gratefully onto the chesterfield sofa, laid her head back on the buttoned leather and sighed in relief. Home. It was wonderful to be home again, in her peaceful little cottage with the river rushing by. She could hear that river now, its constant babble as it scurried by the cottage was the loveliest sound she had heard after the past week of book promotion with its interviews, radio talk shows, bookshops, cities, airports, flights, buses, cars, hotels. The peace and the river were what she craved.

Her eyes stole around the living room, looking for dark shadows. The little room was cosy, and bright. Well, as bright as it could be from its lower than the ground position, and the small picture window at the front which didn't catch much light on a grey, murky skied afternoon. But the lamps were lit, the automatic timer had seen to that – and the heating on; the whole room seemed to sigh a welcome to her as she reclined there, exhausted, and happy.

The book launch was going well for Honey L'Amore. Another best seller. More nice royalties to help her to keep the home fire burning. She'd light the fire later, she thought, casting her eyes out of the window at the gathering dusk. Mushroom clouds of grey cotton candy gathered, laying low in the gathering darkness of a winter evening sky. She'd heard the mention of snow, and whilst she still held a former city dwellers romanticist view of a stone cottage in a tiny village nestling in the snow covered hillside, she was fully aware she didn't own a car, and that the village often got cut off in very bad weather. The nearest shop was a couple of miles arduous walk, which she didn't relish in icy and snowy conditions. She'd better not sit here much longer.

She heaved herself up off the sofa, lumbered upstairs with her case and a determination to have a long hot soak in the roll top bath. After which, she would put on her thickest, warmest pyjamas and socks, and go downstairs to light the wood-burner. All that done, she would arm herself with a whisky and a laptop and get herself onto the internet to do some "serious stocking up of the food cupboard" shopping.

The bath was full, hot, and steamy, and restored her equilibrium. Feeling content and happy, she leapt downstairs two at a time, through the door from the office and into the living room again. It was warm and glowing. She stood shock still, the hairs on the back of her neck rising; her blood rushing cold through her body. Fear was always cold, she thought, randomly. No-one ever had a hot flush when they were terrified.

The fire.

The fire was lit.

The little wood-burner was alive with leaping orange flames, dancing brightly, dispensing warmth and light around the homely, warm room. The cushions on the chesterfield were plumped again, orderly, and neat at either end of the sofa, where just over an hour ago they had been cast aside in messy disarray as she'd heaved herself up to have her bath. Her watchful eyes skimmed the room, and her heart began to beat faster. Her breath caught in her throat as she waited expectantly for something, she knew not what. Glancing at the small oval occasional table, next to the stone fireplace, she noticed that there was a glass of sherry poured out. She had not done that. She knew she had not done that. The fire, maybe. She was tired, she might have laid and lit the fire on automatic pilot. The cushions, yeah. Maybe she had just straightened them absentmindedly before heading up the stairs.

She knew she had not poured a glass of sherry.

She walked over to the table, picked up the glass. The light blonde aroma from the fine *Fino* sherry that she so loved, smelt crisp and tangy. She took a sip, eyes keeping watch on the room for any movement, any giveaway that she was not alone. She put the glass back down on the coffee table and went to sit on the sofa. A soft cool touch suddenly on her neck made her leap across the sofa and flinch in a small terror.

Suddenly, a cascade of odd things which had happened in the cottage tumbled into Vera's mind – papers being moved on her first day; the feelings she got that someone was sitting beside her, touching her. Oh, God! The orgasm! That first night in bed, when she had been taken to the sheer heights and delights of sexual pleasure, which she had put down to an erotic dream. The bath, the touches, the quivering; waking up in the night and feeling a cold breath, a whisper, a gossamer touch beside her. What was happening?

She looked at the sherry again.

Was the cottage haunted?

A gasp seemed to fill the air. A rush of cold made her shiver, and the fire leap. A draught unfolded in the room, like dripping ice.

She stood up, shaking.

'Who's there?'

Her own voice echoed around her as she called into the nothingness around her. She raised her voice again.

'Who's there and what do you want, frightening me like this?'

The room was still. The coldness evaporated. The fire danced and gradually the room relaxed.

Vera dropped her stiff shoulders and collapsed onto the sofa. Obviously, she was overdoing things. Maybe this book tour had been a little too long, a little too much. Perhaps she needed a rest from writing, from overtaxing her brain. She passed a hand over her forehead and sighed. Her calmness returned, she lay down on the sofa, burying herself into the small mountain of cushions.

A long while later, he gently draped the check fleece blanket, which she used as a throw, over her sleeping form before he disappeared into the darkness of wherever.

***

Her neck was stiff, and the fire was out when she awoke in the early hours of the next morning. A pale, sultry winter light was filtering through the curtains. She couldn't recall closing the curtains last night, or was this just another stupid, creepy thing that kept happening in the cottage. Moving painfully into a sitting position, she groaned and absentmindedly grabbed the wine glass, taking a slug of sherry, left over from last night.

'Fuck!'

She grimaced. Sherry definitely wasn't a nice taste before five o'clock in the morning. Pushing the blanket aside and shrugging because she couldn't actually remember putting the blanket over herself, she headed for the shower, and to clear her head enough to be able to start the day and write.

*****

At the other end of the day, when it was once again growing dark, she raised her eyes from her laptop, stretching her hands above her head to unknot her back after being crouched over the computer for several hours. Smiling with satisfaction at her progress, she was content with her writing for that day. The new novel was going well, the change of scenery and living in the cottage certainly had her creativity flowing.

Looking around, she decided that there was no coldness, no spooky atmosphere for her to fear. She relaxed visibly, shut down the laptop and went about her business happily.

FIVE

Weeks passed – happy weeks – she attended events, book launches, literary lunches. She had a survey carried out on the bathroom and agreed with a local builder to have it refitted, changing the layout slightly and borrowing some space from the landing so that a corner shower unit could be installed. The roll top bath with the ball and claw feet she kept, liking it for it being sympathetic to the age of the cottage, although the antiquated taps, wash basin and water closet were replaced with some very pricey but very modern and worth the money, *Armitage Shanks*.

She changed the lighting in the cottage too – added more ceiling lights, bought more floor and table lamps, invested in daylight mimicking bulbs with a higher CRI which, she was told, should help alleviate the dark spots and the ghostly effects she saw in some of the cottage's nooks and crannies.

With the major renovations done to the bathroom, and the additions of lighting, and fresh décor in the office and the lounge, Vera was satisfied that the cottage felt less, what? Sinister? Too harsh a word for it. Creepy. Maybe the brash, young estate agent had been right – it had been a creepy cottage, but it wasn't any longer, she thought with satisfaction. She had been writing well, and she looked forward to arriving home from one of the many events a book launch demanded of her. There were no shadows. No echoes. No breezes or cold spots. Vera was happier than she'd felt for a long time on the run up to Christmas.

She had always loved the festive season. Her thoughts often strayed at this time of year to her childhood; to memories of her father, a soldier, returning home on Christmas Eve. She saw herself being swept up into his arms as her mother watched and laughed as he kissed both of 'his girls'. She remembered the plastic Christmas tree which stood in a tardy pot on the hall table; the paper lanterns and gaily coloured paper chains cascading above them. For a moment, she could hear the sound of carol singers in the distance and smell the delicious aromas of spiced mincemeat bubbling in pastry cases; the turkey cooling on top of the cooker, wrapped lightly in foil to prevent the administrations of a curious cat; the pot-pourri of cinnamon, cloves, and ginger on the top of the bookcase.

Vera's first Christmas in the cottage was spent with Mortimer, whom she'd invited because the two of them otherwise would have spent Christmas alone. He'd bought gifts, festive foods, good wines, excellent sherries. Arriving two days before the festive break, he bustled into the cottage with his arms laden; gaily wrapped parcels containing perfume, jumpers, lingerie, books ('bit of a busman's holiday, Vee, but I know you will forgive me'). Christmas Eve was spent listening to carols on *Radio 4,* then trampling out into the crisp, winter night to attend midnight mass at the small church which stood at the top of a steep and aptly named Cliff Road.

Christmas Day was a lazy indulgent affair, with dinner, not lunch and Vera cooked goose, crispy roast potatoes, carrots and parsnips glazed in a smoky honey sauce, fat chipolata sausages wrapped in bacon. They ate in the kitchen, at Vera's ridiculously small, square scrubbed oak table and pulled large, extravagant Christmas crackers before beginning the meal. They placed gaudily awful paper hats on their heads and after clearing their plates, swearing that they couldn't eat another thing, there was a small, heavily brandy laden Christmas pudding, lit by Mortimer; the sixpence or rather, the five pence piece found by Vera who'd very unflatteringly nearly choked on it. They'd laughed together over the port and the cheese board which Mortimer had bought earlier that week in *Selfridges* food hall. Then they kissed over *Godiva* chocolates while they watched *'It's A Wonderful Life'* late on Christmas night before going to bed and indulging in some wonderful, no strings attached sex – which was how they both liked it.

The huge crash that echoed through the cottage just as

Mortimer had thrust his large and still erect cock into Vera for the third or fourth session that Christmas night, made Vera shriek, and throw Mortimer off her as she sat bolt upright in terror. Mortimer, rolling to the other edge of the bed, cursed under his breath, grabbed his boxer shorts, easing his large and aching member into them before rushing down the stairs to see what had happened. Vera followed more slowly, afraid. It was alright for Mortimer. He would go home and unexplained crashes and things that go bump in the night wouldn't affect him after tomorrow.

She peered from her vantage point halfway down the staircase and Mortimer appeared out of the living room doorway shrugging his shoulders.

'Nothing.' He told her, stepping up the stairs until they were level. 'It must have been a noise outside.'

'Did you check the kitchen?' Vera asked, as they headed back into the bedroom. Mortimer, deciding that there was to be no return to their previous amorous state, poured two whiskies from the bottle they had brought to bed with them earlier. He handed Vera a crystal glass containing a generous finger or two of *Lahaphroig*.

'Of course, I did! It was the first place I looked, to be honest. I thought some of the dishes might have fallen off the draining board, but no, everything is intact.'

'Except my nerves.' Vera grumbled, taking a large slug of whisky before replacing the glass on the bedside table, and snuggling against Mortimer, who took her in his arms and let her fall asleep rather awkwardly on his shoulder.

***

Harry was busy. And while Harry was busy, Isabella was growing bored. Having made scrupulous arrangements and excuses to cover her tracks, she had not expected to find herself alone quite so often. Thomas, distracted as always by his varying mistresses, thought she was in Scotland, visiting her sister, Clara, who was more than happy to provide an alibi to Isabella's unfaithfulness. Clara knew Thomas's mistresses upset her sister more than Isabella liked to admit and having Clara so easily and thoroughly pull the wool over her husband's eyes, meant Isabella was able to spend several days only a few miles away from her own home in Harry's little cottage, which he had named 'Enchantment', because he said Isabella enchanted him.

Enchanted Harry might be, she thought, but not enough to spend every waking minute with her. Isabella, secreted away in the tiny cottage, grew restless behind its' stone walls, and walled garden, away from prying eyes. Harry, nonetheless, was coming and going from the cottage to the Big House, to the Mill and back, leaving Isabella alone for long periods of time. Time which she would rather have spent in Harry's company; preferably in his arms, naked and enjoying his rather magnificent body spreading her eagerly compliant legs apart and thrusting his manhood into her warm, wet womanhood making her writhe and groan and beg for more.

Having awoken Isabella's sexual appetite, Harry was not feeding it as often as Isabella had hoped. She glanced around the living room of the cottage, and the bare scrubbed stone walls seemed like a fortress, cutting her off from the world at large, and more importantly, from Harry – abroad somewhere in the mill, or on his large estate speaking to farm managers, or tenants. This was not how Isabella had imagined her precious days away from her husband and her responsibilities.

Casting a petulant glance around her self - imposed prison, she decided she needed some fresh air, that she was not going to remain inside a moment longer because if she did, she would go slowly mad. Fetching a simple cape to put on against the winter chill, she hugged the tweed material close around her thin muslin gown – her smart taffeta and satin ruffles having been abandoned whilst she was with Harry and living so informally – and stepped outside into the crisp December air.

It was nearly Christmas, and Isabella decided that she should decorate the cottage before she had to return to her home and her husband. Harmer House was always decorated by the servants, and she often wished she could have her own little tree to decorate with silver spangles and candles. The idea lodged in her mind, and she trotted off up the hill, past the newly built school, on the left, from where she could hear children's voices reciting the alphabet. She was heading up the hill, onto the open scrubland above, where she knew that there was a tenant farm, and more importantly, a small farm shop. She didn't have any money; she would charge any purchases to Harry's account, not worrying or acknowledging that in doing such a thing, she might firstly, give herself away and secondly, give her little affair with Harry away, too.

It was snowing, and slippery underfoot. Isabella's smart lace up boots were not really suitable footwear to climb a steep cobbled hill, which gave way to a dirt track at the top and upon reaching the top of the hill, she began to slip and slide on the icy snow underfoot. Finally, she lost her balance and stumbled to the ground with a cry.

Suddenly, she felt the grasp of strong hands beneath her armpits, as she was hoisted upright, and placed onto her unsuitably booted feet. The hands removed, and one of them lifted a bowler hat off a dark head.

'I trust you are not hurt, Ma'am?'

The voice was quietly concerned, melodious. Isabella looked up at the face beneath the dark, almost raven hair. The eyes, again dark as night smiled back, returning her look. She coughed.

'No, thank you,' she replied, 'a little shocked, but unhurt.'

'George Avery, Ma'am, at your service. I teach at the school a little further down the hill.'

Isabella nodded, then realised he was waiting for her to introduce herself. She was careful not to reveal her identity, not thinking for one moment that George Avery already knew full well who she was.

'Isabella,' she introduced, not eliciting her surname.

If George Avery noticed the omittance, he did not comment on it, merely took her cold, ungloved hand in his and kissed it gently.

'Enchanted,' he murmured, and Isabella gasped at the use of the word, suddenly remembering Harry, and the cottage and the need for some propriety. She stepped away from George Avery, dragging her gaze from his rather bewitching dark eyes. Handsome, he was not, Isabella thought; he was thin, almost reedy looking with a sallow complexion which reminded Isabella of cold coffee, but the dark eyes distracted her from his plainness. The interest in her that she saw in those eyes interested her.

'Thank you, Mr Avery. I should go. I was going to the farm shop. I must get on.'

He tipped his hat towards her and bowed.

'As you wish, Isabella. You are sure you are able to continue, bearing in mind the conditions underfoot? I can accompany you, should you wish?'

Isabella shook her head, and her auburn curls escaped the hood of her cape.

'I shall be fine. I shall take more care. Thank you, Mr Avery.'

She risked another look at those eyes, and saw only undisguised interest, and something else which Isabella could not place, but which George Avery knew all too well. Lust.

'Then I shall bid you good day, Ma'am.'

With that, George Avery turned on his heels and disappeared down the hill, leaving Isabella staring after him, the encounter being recalled in her mind. The feel of his strong hands, lifting her upright. The touch of his lips against the back of her hand. His eyes.

She smiled, and continued more carefully up the hill, knowing with certainty that she would encounter George Avery again.

***

His distress permeated the whole cottage, seeping into the stone walls and entrapping his sorrow in the very fabric of the tiny house. He wandered aimlessly, unseeingly from room to room. Vera's chronologically arranged notes lifted and scattered over the desk in the breeze which followed his distress around like a faithful lapdog. The warmth of the radiators cooled like icy tears on a frost encased cheek; the Christmas roses died in their vases on the kitchen window ledge and on the living room coffee table, as the pain and sorrow he felt turned into a raging anger. Rising like a tsunami in a once quiet ocean, wave upon devastating wave of pain and sorrow drowned the peaceful illusion of the shore. The cottage grew tense as his hatred, once dormant, now awakened in a terrible and vengeful torrent ready to be unleashed on another unsuspecting female.

SIX

Mortimer left on Boxing Day evening. He edged his Bentley gingerly up the tiny single-track lane, his arm extended out of the tinted glass window, one last beep of his horn sounding loudly into the silence which lay over the village like a comforter. Vera stood on the top step which led to the pavement in front of the cottage, almost reluctant to go back in alone. Mortimer had been entertaining, bombastic, fun.

Alive.

Her brain repeated the word over and over as she finally turned and went in through the solid wooden door to the living room.

Alive.

Whilst Mortimer had been at the cottage, there were no shapes, no blankets being moved, no sherry being poured, except by Mortimer himself. Now she was alone again, the atmosphere in the cottage became crowded, as if an unwelcome guest were refusing to leave. She looked around and sighed. Did she believe in ghosts? She was beginning to!

It was growing late, and she was tired, yet she climbed the stairs to her bedroom reluctantly, aware as she was of the return of the cold spots, the shadows, that feeling that there was something, or someone, lurking in the corners. Opting for the shower, and not a late night soak in a bath full of bubbles, she washed quickly, then stepped out of the shower cubicle into the newly refitted bathroom and dressed in her habitual fleece pyjamas, the lace robes and satin chemises put away now that Mortimer had gone back to London. There was still a bottle of whisky on the bedside table –Mortimer's habitual nightcap – so she poured a slug of the amber liquid, climbed into bed, and sat with a book, taking a sip of scotch every so often as she devoured the words.

Reading tired her eyes, and she realized that she was falling asleep with the half empty glass of whisky still in her hand. Somewhat reluctantly, she put down the glass, turned down the corner of the page she was reading, a habit she hated herself for but could not break, and switched off her bedside lamp. Shuffling down into the duvet which she hadn't yet changed, and which still smelt of Mortimer's aftershave and sex, she slept.

***

Waking the next morning, replete after a good nights' sleep and the easing of the pleasant excesses from two nights of extremely long and intense sex sessions, Vera smiled to herself as she pottered around the cottage, making breakfast, changing the duvet, putting the washing machine on. She swept up the pine needles, throwing them into the wood burner, cleared away remnants of Mortimer's stay, the cigar butts, a pair of cufflinks which he'd forgotten. Finally, she polished the table and her desk and then, armed with a pot of strong coffee and some panettone and mince pies left over from Christmas Eve, she settled herself at her laptop to begin writing.

Trudy McAlister was well on the way to exposing Donovan. Pillow talk was very loose, and he had a tongue which couldn't be bound. Trudy now had enough potential evidence for her to be able to approach his bosses and reveal to them that she knew for sure that he was embezzling money through fraudulent accounting. The only trouble with this plan, was that Trudy was in love with Donovan by now, so what did she chose? Love or Career?

The crash which resounded through the cottage made Vera jump so violently she almost dropped her laptop. She has been working in the living room, and the sound had come from directly overhead – her bedroom. Shutting the laptop, she put it on the sofa, and ran up the stairs, heart pounding in terror, so scared was she at what she might find there.

Her bedroom always had been an oasis of calm femininity,

pale pastels, shimmery materials, fairy lights strung across the deep recess of the window, pretty prints in shabby chic frames gracing the walls. It still was.

Nothing was out of place.

Nothing had been disturbed.

Nothing had moved.

There was no reason she could see which accounted for such a loud and sudden noise. In fact, the only noise she could hear now was her heart, still pounding fiercely against her rib cage. Moving across the small landing, she checked the spare bedroom, with its floor to ceiling bookcase taking up the whole of one wall, and the pretty, wrought iron, white day bed pushed against the other, overlooking the window. Everything was as it should be, the quiet calmness only punctuated by the river rushing by below and a creaking sound, which Vera couldn't place. It sounded as though something was swinging from the beam overhead; however, the cottage was old and full of strange creaks and groans. Mortimer said it was the wood expanding and retracting in the heat. Maybe that had been the noise she heard, or something outside.

She looked out of the window, waiting for her heart to return to its normal beat, enjoying the quietness, trying to forget the loud bang which had brought her running up the stairs in the first place and trying to convince herself that the noise had been something external. She had almost succeeded when there was another loud rapping. The sound made her jump and her heart pound again, but at least this time, she recognized the sound of the heavy pewter door knocker.

'Hello. It's about time I introduced myself – I'm Hal Winterton. I own the land at the back of your cottage, and some of your neighbour's houses, too. I've been meaning to say hello since you moved in, but you seem to be away a lot.'

Vera blinked at the directness of the odd looking, pale stranger. Tall, with floppy brown hair which he kept brushing impatiently away from his forehead, Hal Winterton carried an old-fashioned air about him. His clothes were not modern, an odd combination of eccentric mingled with brightly coloured hues – he reminded her of a popinjay. He did carry it all off very well though, she thought to herself, taking in his demeanour; his stance and the confidence he exuded. He was pale, but interesting, she thought, quickly imagining herself in bed with him – a terrible habit which her job as a writer of erotic novels had produced. She shook her head, to remove the image of her legs planted on top of his shoulders, and his cock driving into her very wet, and willing pussy. She coughed in embarrassment of her own thoughts, brushed her own hair back from her face and smiled up at the new visitor.

'Vera Matthews,' she said. 'Veronica, but no-one has ever called me that since my parents died.'

She extended her hand, and he took it, almost in a caress rather than a handshake and she felt a tingle of sexual desire slick through her body as their eyes met. His hand was cold, and she suddenly remembered her manners, pushing away the very tempting thought of her mounting him in her wrought iron bed.

'Would you like to come in?' Vera smiled at her visitor. 'I don't often have people call, well, except Mortimer, but he's just left. I was thinking it was time for a sherry; if you'd like to join me?'

Hal smiled and said he would be delighted to join her. They both walked back into the cottage.

***

Sipping his sherry, Hal gazed about the cottage. The intensity of his roaming eyes unnerved Vera who found herself nervous under his scrutiny for reasons she couldn't yet fathom, although she was drawn to the sexual magnetism he exuded. His eyes came back to rest on her, and she looked away from him, cursing herself for being so open in her curiosity that he had caught her looking at him interestedly.

He placed his empty sherry glass on the wooden coffee table and leant back against the leather button back of the sofa, crossing his legs in a lazy, relaxed movement. He knew she was his. He knew that one day in the not too distant future, he would return, and they would go upstairs; they would go into the very pretty, feminine bedroom with its pastel prints and fairy lights and he would simply fuck the brains out of her.

She watched him place the glass on the coffee table, his movements lazy and languid but strangely sensual, exciting. A frisson of sexual desire passed through her whole body and she had an inexplicable thought that he would be back and when he came, she would simply take him upstairs to her bedroom and fuck the brains out of him.

He smiled at her now, almost knowingly, as if he had somehow read her thoughts.

'Tell me, how come a writer has to go away so often?' Hal asked her, breaking the slight sexual tension in the room with his question, as his eyes danced on her.

'How did you know I was a writer?' Vera answered the question with a question.

He waved his hand around in a vague manner, as if in answer, but offered no explanation.

'I attend promotions, and launches,' said Vera, 'books strangely don't sell by themselves. Most authors have to help the publisher to promote their books in order to improve sales.'

Hal's face took on a distasteful look for a split second before he asked, 'And is *he* your publisher?'

Vera looked puzzled for a moment, then realised Hal was looking at the whisky, which she had placed back on the occasional table next to the fireplace. Mortimer's whisky, which she had drank in bed with Mortimer at Christmas.

'No, Mortimer is my agent.'

'And your lover?'

The question was sharp, like the tips of the icicles that had dangled down from the drainpipe in the recent frosty weather.

'That's none of your business, really,' came Vera's curt reply, 'although no, we are merely loving friends as well as colleagues.'

Hal broke the tension by breaking his pale face into a smile.

'Just what I wanted to hear, Miss Matthews!' He leant forward towards her. 'I take it that you are a Miss, and you are unencumbered? That there are no husbands, erstwhile or current, lurking in the loft, or banished to the basement? That my pathway to your affection is clear?'

She realized that he was flirting with her now, and again, that desire to simply lead him upstairs and fuck him hard, for a long, long time snaked through her body, and she shivered involuntarily at the thought.

Smiling at him, she stood up, indicating that the visit was at a close.

'The pathway is clear, if you should so wish to walk down it, Mr Winterton!'

He took her hand. He still felt cold as his fingers played delicately with her palm before he kissed it with equally cold lips.

'I am sure I shall meander in the extremely near future, Miss Matthews, and I shall take my leave, for now, but I may return and expect us to take the first steps, jointly.'

Not leaving Vera time to reply, he departed, vanishing as quickly as he'd arrived, but leaving behind an air of sexual anticipation, and Vera's growing desire.

SEVEN

Somewhat disappointingly, Hal Winterton did not come back immediately. Weeks passed; peaceful weeks, no unexplained banging, no shapes in the corner, no cold spots in the bedroom, and Vera, relaxed and happy, wrote. Trudy and Donovan's little adventure was nicely completed with Trudy giving it all up for love and choosing to utilise her detective's brain to turn rogue with Donovan, who after all, was a fantastic fuck. Having thwarted the efforts of law enforcement agencies, they had both skipped away with the fortune Donovan had amassed and took off on a long haul flight to enjoy a luxurious lifestyle somewhere hot and remote where they could live happily ever after.

Putting the final touches to the pair's last erotic adventure in the penultimate chapter of the book, Vera became aware of the weeks that had passed, and the lack of erotic adventures in her own life, either in her dreams or more hopefully, in real life, being delivered to her by the enigmatic Hal Winterton. The tall, pale stranger who had entered her life and whom she still wished would enter her body occupied her thoughts more often than she should let him. She sighed as she snapped the laptop shut, and as always, when a novel was nearing completion, she felt dissatisfied, at a loss. Loose ends dangling contemplatively before her. What would she do when the final chapter was written?

She looked up and gazed out of the office window, across the tree-tops now beginning their spring renewal. Young green buds and leaves were sprouting forth abundantly, obliterating the winter bareness of their branches. A pale February sun cast a weak warmth through the double-glazed window and as she felt it caress her cheek, she decided. She grabbed her mobile phone and stabbed in Mortimer's number.

'Now Miss L'Amore,' Mortimer growled, his voice thick with affection. 'I take it there is nothing wrong with your latest deadline for the McAlister novel?'

Vera let out a growl of her own – of exasperation!

'Mortimer! I'm not bloody Honey bloody L'Amore – I'm Vera. There's nothing wrong with the book. It's nearly finished and well before deadline day. I was wondering what you were doing this weekend?'

'Do I sense an unspoken invitation in your voice, Miss *Vera* Matthews?' Mortimer emphasised her real name and she smiled at his teasing tone. 'If I do, then I have nothing planned which cannot be unplanned and postponed to another time in preference of your company.'

'Bring some whisky with you, Mortimer, I've nearly finished that bottle you brought with you at Christmas.' Vera instructed, imagining him smiling at the still unspoken invitation and of course, the thought of some very pleasing and more than satisfactory sex.

'Expect me at lunchtime on Saturday,' came Mortimer's acceptance.

***

Vera was sleeping soundly on Friday night, as yet blissfully unaware of the change in the atmosphere. The pain seeped once again through the stone walls of the cottage; the dark shadows reappeared and shifted sullenly into place in the bedroom, the lounge, the kitchen; the barely controlled rage simmered in the very foundations of the house.

From his vantage point, he stared down at the sleeping woman, and reached out a cold, blue hand, gently caressing her cheek. In sleep, she put up her hand, and brushed the feeling away off her face, sighed and resettled back into her mound of pillows. He felt the rage built again as he imagined the other man arriving, kissing her, being familiar with her. He thought of the two of them going to bed together, of him undressing her; hands tracing contours of her body; lips kissing the delightful cupid's bow of her luscious mouth. He could almost feel her wetness as her desire for another grew between her legs and he could not bear it. He simply could not bear it. He let out a silent scream of pain and the cottage moaned, the stone wept, and the wooden beams bowed in sorrow.

It had begun again.

***

Saturday was a pale, glittery winter morning, with a shimmer of sunlight streaming through Vera's bedroom window as she drew back the curtains. She watched one of the neighbours walking down the hill with a black Labrador bouncing along beside him. He spotted her at her window and threw up a hand in greeting before disappearing from view, on his way to the riverside pathway, at the bottom of the hill beneath the viaduct.

Vera turned from the window and stared around the bedroom. She thought she heard a rustle from the corner by the door but shook her head, shrugging the slight movement away as she trotted downstairs to get coffee and get ready for Mortimer's arrival.

Around midday, the dark green Bentley edged truculently down the narrow country lane, with its limited passing places which Mortimer resolutely refused to back into. He stood his ground and eventually whoever was coming in the opposite direction simply gave up and reversed their car so that the Bentley could continue to its destination. Mortimer glanced at the cottage now, and was surprised at how dark, how malevolent it seemed. It looked like an evil old man, with his shoulders hunched, glowering at him from the crest of the hill on which it stood. He thought back to the strange unexplained crashes at Christmas and felt some sympathy for Vera, living alone in this dark, unfriendly little house.

Turning his attention back to the road, he eased the large car into a parking space just opposite the cottage, which continued to brood, silently, resentfully, as the man got out of the driver's seat, opened the boot lid with a click of the electronic key fob and began unloading bags, a *Samsonite* overnight bag on wheels together with an array of designer labelled shopping bags. Locking the car, Mortimer and his assorted possessions headed for the stone steps which lead to Vera's cottage.

The door flung open, and Vera stood on the threshold in the tiny lobby, grinning up at Mortimer as he stepped gingerly down the steep steps, laden with parcels. She was dressed in check leggings and a tight camisole top which made her breasts look voluptuous. Her pale pink bolero style cardigan she wrapped around herself, because the pale February sun was not strong enough for warmth, and there was still a winter chill in the air despite the buds on the trees.

Mortimer, having successfully made it down the steps, handed several parcels to Vera, and kissed her quite greedily on the lips for quite a long time before an enormous bang from within the cottage made them both jump apart, startled. Vera, thrusting the parcels Mortimer had just given her back into his hands, ran back into the house with Mortimer following more sedately, hampered as he was by his parcels and bag.

Vera was staring in despair and shock at her smoking laptop, sitting where she had left it on the coffee table, its screen now splintered. Nothing else was disturbed.

'Short circuit?' Mortimer asked, setting his encumbrances down.

'It wasn't plugged in, Mortimer,' said Vera, shakily. 'Why on earth did it blow up like that?'

She started to gather together her notes and tipped the broken shards of glass which had landed on the papers, into the waste bin by the fire.

'They don't make things to last anymore, Vee,' came Mortimer's reply. He was rummaging in his numerous parcels until he found the *Whisky Shop* bag and pulled out a bottle of

1969 Glen Mhor.

'Why do things always go bump and bang when you appear here!' Vera laughed shakily, moving the laptop aside as Mortimer settled two tumblers with generously poured slugs of whisky onto the table.

'Do they?'

He sat next to Vera on the sofa, one arm flung onto the button back, an invitation for Vera to slide into the crook of his arm, which she did.

She leapt away from him as a second banging noise filled the stillness of the room.

'Vee, it's the door!' Mortimer chuckled, reaching for a glass of whisky, while she stood up and headed for the lobby.

Opening the front door, Vera nearly fainted. Hal Winterton, dressed as eclectically as she remembered from their last encounter, stood in the doorway. Still pale and interesting, she thought, temporarily forgetting about Mortimer, sipping whisky in the lounge. She blinked, pushed her blonde hair out of her eyes and smiled at Hal, who returned the look with an enigmatic smile of his own.

'Miss Matthews. How delightful it is to see you again.'

'Oh, well, I'm glad you think so, Mr Winterton. How are you?'

Hal smiled evilly; a look which did not register with Vera, who was flustered by the appearance of one man whom she would willingly go to bed with, whilst in the company of another whom she was definitely going to go to bed with.

'I'm cold!' Hal hinted, looking beyond Vera into the warmth of the cottage.

She smiled at the unspoken hinting in his voice.

'And I've got company,' she told him, apologetically.

'It's alright Vera,' came Mortimer's voice from the lounge, 'bring your visitor in.'

Vera stepped aside and with a breeze of cold air, Hal stepped into the lounge. Mortimer stood up in greeting and held out a hand, which Hal did not take, but merely nodded in his direction.

'Whisky, Hal?' Vera asked, nodding towards Mortimer to pour a third glass.

Hal took the whisky and settled himself into the wing chair by the window, as Mortimer and Vera sat back down, very close to each other, on the sofa.

There was an awkward silence. Hal sipped his whisky, Mortimer cracked his knuckles and Vera played with a strand of blonde hair which had escaped its ponytail; an action unconsciously erotic, which both men did not fail to notice.

None spoke. Hal downed his whisky, then stood up.

'Miss Matthews, thank you. Most welcome. The weather outside is changing. I can smell snow. Perhaps you and your visitor should get firewood, and stock up. It tends to be quite harsh around here in adverse conditions. Now, what are you two doing for dinner? Shall you attend with me at the Big House?'

Vera declined on their behalf, but seeing the hurt in Hal's eyes, and a slightly impatient look, she found herself asking him if he would like to have dinner with her and Mortimer in the cottage later, say seven-thirty, for eight?

Hal's rather long face broke into a smile, and he accepted before taking his leave, disappearing into a distinctly changed atmosphere outside. The surrounding countryside brooded expectantly as thick, greyish white clouds swirled overhead.

Mortimer looked in the direction he thought Hal had taken and wondered how the other man had managed to walk up the steep hill so quickly. He was nowhere to be seen.

'Smells like snow, Vee.' Mortimer said, sniffing the air, before going back into the lounge and shutting the door.

Vera laughed. 'You're beginning to sound like Hal!'

Mortimer noticed the use of Hal's first name and raised his eyebrows.

'Shush, Mortimer. And if we really are going to have snow, perhaps you'd take that monolith of a car of yours to the garden centre for me, and fetch some logs and kindling for the fire?'

Mortimer grumbled under his breath, but did as he was bid, and a good job too. By the time he returned to the cottage with the logs and kindling, some dinner candles, and delicacies from the wonderful delicatessen within the garden centre, not only had it grown dark, but the anticipated snow had indeed begun to fall. Silently the swirling flakes blanketed the village in a fast laying winter white cloak, its folds and curves obliterating the landscape.

'You'll get snowed in, Mortimer,' said Vera, happily, coming up the stairs from the kitchen, from where there came a delicious smell of roasting venison, rich and full bodied.

Mortimer waved his hand and muttered something about four-wheel drive as he handed his parcels to Vera.

'Although Mr Hal Winterton, turn-up-at-the-wrong-moment-man might have a problem getting here.' Mortimer looked almost pleased at the idea.

'I don't know if he drives, I've not seen him in a car, ever.' Vera replied. 'Check that meat in half an hour, Morty, will you, please? I'm just going to change for dinner.'

EIGHT

By seven thirty, the meat was resting, and the potatoes and vegetables keeping warm in the oven. Mortimer had opened an excellent red, and it was breathing quietly on the kitchen table. Vera, returning resplendent in a clinging, spaghetti strapped silver and black dress and subtly made up, tottered downstairs in her Louboutin stilettos. Rushing, she almost lost her footing and Mortimer held out a hand at the bottom of the steep wooden staircase.

'Careful, Vee,' he said, casting a lascivious glance over her curvaceous body. 'We don't want Death Wish Stairs to claim their first victim before dinner!'

She laughed. 'It's alright, Mortimer, I shall be careful and make sure they don't get their wish.'

Vera began setting the table, using her antique crystal glassware, and the beautiful, over-the-top *Royal Albert* dinner service, which she had espied in a local second-hand store in Ramsbottom and bought for next to nothing. She often wondered if the person who had donated the goods had actually known their value.

The tiny table set, Vera stuck breadsticks in a jar in the centre, next to the wine and instructing Mortimer to carve the venison, she went upstairs. A moment later, the doorbell rang its ding-dong song. Hal was a "seven thirty on the dot" type of person then, thought Vera, glancing at the clock on the mantlepiece as she pulled open the door, letting a gust of cold air and a swirl of snowflakes into the vestibule.

Hal smiled appreciatively at Vera's appearance, and handed her a bottle of *Grahams Ne Oublie*. Vera, knowing nothing of port, smiled gratefully, said nothing, and placed it on the side table by the fireplace.

The two went downstairs to the kitchen, where Mortimer looked slightly cherry cheeked from the heat. The venison rested on the serving platter, there were just the vegetables to get ready after the starters of winter salad had been served. Vera was a good cook. It was one of the things she did to relax after a hard day of writing. When the adrenaline flowed and the ideas taxed her brain to the limits, cooking released a feeling of peacefulness within her and she enjoyed experimenting with recipes as much as she did with sex. The thought made her smile as she served the salad, whilst Mortimer poured a chilled and splendid *Riesling* to accompany the starter.

Conversation flowed, mainly about Mortimer, because Mortimer loved talking about himself if he could, and Hal, whilst neither talking nor eating much, proved to be a willing listener. Vera served the main course, watching the two men, how relaxed Mortimer appeared in her cottage, and her company; Hal seemed tense and ill at ease, perhaps because Mortimer was slightly bombastic. He did tend to overtake proceedings somewhat. She turned to the table, placed a hand on Mortimer's forearm and was about to tell him to let Hal speak, when there was a crash, and two of her antique glasses splintered onto the quarry tiled floor.

'How on earth did they fall off the draining board?' Vera asked, shakily while Mortimer fetched a dustpan and brush to clear up the mess. 'Things are always going bump in the night or crashing in this place!'

Hal looked up. 'I'm not surprised,' he said, 'it's supposed to be haunted, this cottage. Didn't you know?'

His face took on what Mortimer thought was a very unpleasant expression as Hal watched Vera's discomfort. Clattering the dustpan and brush in the corner, Mortimer turned to take the plates from Vera, plonking Hal's in front of him unceremoniously.

'I don't believe in ghosts,' he said flatly to the other man.

Hal raised his eyebrows. 'Really?'

He turned his attention to his plate of food. 'Venison! How delicious,' he declared, whilst not eating any of it, as the now stilted conversation stumbled through the meal.

After a delicious dessert of poached pears, Vera remembered the port.

'Shall we go upstairs, and have the port? Hal brought some for us, Mortimer.'

'How kind,' growled Mortimer, although his temper mellowed at the site of the expensive, and extremely rare bottle of tawny port on the side table.

This time, Hal made certain he was sitting next to Vera, and Mortimer, slightly put out, heaved himself into the club chair, which at least gave him a great view of Vera's very shapely legs.

Vera sighed.

'I'm worried about you getting home in the snow,' she said to Hal, as she sipped the beautiful liquid from its crystal glass. 'It certainly is coming down.'

Hal smiled, poured a second glass. 'We'd better batten down the hatches, and get this down our hatches, in that case. It will be a shame to waste it, by letting it spoil.'

Sitting in the cosy, dimly lit room with the delicious smell of applewood logs burning in the stove, the atmosphere became more convivial. Vera relaxed, and took off her shoes, curling her legs up on the sofa. Hal leant back against the button back and watched her, his eyes resting appreciatively on her cleavage.

'Nice, aren't they?' Mortimer grinned, lecherously. He had been watching Hal and decided it was time to show him exactly who Vera was going to allow to fondle her breasts.

'Mortimer!' Vera spluttered, almost spilling her drink.

'No worries,' said Hal, placing his glass on the coffee table, and turning to Vera. He put out a tentative hand, towards her left breast, as Mortimer continued to caress the right one.

Vera let out a gasp, and then smiled to herself as she leant back and let herself enjoy the excitement that the touch of two men gave her. Two men whom she wanted desperately to go to bed with. Mortimer because she always did go to bed with Mortimer, and Hal, because she knew she wanted to go to bed with him.

Mortimer kissed Vera's cheek, as he slipped his hand inside the silver and black dress, lifting her right breast out. He bent his head to take the pert brown nipple, visibly hardening now, into his mouth and he sucked steadily, greedily. Vera gasped again and heard Hal groan. She turned her head, and saw Hal, unbuttoning his trousers to reveal a very erect, large cock, which he started to masturbate as she kissed his lips.

It was going to happen – was all she could think of as she kissed first one man, then the other and both men were worshipping her breasts – it was going to happen.

Mortimer pulled away and raised Vera to her feet, indicating to go to the bedroom. He led, she followed, with Hal behind her, his hands running over her undulating bottom.

In the bedroom, Hal stood behind her and pulled the dress off her, easing it over her head until she stood naked except for her black hold up stockings and her silver and black shoes. Mortimer was undressing as he knelt down before her and his tongue, his eager wet tongue sought out the swelling nub of her clitoris. She groaned and leaned into Hal as the sensation of Mortimer's tongue gently circling around her sex overtook her and she shuddered gently as he took the hard bud in his mouth and sucked her. She felt a rush of wetness trickle down her inner thighs as she drowned in the delights of his mouth.

Hal, also naked now, was cupping her ample breasts in his hands from behind, rolling his fingers over the hard, swollen nipples, pinching them between thumb and forefinger whilst

Vera thrust her bottom into his groin. She could feel how big and hard his cock was for her, and she shuddered again.

Mortimer stood up and walking backwards, pulled Vera towards the bed. He lay down and pulled Vera on top of him. Her legs were either side of him as she straddled him, and she felt him guiding his cock in between her legs. Slowly she lowered her aching, gushing pussy onto his fat cock; she threw her head back in delight as she felt him push upwards, opening her roughly. At the side of the bed, Hal grabbed a handful of her blonde hair and pushed her face onto his cock. She opened her mouth eagerly to receive what he had to offer and as Mortimer moved inside her and thrust into her pussy, Hal thrust a large and engorged penis into her small, hot mouth.

Her tongue rimmed the head of his cock, lapping at the folds of his foreskin, pulled back so the bulbous head of his manhood enjoyed the feeling of Vera's tongue licking. She ran her tongue down the shaft to his heavy balls, and up again to the tip and tasted pre - cum on her lips. Taking the whole of his cock into her mouth, she gently sucked as Mortimer thrust.

Groaning, Hal held the back of her neck as he pushed his cock down her throat. He felt her gag and held it there for a moment before he pulled his aching cock out of her mouth and he knelt behind her, slapping her bottom.

In an almost orchestrated movement, Vera pulled herself off Mortimer's cock, and shimmied down the bed so that she could take him in her mouth, still wet with her juices. As she sucked Mortimer greedily, she felt Hal fingering her pussy, holding the outer lips apart and then she felt him push roughly into her. His cock was harder, and bigger than Mortimer's and he was much less controlled in his thrusts, making her gasp as she sucked on Mortimer.

Outside the snow swirled against the window.

Inside, the two men had her now, Hal had pushed her down on her back on the bed, and Mortimer had picked up his necktie from the bedroom floor, using it to bind her hands to the wrought iron bedstead. Hal's handkerchief was big enough to blindfold her as Mortimer pushed her legs apart roughly and the two men took turns to use her, to thrust into her aching pussy, to rub their cocks over her throbbing clitoris. She became a quivering, groaning mess as over and over again she was penetrated, first Mortimer with his thick, stubby cock stabbing into her and then Hal, his large, long penis thrusting hard as far up her as he could get.

Vera gasped, the sensations tumbling over her like wave after wave of tumultuous pleasure, rising, falling, bursting. She could feel her pussy contracting, gathering as her orgasm built. Her clitoris ached, and her juices flowed over the two eager cocks pounding her. Mortimer, knowing more than Hal of Vera's habits, reached over into the bedside cabinet, and pulled out a large white sex toy, her "magic wand", as she called it. He switched it onto her favourite setting, and as Hal thrust inside her, Mortimer held the wand against Vera's clitoris.

Vera started to cry out, loudly, her shouts of ecstasy mingling in the silence of the falling snow. The wand vibrated against the hard nub of her clit, and she started to shake. Mortimer moved over her, knelt above her face, nudged her mouth with his hard, thick cock. She took him into her, greedily sucking as she was thrust into by an equally greedy Hal.

Mortimer grunted, ground his pumping cock into her mouth and she swallowed his cum as she felt her orgasm ride over her and her pussy contracting against Hal's growing cock. He thrust again and again against the tide of her orgasm, the tsunami of her sexual crescendo. She went very still, arched her back and screamed in delight as she felt Hal empty himself inside her trembling pussy.

Outside, the snow continued to fall.

NINE

Vera awoke to a white world, to a silence that was almost deafening. Memories of the previous night drifted into her consciousness and she turned her head, expecting to see both Mortimer and Hal in the big, cosy bed.

She was alone.

Outside, the snow continued to fall.

***

She dressed quickly, because the heating hadn't ignited, and the cottage was cold and inhospitable; dark corners leapt at her and the wood burner resolutely refused to light despite the copious amounts of paper and kindling she threw into it.

Shrugging, she picked up the hastily scrawled note left by Mortimer, sometime in the remains of the night after she and he and Hal had enjoyed each other.

'Sorry, Vee,' the note said, *'I had to leave. The snow was getting worse and I can't afford to be snowed-in. I decided to take a chance on the roads and try to get back to London. I'll call you when I get there, Morty.'*

Vera smiled at the note, he'd put an 'x' and a heart at the bottom. Briefly, she wondered if he did love her and whether she did, in fact, love him. She imagined Mortimer trying to manoeuvre his huge car up the narrow, treacherous snow-covered lanes.

Scrunching the note up and throwing it into the un-cooperative wood burner, she pulled on the shrug she had so carelessly abandoned last night and then went to fetch her fleecy dressing gown to put on over the odd assortment of other clothes she'd dressed in, to try to keep warm. Still full of potential love for Mortimer, her mind flicked briefly to Hal. She wondered when he had left and hoped he had got home safely.

Collecting together the empty glasses, the physical debris of the night before, Vera busied herself against the cold, and a slight hangover by tidying up the mess. She cleared tables, scraping away left-over food, and putting it in the waste bin. She couldn't be bothered to go outside into the virginal white world to the recycling bin. Stacking the dirty dishes in the sink, she decided coffee was more important and, abandoning her housewifery, she made a pot of coffee, taking it with her as she ventured upstairs to the frigidly cold living room. Trying again to light the fire to no avail, she sat hunched over her coffee cup, and wondered why central heating and fires in general had decided not to work on one of the coldest days she had experienced in the cottage.

Shivering, she switched on the radio – she didn't have a television, preferring the gentleness of background music and debate to the brashness of a flickering tv screen invading her living room – and tried to concentrate on the news, hoping that it would provide a distraction from the cold. She was in the middle of putting on a pair of gloves to try to keep her hands warm when she heard it.

"...and as the country is blanketed by an unanticipated seriously heavy snowfall, news just in of a major collision involving a lorry and several cars heading southbound on the M62. Initial reports say there are numerous casualties and sadly, one fatality in the crash which happened in the early hours of this morning. Details of the fatality, a male in his late fifties have not been released until family have been informed..."

Sitting in the cold, uncongenial living room of a cottage from which Mortimer would have had to travel onto one motorway, and then join the M62 a few junctions away, Vera was filled with such a feeling of dread and foreboding that she actually screamed.

'NO!'

Her voice sounded very loud in the silent, unsympathetic surroundings.

Suddenly, her ears were filled with laughter – malicious, unfriendly laughter. She leapt off the sofa, almost falling over in fear and she stared around the room, heart beating furiously, as the hairs on the back of her neck stood on end. The back of the neck which Mortimer had kissed last night; warm lips against heated skin, his breath brushing against the tiny hairs, his teeth nibbling beneath her ear, the spot he knew turned her to liquid desire in his arms. Her mind replayed the last sentence she had heard on the radio like a mantra.

"Details of the fatality, a male in his late fifties, have not been released until family have been informed…"

The cold forgotten, Vera was now in a white heat of panic, stumbling around the living room into the office. Tearing the phone handset off its cradle, she dialled Mortimer's number. In a frenzy of impatience and rising panic, she heard a dead tone. Screaming again, she dialled Mortimer's number over and over, tears running down her alabaster cheeks. Flinging the phone to the floor angrily because she was frightened, she stood in the middle of her office, listening to the silence of her surroundings. The freezing air seemed to wrap itself around her in an icy grasp.

How long she had stood there, sobbing and gasping, she did not know. Her body was stiff, rigid with cold and fright. Outside, the treacherous snow continued to fall, obliterating the tiny, cobbled street. It nestled on the footpath, and on the steps down to the cottage. The temperature continued to fall, although beneath her layers of clothes, Vera was sweating. Eventually, she gathered her thoughts together and ran upstairs to her bedside cabinet, where she rummaged amongst sex toys, discarded suspender belts, and various scribbled notes on bits of paper until she found an old address book. As far as she knew, Mortimer had one living relative – a sister he did not speak to very often, but a sister nonetheless – a sister who would probably be his next of kin. Vera had to know; she just had to know.

Leaping down the stairs again, she grabbed the phone from the floor and with hands that wouldn't stop shaking, she managed to dial Mortimer's sister's number as she stood and sobbed in the office, staring out unseeingly at the white blanket that was smothering the landscape.

"You are through to the voicemail of Felicia Blake-Harrison. I'm sorry, I'm not able to answer your call right now but please leave your name and number and a short message and I will get back to you as soon as I am able."

Vera, still sobbing, gabbled a message to the voicemail and then, in a blind panic and sheer frustration, she threw the handset across the room. It hit the wall by the kitchen stairs and shattered onto the floor. *Great*, she thought, *now I'm without a phone as well as heating and hot water.* She walked into the living room and sank onto the sofa, staring at the three quarters empty bottle of port, consumed so eagerly last night and now simply a sad reminder that neither of the men who had enjoyed drinking it were still there. One of them could possibly be dead.

Running her cold fingers through her unkempt blonde hair, Vera swallowed a great mouthful of fear and tried to calm down. She may be over-reacting; of course, it was unlikely that Mortimer was involved, after all, hundreds, maybe thousands, of people used that stretch of motorway every day; she was panicking for nothing. She decided to go and make a cup of tea. Tea calmed her more than coffee could, and she made it in a pot using tea leaves, not by chucking a brand label teabag into a mug.

She clattered down the bare wooden kitchen stairs, shivering again because the kitchen was so much colder than the rest of the house, and she reached for the tea caddy in the wall cupboard above the microwave. She put a large scoop of Rose and Oolong leaves into the china teapot and clicked the kettle on. The blue indicator light did not ignite. Vera started at it disbelievingly. It was a new kettle, for God's Sake! Never mind, she could heat some water in the microwave. She ran the kitchen tap and filled a plastic basin with water, thrusting it into the microwave and pressing the appropriate timer button. Nothing happened and the slow realisation dawned on Vera that the electricity may not be working as well as the central heating. She flicked a light switch. Nothing.

Outside, still the snow continued to fall.

***

It was snowing heavily when Harry came back to the cottage. Isabella was hunched over a meagre fire, which she had managed to coax to life using the kindling which Harry kept in a large metal box at the side of the inglenook. She had spent considerable time rubbing the dry sticks together over the embers of last night's fire but eventually the kindling had caught, and now a tiny, bright orange flame licked up the chimney and cast a welcoming glow towards her lover, as he shrugged the snow off his greatcoat, and came to envelope Isabella in strong arms.

'You're cold, sir,' Isabella turned her pretty face up towards Harry, and waited for him to kiss her passionately.

Harry was a wonderful kisser. His lips were gently coaxing, then more urgently biting until he had made her desire him, and she returned his kiss with fervour. Her lips turned to hot, molten lava in the heat of the passion which set fire to them both. He slipped his hands into her hair and unknotted it, letting it tumble down her back like a titian waterfall, each curl draping downwards towards the vortex of Isabella's passion.

'Then we shall have to warm each other up, Isabella.'

Harry's voice sounded thick and he kissed her again and again, grabbing her by the waist, lifting her into his arms and carrying her up the steep wooden stairs to the tiny bedroom. He flung her down onto the heavy, horsehair mattress, watching her breasts heave with desire as he hastily removed his clothes.

'Touch yourself, Isabella!' Harry commanded, pushing her legs apart, so that she surrounded him as he knelt above her, with his long, thick cock growing visibly as he moved his hand over his shaft, backwards and forwards. He repeated his request.

Isabella hesitated. She thought Harry rather deviant sometimes, in the things he asked of her when they were in bed. Although she enjoyed the feel of his thick set, muscular body enveloping hers as he rose above her and penetrated her, she was often dismayed and slightly embarrassed by some of the things they did together. He had made her take him in her mouth once, the thing that he pushed into her private part! He had pulled her off the bed and made her kneel down in front of him as he sat on the edge; having taken hold of her fox coloured hair firmly at the nape of her neck, he had almost forced her to take his *thing* into her mouth. Commanding her to move her mouth up and down the huge shaft, he had held her head very firmly as he rooted and grunted, pushing his *thing* in further and further until she had gagged. He'd laughed as he spurted hot, foul tasting, creamy liquid inside her mouth. She'd been horrified and spat it out onto the floor, still gagging. Harry had laughed, telling her spitting was very unladylike and she should learn to enjoy the taste.

Harry obviously wanted her to be unladylike now, he was watching her intently as he stroked himself. He snatched hold of her small hand and placed her fingers onto her womanhood. She had never touched herself in front of a man before – it was not seemly to do that. Thomas had never asked her, but she suspected this sort of act would be something one of his many mistresses would perform for him. Harry, however, clearly wanted her to do it, in front of him now.

Tentatively, she placed her forefinger onto the small hot bud, which stiffened at her touch.

'Move your fingers in a circle around it, Isabella, keep your touch firm and enjoy it,' Harry instructed.

Isabella did as she was commanded and was surprised at how quickly the sensation shot through her, licking upwards from her sex – a thrill, a tingling, a strange wanting and she was amazed to feel her fingers getting wet, very quickly. She had never, ever considered that touching herself in front of a man could be so arousing. In private, yes, in her own bedchamber, alone; but not in front of a man.

Harry moaned, and moved down the bed – Isabella wondered what would happen next and how long he wanted her to carry on rubbing, which was not an unpleasant feeling. Suddenly, she gasped, and shrieked. Harry's head was between her legs now, one hand placed over her fingers, still placed on that delicious bud and he was guiding her fingers over the tip which was hard and wet. His hand moved hers over swollen folds of delicate flesh, tingling flesh, pumping with blood as Isabella's body reacted to the coaxing fingers and at the same time, she felt something else – unbelievably – she felt Harry's mouth clamping over that secret place where he entered her.

She let out a small noise, like a distressed kitten – she was half afraid, half wanton as she felt Harry's tongue seek out that place, licking the lips and folds which were now agonizingly sensitive to his kisses and his insistent licking. She found that the sensation, combined with her fingers slicking over the strange, hard wonderful hub was maddeningly good, that she could not keep still and wanted to raise her body and arch her back; wanting Harry, wanting his tongue to give her the release from the buildup of desire that she felt.

'Come, Isabella,' Harry whispered against her wetness, 'come, and let me in while you shudder with pleasure.'

In the back of her mind, Isabella wondered where Harry was talking about. Come where? She could not concentrate, so strong was the pull of pleasure emanating from between her legs as Harry's tongue curled inside her, drinking her sweet juices, which poured out and down his chin. She gave herself up to pleasure, thought abandoned in a heady rush of bright white light and then a drawing together feeling and then, then! Harry pushed the tight, swollen head of his *thing* inside her and she was contracting and swelling around him, a mess of moistness, a delirium of desire. He pumped himself as far up as he could get inside her and she had to do it, she had to scream as he made her body shake in an agony of pleasure; the sound of her triumph mingling with the silence of the snow, which continued to fall.

TEN

The flickering candles, haphazardly dotted around the unbearably cold cottage, made sinister shadows on the wall in the growing light of daybreak. Vera had survived a day and a night at the cottage with no heating, hot water, or electricity. She was huddled in a tight, cold ball, fully clothed, underneath her duvet cover and had slept fitfully, clutching her mobile phone, which thankfully had some battery power left. She waited through the dark, cold night for a call from Mortimer, telling her he had arrived, so that she could share her silly fears for his wellbeing with him. To which, Mortimer would call her stupid, and she would laugh in relief and agree with him, that she was, indeed, a daft cow.

At the start of a second day with no contact from Mortimer; dear, thick set Mortimer, with his mane of black hair, scattered with silver which Vera ordered him never to disguise with any sort of colourant, she sat up and her silly fears grew. She wondered what time it was, knowing she should get up, bear the brunt of the bitter cold which waited for her outside of the duvet. She would go and find her address book to call Mortimer's sister again. She contacted Felicia so infrequently that Vera had not even stored her number into her mobile phone.

She got out of bed and the frigid coldness encased her in a tight, icy grasp. Vera became aware of an unpleasantness accompanying her down the first flight of stairs to the room overlooking the river, her office. The hairs on the back of her neck rose, and a ribbon of fear unfurled down her spine.

The room was still; dark. Shadows leapt at her and the silence deafened her. The snow outside blanketed any sound from the rushing river. The treetops bordering the window were covered in a thick, white eiderdown of snow. Vera padded through the office in her fluffy socks, making no sound – she felt as though she didn't exist, for some reason. It was when she reached the top of the kitchen stairs that she saw it. A shape. A rushing. A blur of something that should not be there.

Vera blinked and when she refocused her eyes in the semi darkness, cursing there being no electricity, the shape had gone and all she could see was what she expected to see, the waxed pine kitchen units, and a tiled worktop, housing the redundant coffee maker, the kettle, storage canisters. As she peered down the stairs, she smacked her head in frustration. She had a gas hob! Oh, the joy! Providing her gas supply hadn't mysteriously stopped working, Vera realised not only could she make a hot drink, but that the gas flame would give off some heat. What was she standing there for? She shook her head, thinking the cold was getting to her and making her start to forget things as well as see things that weren't really there. Did being cold do that?

She discovered her legs were shaking with cold and fear as she went down the steps to the kitchen. The silence was almost tangible. She stood and took hold of the worksurface, just to make sure that it was still there, and that she could feel something, anything. Steadier now, she breathed deeply and exhaled, her breath making a frost trail into the cold air. She rummaged in the floor cupboard, and found a pan, which she filled with water. All the while she functioned, did things, she was aware of the hairs on the back of her neck and on her arms standing on end. There was still that feeling of not being quite alone. Putting a pan of water on the hob to boil, she was grateful for the box of matches she kept in the cutlery drawer, next to the cooker. She watched in some satisfaction, the small, bright blue flame of the gas hob ignite and whilst the pan of water heated, she stood over the gas ring and warmed her frozen hands from the sliver of heat.

Outside was completely obliterated; the snow had erased the garden from view, all she could see were scattered white mounds where trees, bushes and fences might have been. The line of waste bins stood smothered, they looked like a row of sad snowmen, wanting to come in from the cold. She turned her attention from the kitchen window back to the task of heating the water and went to fetch a mug from the wall cupboard opposite the stairs. Before she could get there, the door to the cupboard flung open violently, narrowly missing hitting her on the forehead but causing her to step back sharply. Her elbow caught the handle of the saucepan, which overturned, and the almost boiling water cascaded over the cooker, splashing her legs.

She cried out in fear and pain, bending down to rub her legs, and throw a tea towel onto the floor to soak up the water spillage. Did she believe in poltergeists? What had caused the door of the wall cupboard to open? She definitely hadn't touched it. It had opened by itself.

Slipping on the spilt water, she reached for the pan again, half-filled it and put it back on the hob to boil. She was cold and thirsty. She was going to have a hot drink to warm her up, poltergeist or no poltergeist. Suddenly, Hal's words came back to haunt her, an appropriate choice of word, she thought, as her logic and reason battled with this morning's events.

"The cottage is haunted, didn't you know?"

Mortimer had pooh-pooed the idea and had told Hal off for trying to frighten her. Well, she was frightened now.

'Good!'

The word filled the room, a harsh, breathy whisper which seemed to echo through Vera's mind. Vera spun around, expecting to see the owner of the voice she had heard. Female, petulant, vindictive, and full of hate. Of course, there was no-one there. Vera was staring hard at the boiler, and the fridge; the rustle of petticoats and the sound of feet climbing the bare wooden stairs was just her imagination. Wasn't it?

A hissing sound from the cooker made Vera jump as she realised the water in the pan was boiling over the rim and had extinguished the flame. She turned off the hob and moved the pan to another unlit ring to cool. After she had picked up the sodden tea towel from the floor, she hastily made her coffee, and took herself and the mug back up the kitchen stairs.

Upstairs, the air was full of foreboding. Vera shivered at the rancour she felt, which hit her full force as she padded cautiously across the floor. Staring out of the office window, she wished she could escape to the virginal white world outside, where the world glistened with frozen diamonds, littering the landscape. *Maybe that was the answer,* she thought. Perhaps she should go out, clear her head. Decision made, she wandered into the living room and stood shock still at the sight which greeted her.

In disbelief, she stared at her possessions, her furniture. Books were scattered all over the floor, pages ripped, spines bent. Her two lamps were smashed to smithereens, splintered all over the wooden floor; her wing chair was overturned, the cushions ripped, feathers spilling from the gashes in the fabric. The drawers in the wooden coffee table had been pulled out, and the contents scattered all over the room. The vase of winter roses had been smashed, the stems twisted and broken, petals torn off. A damask curtain hung off the broken curtain pole.

Fear, when it grabs you makes your heartbeat thump loud and fast into the all-encompassing silence. Fear makes your blood cold and your skin hot. Fear makes you break out into a cold sweat and you can feel the beads of perspiration trickle down your back and your armpits. Fear stops you from screaming as loudly as you can, you have no voice. You are rooted to the spot, paralysed with dread and trepidation.

It took Vera some time to catch her breath, and take in the scene before her, which could not have happened without her hearing a disturbance. She put down her coffee cup, on the bare shelf of the bookcase. It could not have happened, despite the evidence being in front of her eyes. Things, THINGS did not fall off the shelves and rip themselves. Furniture did not overturn on its own. Ornaments and lamps did not fling themselves onto the floor and smash.

A rustling noise distracted her from her quiet terror, and she felt an unmistakable pushing sensation, as if someone had just bumped into her. She felt the material, soft and smooth and then a hand brushed hers. The room filled with coldness, menace, and the malevolence. She heard laughter again, high pitched, hysterical. It filled her ears, filled the room and it turned her blood to ice.

Now Vera moved. No longer rooted to the spot, she ran to the front door, searched in vain for the keys, which usually sat on the little hook above the gas meter cupboard. They were gone.

The laughter grew louder, and the atmosphere grew colder, more sinister.

Vera let out a sob and flung herself through the door into the office. Somewhere in the distance, she heard a phone ring. Her landline. She did not want to risk running up the stairs to her bedroom to fetch it. She wanted to get out of the cottage. She headed for the kitchen stairs, knowing a set of spare keys was hanging on the coat hooks next to the door.

At the top of the stairs, in her hurry, the sleeve of her dressing gown caught on the bannister. She tugged at it, trying to unhook herself, then she saw it. An unmistakable human shape, sort of floating towards her. This time she did scream, and she pulled frantically at the dressing gown. Thank God! It had unhooked! In her terror, she hardly felt the pair of female hands, which placed themselves in the small of Vera's cold back and pushed her towards the stairwell. Disconcerted, frightened, she heard another scream, not comprehending it was her own, one last sound.

Vera lost her balance. Her head hit the stone reveal as she fell, tumbling down the stairs she had joked with Mortimer, would be the death of her. She lay, crumpled and bleeding, her neck in a position which told the paramedics when they eventually arrived that it was broken.

As she lay there, all the lights suddenly switched on. Her mind, drifting into death, realised there had been a power cut, and like her life, now it was over. The last thing that she heard, mingled with the laughter which filled her ears along with the blood, was the sound of her phone's answering machine, picking up a call; thankfully still working after Vera had flung its handset at the wall. Too late now, she thought.

'Vera, it's Felicia. I'm so sorry I didn't pick up your call and darling girl, I'm afraid there isn't an easy way to break this to you, so I'll just have to say it. Vee, Mortimer's died – I know you two were close. I'm just so awfully sorry I have to be the one to break it to you, I can hardly believe it myself. He was killed in a car accident yesterday, trying to drive home from your cottage, I think. I am sorry. Ring me back when you can, I'm sure he'd want you at the funeral. We're trying to arrange it now. I'm so very sorry, Vera. I know Mortimer loved you dearly.'

***

Once again, the cottage was empty. The cobwebs gathered and the pain returned to his very soul, if he still had one left. She had gone. He did not know why. The sadness which filled his days hung over the cottage like a long, winters day. The emptiness echoed around the stone walls and the whispers from the past were silent once more.

MADISON

ELEVEN

Madison Cooper – Clarke stood shaking her mobile phone in frustration, unable to get a signal inside the living room of the small, stone - built cottage which was now hers. She strode outside, leapt up the uneven stone steps and tried in vain to make a call to her husband. Well, she supposed he was her ex-husband now; technically they were divorced, but a ten-year habit was hard to break. They got along well enough. She didn't worry too much about their marital status anymore, she was more concerned about being able to check on the welfare of their daughter, Phoebe, currently in the sole charge of her father, whom Madison doubted could look after himself, let alone a three-year-old.

Suddenly, miraculously, the call connected, and Madison gratefully heard the ringtone shrilling and then Perry's upper class nasally whine.

'Madison! Why the fuck will this child only eat spaghetti hoops?' In the background, there came the sound of tears, and a great deal of shushing going on.

Madison grinned.

'Blame your nanny, Perry, darling. I wasn't overseeing Phoebe's diet, remember? I was told I was only her mother! Anyway, let her eat spaghetti hoops if she wants them. It's no big deal.'

Madison's rich, old money Boston drawl rang through the small, cobbled street and sounded out of place in this quintessentially northern English village. 'Anyway, Perry, I'm here. It's *gorgeous!* So clever, finding this!'

'Hang on, hang on, Madison, let me wipe this child's face and send her to my mother.'

Walking up the hill to the left of the house, Madison basked in the heat of an unseasonally warm early April day. Halfway up, she realised she was out of condition, and she would need to do some serious workouts if she had any hope of walking up the hills and dales of her recently acquired surroundings. Perry's voice came back on the line.

'I'm glad you like it, darling,' he replied, having divested himself of his small daughter. 'Got it for a song, off an estate agent chum. Enjoy yourself, that was some case you defended. Well done, old girl. Bea will be fine here for a couple of weeks, till you settle in.'

Madison agreed, and disconnected the call, walking back to the cottage. The front door was open, and the removal men were carrying boxes in and out of the living room, working around the home stagers who were unpacking and creating order from the chaos of moving in. There was little furniture to move, Perry had told her that the cottage had been offered practically fully furnished, but Madison had insisted on replacing the beds, and all of the white goods in the kitchen.

She placed her mobile phone on the bow fronted china cabinet in the living room, and walked through the cottage, inspecting what the home stagers were doing. She had told them to remove the old wooden bureau from the back room, and it had now been replaced by stark white desks, upon which sat several computers. As a successful criminal defence barrister, Madison split her time between working remotely, reading briefs, taking instructions, and holding case conferences via *Skype* before returning to her room at one of the country's leading barristers chambers, One Deansgate, only if she was at a local court.

The road to her success had not been an easy one. Rather like the roads outside, it had been an uphill struggle to establish herself on the Northern Circuit, having had a brief, but illustrious rise to barrister fame within her London chambers. Upon realising she and Perry were never going to live happily ever after, she took the decision to divorce him and put some distance between them both. When she was accepted for a room at One Deansgate, she had been told by the Head of Chambers that she'd have to work hard for a living. Madison worked.

Turning, she ran up the stairs to the bedroom floor, and peered into the smaller room, which overlooked the river. It had been painted a soft, pink colour, and a matching single four poster bed with drapes the colour of old roses had been installed together with a patchwork quilt bunting. Strings of fairy lights were festooned over the window, a tiny pink desk and chair sat in the corner and built in shelving had been installed for Phoebe's designer clothes, which were being unpacked now.

Madison strode into the large front bedroom, with its pastel painted wooden bedroom furniture, and her new king-size sleigh bed with its almost masculine style duvet and check throw. She instructed the stagers to remove all the ornaments and the pretty, feminine prints which adorned the walls. Madison preferred her surroundings perfectly uncluttered, like her mind.

She stood for a moment, looking up the hill opposite the cottage, at the bright, uncluttered blue of the sky and the perfect uninterrupted view of the surroundings, so far removed from the smart, large terraces of Tufnell Park. She was going to enjoy being here, and when her future detached five-bedroom house had been built in one of the neighbouring villages, maybe she would keep the cottage as a weekend retreat for her and her daughter.

***

Thomas looked down at his small daughter, curled up against his wife's bosom. She was swaddled in blankets and coverlets, and her tiny face was screwed up in righteous anger at being so tightly bound. Tentatively, he reached out a nervous hand and brushed the pink, indignant cheeks with the back of his fingers. The baby let out a mewing noise and turned her face towards his fingers, her mouth seeking sustenance. Thomas laughed and his eyes met his wife's over the head of his new daughter.

'She wants feeding,' smiled Thomas and awkwardly, because she was unused to handling a baby and because the occupant of the swaddling was so precious to her, Isabella passed the baby to the wet nurse, wincing at the small stab of pain in her undercarriage, which she doubted would ever recover from the trauma of her daughter's arrival into the world.

Having borne the baby away, the wet nurse left the Master and Mistress alone and Isabella lay back against her feather filled pillows and comforters, exhausted.

Thomas smiled again, but this time, the smile was not a friendly one.

'So, Lady Harmer, we have a daughter,' he addressed Isabella, who had her eyes closed against the pain, and exhaustion and fear. She did not see Thomas's look.

'I'm sorry,' she whispered.

'What for, Isabella?' Thomas was heading towards the door to the master bedroom, now an entirely female domain during his wife's laying – in period. He would sleep in his Gentlemen's Quarters.

'A girl. I'm sorry.'

Thomas smiled unpleasantly again.

'Oh, I am not at all perturbed by the baby's *sex*, Isabella,' he informed her and with a touch of his fingers against his forehead, he turned and let himself out of the bedroom door without looking back at his wife, as she lay sadly against her pillows.

***

Henry's mother stared at the stiff card requesting the presence of Sir Peveril and Lady Winterton, Lord Henry

Winterton and the Honourables Charlotte, Grace and Amelia Winterton to the christening of the Honourable Arabella Henrietta Eliza Harmer, firstborn daughter of Lord and Lady Thomas Harmer. She sniffed, told the waiting footman to advise the relevant staff of the date of the christening, and dismissed the servant with a wave of her hand. The invitation card she placed on the mantlepiece, wedging it between the wall and a large brass candlestick.

Returning to her chair by the window, overlooking the courtyard where she had seen Henry sitting with Lady Harmer, many months ago, she sat with the baby's name playing over and over in her mind – Arabella Henrietta Eliza – and she wondered; hoping desperately, that the name had no connection with Henry.

***

Harry wondered, time and again, why this dirty little mill girl appealed to him so much as he unlaced a grimy corset and pulled out an equally grimy breast, which, actually tasted rather delicious- all warm and cotton like. He supposed that the cotton association came from the atmosphere inside the mill; a huge, cavernous building which was kept warm and damp in order to keep the cotton strong, but which produced a huge amount of dust from the yarn, and it was this that Harry could taste as he sucked on the pert, hard nipple. The dust got into the back of his throat and caused him momentarily to gag, and he had to suppress a cough. As he sucked the delightful little breast, he felt a brief pang of chagrin that his mill workers, like Elsie, were subjected to these sorts of conditions on a daily basis.

He often wondered where Elsie got her energy from, considering that she worked a twelve hour day at his mill, and then had to go home – one of his tiny cottages opposite the mill which was quite near to Enchantment Cottage – and prepare a meal for her father and her brothers, her mother having died in an accident at the mill a few years ago.

They were in Enchantment Cottage now, and it was fair to

say that Harry was quite enchanted by his grimy little mill girl. Her tiny, almost childlike breasts were exposed, and she was standing half naked in front of Harry, the Master, whilst he sucked on one nipple and caressed her other breast.

Elsie whimpered slightly as Harry took her whole breast in his mouth and sucked hard. Releasing her breast, his hands covered her buttocks, and he slapped her rounded bottom with the palm of his large hand. She let out a cry and Harry smacked her again, rather harder. He liked being rough with Elsie, she was young and malleable unlike Isabella, who after all was a gentlewoman and quite well educated despite being a woman. He had not bitten or smacked Isabella.

He had not moved around behind Isabella either, as he was doing to Elsie now. He could feel her tentative tension, her fearful reluctance at what he might be going to do to her, and her fear made him harder, and encouraged him to treat her more roughly, with little disregard for her pleasure because he simply wanted his.

'Lift up your skirts, woman,' he commanded thickly, as he started to undo buttons and pull down his trousers revealing a long and erect cock, foreskin pulled back, juices already spilling onto the large head. God, he wanted this girl, and he wanted her whatever way he could get her.

Elsie risked looking over her shoulder at the Master and saw him unbuttoning his trousers – he had taken her before and entered her, but never from behind. She was not entirely sure she wanted him to do this, but there was no way she could refuse him, being the Master; her and her father and brothers' employer and also their Landlord. Besides, she reasoned to herself as she glanced at his hugeness, the few extra pennies Harry tossed her afterwards, allowed them to eat meat once a week and she was able to take home scraps of cotton from the mill, which she could sew into petticoats or collars for the men.

Harry was behind her now. He made her bend over the feather pillow filled bed, and he pushed her head down amongst the blankets which smelt of lavender, and something else – another woman's aroma. His hand rested menacingly on the back of her neck as she felt his other hand guiding his huge manhood inside her very tight little fanny. She cried out as he thrust roughly inside her. Whilst Harry was turned on, Elsie was not, hardly knowing what to do and not being important enough to Harry to spend time on such delicacies as ensuring their coupling was pleasurable for her. He grunted, pulled out, spat on his hard cock, and plunged it back inside her.

She was wet now, and he was able to pump himself inside her, ride the grimy little bitch, and give her what he thought she deserved. Elsie's cries were not like Isabella's – moans of delighted pleasure – but the thought of the girl's discomfort just made Harry treat her more roughly. He slapped her bottom as he thrust, his hand on her neck tightening each time she cried out. Her small bottom grew red, his handprints visible on the dirty, creamy skin. He loosened his grip on her neck suddenly, and placed a hand on each red raw buttock, pulling the cheeks apart. She felt his manhood push into her back passage, and she cried in pain as he thrust in, over and over again. Each time she cried, he would let go of her bottom and smack her around the head. She pushed her mouth into the feather filled pillow and grabbed hold of the comforter, determined not to cry out again as Harry's cock stabbed into her anus and almost broke her.

Spasming suddenly, Elsie felt a hot wet sensation as Harry spilt into her bottom and over it, as he suddenly pulled out. She gasped, and he pulled her up, kissing the back of her neck.

'Go!'

Harry commanded, pressing two pennies into Elsie's clammy, dirty hand. Now he had taken what he wanted he did not want her in his presence. He heard her stumble down the wooden stairs and pull the door open. When her footsteps faded, Harry heaved a sigh, and sat on the bed thinking of Isabella.

TWELVE

Madison sat on the bed, thinking how much easier life had been living with Perry in his large, staffed house in Tufnell Park and at the same time she was trying to console a sobbing Phoebe, who'd woken in the night, screaming about a 'nasty lady,' in her room.

Making soothing noises at her small daughter, who was now clinging to her like a vine wraps around a tree branch, Madison realised that there was little chance of her getting back to sleep. The clock on the landing table told her that it was twenty - five past three. Having only managed to crawl into bed at one o'clock, after reading briefing notes till midnight, she had heaved herself tiredly into the old fashioned roll top bath to soak away the stresses of the day. Once in bed, sleep had not come easily, and she had begun preparing her opening statements for the defence she was working on. Madison sighed, and resorted to going downstairs to the kitchen to make warm milk for Phoebe and a jug of coffee for herself.

Tired, scared, and overwrought, Phoebe clung to her mother as Madison made her way down the precariously steep kitchen stairs. Halfway down, she lost her balance and stumbled, grabbing hold of the bannister in terror at the thought of falling with Phoebe in her arms.

'Lady pushed you,' said Phoebe, tearfully, tightening her grip around her mother's neck.

Madison was tired. Standing straight, she got to the bottom of the stairs, pushed Phoebe onto a kitchen chair and said quite firmly, 'Enough talk about a lady, Bea. There's no-one here except you and me. So, we are going to make a drink and go back upstairs to the sitting room so you can go back to sleep, and I can read before we have to get ready for work and nursery, okay?'

Phoebe stuck her bottom lip out at her mother, in defiance, but was then momentarily distracted by a flash of blue and the rustle of a long, pretty dress. Mesmerised at the small movement, Phoebe did as she was told, and stayed quiet, allowing Madison to make the coffee and the milk. Noticing that her mother put cookies onto a plate on the tray, Phoebe decided that the lady wasn't worth risking an early morning treat, and mother and daughter returned upstairs with their goody laden tray.

**

Walking into the robing room, Madison managed a weary smile back at her opposition. Having been on the road since seven that morning, transporting her daughter to nursery school, Madison had then driven at breakneck speed into Manchester city centre. Finally finding a parking space, she had arrived at Court slightly late, at half past nine, which accounted for her demeanour. Now, she was so tired, she simply wanted to lay down on the benches and sleep. Juliet, noting the other woman's distraction, snapped her fingers in front of Madison's face, returning her to the conversation.

'Yes, this should give old Harrington a dilemma, shouldn't it, two women Counsel?' Madison smiled.

'Misogynistic old bastard! Soon, there will be too many female barristers for him to discriminate against.' Juliet replied, speaking of the presiding judge, Lord Justice Harrington, who was well known within the circuit for having a tendency to direct the jury in favour of male Counsel.

'Bit of fun, eh, Maddie?'

Juliet gathered her notes and bags, and with a flourish and a slap on Madison's shoulder, she headed towards Court Two, where she and Madison were opposing each other in the case of *R – v – Carvell, Clayton and Bennett.*

Madison watched Juliet in her high heels, clip clopping down the long, dark corridor and finally disappearing around the corner, towards the lift. She enjoyed trials which involved Juliet. It had been a long time.

She turned her attention to getting robed, and then going to the cells to have a quick word with her client before the trail started. After that, she would just have enough time to find which conference room her co-defending Counsel were convening in and have a word with them to ensure that the everyone was all singing from the same hymn sheet, because only prayers were going to keep her client out of prison this time.

Thomas Carvell, or 'Tommy the Carver' as he was known to his contemporaries, was a nasty piece of work, and was facing a possible life sentence for his part in a series of bank and building society robberies committed over a two year period. Madison didn't particularly like him; she didn't like many of her clients but her dislike for Tommy Carvell was one that her professional mask of indifference failed to disguise. Looking at him now, bald, hook nosed with a small gold earring in his left ear, Tommy returned the look with a hint of menace.

'Where's the bloke? The one who usually looks after me? He usually keeps me on the outside. I hope you do, Miss.'

Madison smiled her best Barrister - Client smile, thinking that he looked rather like she imagined one of Oswald Mosley's Blackshirts to look at. Sinister, was a good way to describe it. His use of the salutation "Miss" – used traditionally in Court and chambers to address a female of the profession as "Sir" was used to address a male barrister – was deliberate, she understood, to let her know that he knew the ropes. Well, he wasn't going to intimidate her.

'If you are referring to Simon Latymer, he is working on another case. Your matter was returned and given to me.' Madison gave her client a cool look.

Tommy shrugged. 'You're better looking.'

'Oh, Simon's alright in a dark room.' Madison pulled some

paperwork out from her briefcase and scanned the documents relating to the case.

Tommy smiled. 'You'll do.'

'Thank you.'

'I would like to stay outside,' he told her.

'I shall do my best, Mr Carvell. Although I am sure that both Mr Latymer and your solicitor will have advised you that a custodial sentence is highly likely, given the evidence which has already been listed in the prosecution's disclosure. I suspect that unless you decide to alter your plea to guilty or tell me something which you have not already made your solicitor or Mr Latymer aware of, then the best I can do is aim for minimum sentencing. Thirteen years, in this case Mr Carvell.'

'Do your best. I'd rather be outside than in.'

Madison smiled, swept up her papers and nodded briefly to her client. Why did what he say sound like a threat?

***

Why did what he say sound like a threat, thought Isabella, staring down at her daughter, now officially named, and sleeping quietly in her arms still dressed in her christening robe.

Only the family had been invited back to Harmer House, for which Isabella was exceptionally grateful. The close proximity of Harry and his family in church, was unnerving. In particular, Isabella felt nervous of Lady Winterton, who kept shooting the most curious glances in her direction every time Harry approached her, which strangely, considering the nature of their past together, was not often. He had contented himself with striding over to the nurse holding Belle and simply looking at the baby before making an excuse to depart as early as politeness would allow.

Arabella, or Belle - her name had been shortened quite soon after her birth when Isabella's parents had arrived to inspect their new granddaughter – was growing heavy in Isabella's arms. She kissed the top of her daughter's head, remembering her parents visiting the baby for the first time. Isabella's father, Sir Graydon Mountbatten had stolen a peremptory glance at the baby, asleep in her wicker basket at the foot of Isabella's bed. He had looked at his daughter then, his usually stern face replaced by a look of loving pride and said to her, 'Lovely. What a little beautiful Belle she is, rather like her mother.'

Isabella had smiled and then cried at her father's approval of her daughter, whom she now handed back to an eager nurse and who was swept away to the nursery, three floors above the Morning Room, which was being used for the Christening party on the return from church.

Sighing, Isabella tried to stop feeling so afraid of her husband, who she saw making his way to her side. He must never find out, she thought, suddenly recalling how, after Belle's grandparents had departed, Thomas had smiled delightedly at his daughter and repeated her name as he cradled her, before handing her to her mother.

'Isn't she beautiful, Isabella? She is certainly deserving of the name Belle – my beautiful little Arabella *Henrietta* Eliza!' He beamed at Isabella, but it was not a pleasant smile and Isabella had blanched at Thomas's emphasis on Belle's middle name.

Now, as her husband took her hand at his daughter's Christening party, for the first time, Isabella wondered whether her husband was smarter than she had given him credit for.

***

Did she think he was stupid? Calling the baby Henrietta? Did she think he would not make the connection? He had left the Christening party, not caring for the breach of etiquette, and had ordered a groom to saddle up one of the horses. Now, sitting astride his chestnut Tudor, he surveyed the landscape that stretched out beyond Harmer House. Standing stoutly and defiantly above the moorland at Holcombe; the honey coloured stone house seemed to rise up to the horizon above the craggy course hills and green pasture, towering over ochre and brown scrub which dotted the rather foreboding hills and peaks. Beneath the house, the village of Holcombe Brook huddled rather humbly. Legend spoke of a strong-hold, or settlement, having been there on the site of the house since Saxon times. He had seen records dating back to the early thirteenth century, which indicated a scattering of farmhouses on the site where Harmer House now stood.

He couldn't understand why he was thinking of this now, perhaps it was because he didn't want to think of anything else. Reluctantly, he turned Tudor away from the ridge of the hill on which they stood and turned back towards his home, to his wife and the baby, planning his revenge for their causing him so much pain.

THIRTEEN

Phoebe was screaming again. The sound made Madison leap out of bed and almost trip up on the bedclothes and discarded case notes and files which had found their way to the floor once Madison had eventually drifted off to sleep in the early hours of the morning.

She threw herself across the small landing and into Phoebe's room. Phoebe, still screaming, was standing in the middle of her pretty pink bedroom, tangled up amidst the pink and cream bunting, which had been festooned around the drapes of her four-poster bed. Madison gathered her small, terrified daughter up in her arms, tugging at the bunting, trying to free her daughter from its grasp.

Phoebe was coughing now. Madison, realising the string was fastened around Phoebe's delicate neck, frantically tugged it off her daughter's skin with the superhuman strength terror gives you. Finally, thankfully, having made enough space between Phoebe's neck, Madison gave the string a final pull and it snapped, letting her untangle the sobbing child.

Gathering Phoebe's small, terrifyingly vulnerable frame close to her chest and nursing her against her mother's heaving breasts, Madison started to calm down. Kissing the top of Phoebe's head, the blonde curls damp with distress, she picked her daughter up in her arms and carried her back to the main bedroom. The small body relaxed into her caress.

Madison did not talk, apart from uttering soothing sounds, and soon, Phoebe fell asleep again, tucked against her mother's tartan check pillows. Drawing the matching duvet over her daughter's form, Madison got up and padded into the small bedroom at the back of the house.

The hairs on the back of Madison's neck stood up and she felt icy rivulets of foreboding trickle down her spine. Since she had moved here, Phoebe had been unsettled and her sleep patterns were erratic; she refused point blank to be put to bed to go asleep.

Madison, often tired and cranky herself from an arduous day in court, did not fight her daughter on this point, and usually let her fall asleep on the sofa downstairs, carrying Phoebe to the small pink bedroom once she herself was ready for bed.

Now, Madison understood Phoebe's reluctance. The room was not a pleasant place, she felt uneasy and, staring at the bunting, which *could not* have unknotted itself and placed itself around her daughter's sleepy form, Madison knew why. Something was wrong with this room. She shivered, and for the first time, noticed how cold the room seemed compared to the temperature elsewhere in the house.

Returning to her own room, and slipping back into bed, she felt Phoebe roll into her arms, and they slept, as the temperature in the small pink bedroom dropped once again and the shadow filled the room with hatred and fear.

***

Juliet grinned at her.

'Come on Madison, it'll be fun. You can't not come, everyone else is going. This trial is the pits, we need cheering up!'

It was tempting, thought Madison, her mind rushing to the small pink bedroom, to the bunting wrapped tightly around her daughter's throat, and to another night filled with sleeplessness and Phoebe's distress. She grinned back at Juliet.

'Alright, then. But I have to make a few arrangements first.'

'That's my girl!'

Juliet gave Madison's arm a squeeze and left her alone in the robing room to make the arrangements for a babysitter to collect Phoebe from nursery school, and bring her to *The Gotham*, where Madison booked two of the suites - one for herself, and one for the sitter and her daughter. She arranged for a change of clothes for herself to be couriered to the hotel from her room at Chambers, so that she had fresh clothes for the following day in Court. She instructed the sitter to collect clothes for Phoebe from *Millymog* in Chorlton, where Madison bought most of Phoebe' eclectic, bright and fun fashions.

All this done, Madison beat a hasty retreat to Court number two with a spring in her step and thoughts of a night out, away from the cottage, in her head.

***

Isabella could not get the cottage out of her head. Following Belle's birth, she found she missed Harry far more than she wished she did, and somehow, the thought of seeing the tiny little stone cottage again would make her feel closer to Harry. She had been utterly distraught when she had discovered Harry no longer wished to continue their relationship, after the baby had been born. Spoilt, greedy and selfish, the youngest daughter of over-indulgent parents, Isabella had simply assumed she could tell Harry Winterton to put their love affair on hold, while she gave birth to her child, and when she was ready, she could expect Harry to return to their former status. She had been wrong.

'*Isabella,*' Harry's curt note, returning her calling card had said. '*Whilst I hold you with great affection and I shall remember our time together with fondness, I am aghast that you should think we could return to the arrangement we had before your daughter was born. You have given birth to another man's child. Sadly, during our dalliance, I had believed you faithful to me. I had no idea your relationship with your husband had even been consummated, let alone that you would allow yourself to be impregnated by him whilst sleeping with me. Goodbye, Isabella. I wish you well. Congratulations on the birth of Lady Arabella.*'

That was it. No protestations of love, or even affection, just a callous ridding himself of something he no longer wanted.

Isabella had been incandescent with rage and almost took the decision to tell Harry the truth about Arabella, until her sister Clara had told her in no uncertain terms that doing so would only cause shame and embarrassment for the family, and how could she even think of such a thing? Angry at everyone and everything, Isabella raged until she felt that she simply had to go to the cottage, just to see it, to possibly see Harry.

She made plans over the next few days to visit the little house where she had spent so many blissfully happy hours with Harry, wrapped up in his adoration, and his body wrapped appreciatively around hers. Dressing with utmost care, wearing the peacock blue dress which she had worn the first time Harry had actually taken notice of her, when they had kissed in the courtyard of his parents' home. Then, telling her husband that she was going back into society after the birth, and making a few social calls, she took a carriage to the tiny village of Winterton, beyond excited at the thought Harry might actually even be there, and they would meet again. She knew she would be able to persuade him to resume their relationship and her visits to the cottage again.

In this, Isabella was wrong. Harry Winterton, having lost his heart and had it irreparably broken, would not be so easily won over. Having considerably hardened what was left of his heart, Harry's way of forgetting he was ever in love with one woman, was simply enjoying the pleasures of the flesh with another. It didn't matter who, none would ever be what Isabella had been to him and what she had been, he would never have again with anyone else. The baby might have made a difference, Harry had reasoned one lonely night at his cottage. If only Arabella had been his, he thought, over and over again, but he knew now that it was too late for any "if only's." Isabella had lain with her husband and had given him a daughter; Harry had given his heart and would never again lay with the person he had given it to.

Isabella enjoyed the carriage ride to the village, which lay betwixt open countryside and the river where the Mill stood, its grey grit walls shone peacefully in the summer sunshine, belying the rather dank and dour conditions which prevailed inside. She took pleasure in the journey from Holcombe, along the tiny dirt track which wound steeply down the hillside leading to the row of stone cottages where Enchantment Cottage stood stoutly at the end, larger than the others, separating it as the Masters. Isabella got out of the carriage and stood for a while arranging her skirts and gathering her wits and her courage.

A bay horse stood tethered to the stone wall opposite the cottage, and Isabella's heart leapt as she recognised Blaze, Harry's horse named so because it had a large white blaze running down its rather roman nose, and four accompanying white socks. Stopping to stroke the horse's nose, Isabella heard peals of laughter ringing out into the quietness of the surroundings. Harry! Her heart lifted; Harry was there!

She strode towards the cottage, not pausing to think why Harry would be laughing in the cottage if he were alone, when suddenly, there came the sound of a slap and a giggle and then the laughter again. Isabella stood in disbelief, and heard by more slaps. Then unmistakably, the sound of a woman's voice carrying out from the slightly open window of the bedroom where Harry had, once upon a time, entertained Isabella. Where he was now obviously entertaining Isabella's replacement.

Bitterly hurt, and embarrassed, Isabella almost ran past the cottage, up the hill to the right. Blinded by her hurt, she did not see the man walking down the hill, in the opposite direction to her. In her hurry, she cannoned into him, losing her balance. A strong hand grabbed hold of her arm and steadied her so that she did not fall to the ground.

'Dear me, Isabella,' said the man, still holding onto her arms, 'it seems to me that you are forever falling at my feet, dear woman.'

Isabella blinked, and suddenly the face fell into context in her memory and she smiled unsteadily at George Avery, the teacher at the school just a little farther up the hill.

'Mr Avery, I believe, Sir. Thank you, I do seem to always be tripping whenever you appear!'

George Avery smiled benevolently at her and finally let go of her.

'How fortuitous then, that I am here to catch you when you fall. I am afraid Lord Winterton is entertaining.' George looked at her with concern.

Isabella blushed. She had not contemplated that people might know of her affair with Harry and the thought unnerved her slightly. She waved her hand as if it were of no consideration.

'I do not need to see Lord Winterton,' she said, decisively. 'I am recently returned to society after the birth of my daughter, and I am simply taking the air.'

George Avery raised his eyebrows, but simply let the allusion pass, bowing to her.

'Of course, Lady Harmer, and may I offer my congratulations. Although it is a little early to consider, but I do hope I shall have the pleasure of tutoring your daughter, as the time comes.'

Isabella smiled graciously, shaking her head. 'Mr Avery, Arabella is the daughter of Lord Harmer, Sir. I do not think she will be needing an education within a poor school.'

'Education will change, Lady Harmer, by the time your daughter is of an age to require learning. Rest assured, one day all children will be required to be taught properly. Education shall not be limited to those who think they are entitled to it for much longer.'

George grew ruddy in his passion, and Isabella's interest was sparked by such. She smiled again, this time the smile was warm and encouraging.

'You speak with such passion, Mr Avery,' she told him, 'I have no doubts that your vision shall become more than the bounds of fantasy when spoken of in such a way!'

George Avery returned her smile. 'I do a lot of things with much passion, Lady Harmer – Isabella – perhaps one day you should care to find out?'

Isabella watched George Avery thoughtfully, as he bowed, and took his leave of her to carry about his business. She had been greatly moved by the passion he displayed and she, having discovered a passionate nature hidden within herself, decided that she should like to find out more about the other things George Avery was passionate about.

***

Madison was drunk – or at least very tipsy, she decided, as she carefully poured another generous slug of Jack Daniels into her glass. Juliet watched her quietly, from the other side of the booth and shimmied around the leather couchette until she was sitting next to her opposing Counsel.

'Hey, steady old girl, we're still in Court tomorrow, you know,' she cautioned, as Madison took a large mouthful and swallowed, savouring the taste of the American Bourbon. She drank it neat, Juliet noticed. Madison was a neat kind of person altogether.

Madison looked up at Juliet. She was blurry around the edges, like a caricature. Juliet's raven hair spilling across her face like ink dripping from the artist's pen; Juliet's red lips were luscious cherries, juicy and shiny, ripe for biting. Madison shook her head and announced her intention to go to bed. Unfortunately, her legs didn't seem totally co-ordinated with her brain, and as she stood, she fell forward onto the table. Juliet grabbed her and grinned.

'Whoa, lady! You need some help!'

Juliet stood up and let Madison lean against her and with

her arm around the other woman's waist, she managed to half drag her drunken colleague towards the lift. Once inside, she hoisted Madison against the wall of the lift compartment and stabbed at the appropriate buttons to take the lift up to the bedrooms. Madison groaned, and sort of slithered down the wall, landing with a thump on the lift floor with her legs crumbled underneath her.

The ping sounded, announcing that the lift had arrived at its destination and Juliet somehow managed to haul Madison upright. Together they sashayed across the foyer to Madison's room. Pushing the door and half stumbling, half walking, the two women clutched each other, giggling together at Madison's ineffective gait. They threw themselves in a half drunken heap onto the huge sofa in the living area. A sixty-inch television dominated the room, thoughts of kissing Juliet dominated Madison's mind.

'Coffee, Mads.' Juliet said firmly, as Madison flung her arm around Juliet's shoulders. 'We are in Court in the morning and I will make mincemeat of you in cross examination!'

Madison made a noise which sounded like a balloon deflating and then laughed.

'Never, Miss Harper. I shall have you know I am a shit-hot defence barrister!' Madison stood up, pulling Juliet with her, then lost her balance and fell to the floor, her head narrowly missing the rubberwood coffee table. Juliet also overbalanced, landing on top of her friend.

'Fuck the coffee, Jules,' drawled Madison, 'because I am going to fuck you!'

It had been a long time, but it was surprising what Madison remembered of Juliet; the way she liked to have the back of her neck caressed as Madison's full, eager lips crushed hers; the way she liked Madison to suck on her bottom lip, and bite it gently in between urgent, hot, hungry kisses, both women wanting to devour each other in their need.

The need now was overwhelming Madison. Pulling away from the deliciousness of Juliet's mouth, Madison ordered her to turn around, so that she could ease Juliet's dress off her slim, undulating body which moved in a frenzy of eagerness. There she was, thought Madison, drinking in the sight of her friend sprawled out on the carpet with her small, neat breasts and dark nipples standing erect. Juliet's legs were spread invitingly open, waiting. Waiting for the moment, the tempered, excited, moment of surrender to Madison's lips; when Juliet's swollen, engorged clitoris would be devoured. Madison felt a tremor of desire shiver through her body, her own breasts heaved at the thought of touching Juliet's and Madison knew that her own pussy and clit were slick with excitement; ready and willing and wanting.

Her eyes never left Juliet's as Madison undressed herself, throwing off her blouse, her skirt, revealing nakedness beneath, clad now only is sheer hold up stockings and high, pointed shiny stiletto shoes.

Juliet grinned. 'Just how I like you,' she whispered, hoarsely, her voice low and urgent with desire, 'get that body back down here!'

Madison lay herself on top of Juliet, feeling the softness of her breasts at variance with the hard peaks of her nipples. Madison's larger, pinkish brown tipped orbs spilled over Juliet's chest and then, they were kissing again, tongues winding around in one mouth, one heat. Madison's hands strayed down the other woman's body, which was now shaking with desire and anticipation. Reaching that secret place, Madison felt Juliet shudder as her fingers slid insistently across that slick, hot, throbbing wet nub.

In one part of her mind, Madison acknowledged how instinctive it was, the sexual act, between two women. She knew without Juliet having to guide her hand to the pulsing bud of her sex. Madison's fingers circled the hood of Juliet's clitoris, catching her desire so precisely. Juliet arched her back as Madison caressed her, large circles of lust played around a dripping wet, hungry pussy. With each firm stroke on Juliet's clit, Madison felt Juliet contract and without waiting any more, Madison plunged two fingers inside Juliet, pushing and feeling her pulse around her exploration.

Juliet let out a sign and a groan against the other woman's lips, and Madison felt her body being pulled harder, closer. Their hips locked together, and they gyrated against each other as Madison withdrew her fingers from inside Juliet and held them to her mouth. Juliet watched her friend suck each finger clean of the desire of the juices which had poured from her body.

Scissoring each other now, clit touching and pressing against clit. Juliet's dark, heart shaped pubic hair a stark contrast against Madison's completely shaven pussy. Looking down, Juliet groaned again as she saw the wetness, the droplets of Madison's honey glinting on the outside of her pussy lips; swollen, wet, full of promise. Juliet pushed against her friend again, her clit pushing harder against Madison now, frantically kissing her as Madison's hands sought Juliet's breasts and greedily pinched and pulled at her stiffening nipples.

Wanting to satisfy Juliet more, Madison's mouth meandered over her friend's delicious body, breasts, stomach and then her pubis. Her lips were against Juliet's labia, both could feel the heat from each other. Juliet groaned as she felt a kiss on her pussy lips. Madison kissed gently all over Juliet's outer labia, saliva mingling with juices which frothed from Juliet's pulsating pussy. Madison sought Juliet's inner lips and clitoris. Sucking hard, Madison took both full in her mouth and she heard her friend scream in ecstasy at the slow, rhythmic sensation, her tongue flicking out over the hard bud of Juliet's clit.

Long into the night, the two women satisfied each other, first with just their bodies, and later, Madison retrieved her bag, abandoned in lust, rediscovered in desperation, as she took out the small silver vibrator to use on her friend's clitoris. The buzzing toy when pressed against her sensitive bud built each sensation, each orgasmic pulsation to the point of it being unbearable and Juliet screamed. Madison enjoyed the feeling of power it gave her, seeing her friend a quivering, wet mess beneath her.

Eventually, sore, swollen and spent, both women crawled into each other's arms and slept soundly and safely, the court and the cottage forgotten amongst the debris of their desire.

FOURTEEN

Thomas paid the messenger the shilling he had promised him and waved the boy away so that he could cast a disagreeable backward glance at the debris of his life, his marriage, and the façade it had become.

He remembered Isabella as his bride and smiled briefly at her fresh-faced beauty on the day of her wedding; a slender, shy girl of eighteen, coming to him a virgin for him to make his own. Despite Isabella's lack of prowess in bed – virgins did not appeal to Thomas's rather eclectic bedroom habits – she was, he reflected, a fast learner. Thomas wondered where she had been receiving lessons. Mathematics had never been Isabella's strong point and her adding up so far as the conception of her eldest child was somewhat scanty in relation to the rare couplings they had partaken of. However, she was, and still looked, beautiful. He remembered winding his hands into her hair, the colour of a golden autumn afternoon, rays of sunlight shimmering within the long strands uncoiled now that she was a married woman in bed with her husband. His smile turned sour as he wondered how many other hands had uncoiled her braids and made her theirs whilst they held her hair and sought out places which only, he, her husband, should know how to find.

His hands curled into tight fists and he beat his own brows in anger and frustration. Thomas was a man of the world. His marriage had been a business deal, he accepted Isabella in return for the growth in the mills – his two merging with the pre-existing connection between Mountbatten's three and the Winterton's empire. He knew that love was not part of the arrangement, but he had hoped that Isabella would have given him respect, courtesy and discretion.

Switching his thoughts to the nursery, and how quickly Isabella was filling it with her brats, a wave of disgust swept over him, a silent burst of hatred for his wife and the children she had borne; children he had given his name to, whom he fed and clothed and who would one day inherit his estate and everything that he stood for, should she ever give birth to a boy. He stood up, unable to contain his loathing and he paced up and down the drawing room where he had sat doing his accounts, having dismissed his bailiff from the job because he needed the distraction from his hatred.

***

Isabella hated being pregnant. Forced to genteel occupation and curtailed from activity of a sexual nature, she was bored and resentful, as well as frustrated that she had had to withdraw from society until the birth of the third baby. She sighed heavily, moving her bulk to a more comfortable position as she watched Belle trying to entertain her baby sister, Georgina, with a silver rattle.

The girls painted a pleasing scene, Belle gave every indication of living up to the nickname given to her by Isabella's father, Sir Graydon Mountbatten; she was a pretty little thing with flaxen curls framing a heart shaped face. At two years old, she was destined to beauty. Georgina's looks were still undefined as yet, being only one and having the baby chubbiness which hid definition of her features. She was a complete contrast to her older sibling in that Georgina was dark, and sallow complexioned. When Isabella had given birth to her, she had thought her alien, so unlike her other daughter was she. Only the dark colouring of Isabella's father prevented those in society casting their own conclusions about whether or not Georgina and her sister had been fathered by the same man.

Thomas seemed not to notice. He spent the requisite amount of time with the girls, appearing first thing of a morning in the nursery to accept Belle's polite "Good Morning Father," and Georgina's baby chatter, and he kissed Isabella on the cheek before departing either to the mills, or to the large estate which surrounded Harmer House. Isabella could not fault him in his treatment of the children, and she fervently hoped that she would be able to present Thomas with a child who would be his son, this time.

She did not for one moment consider Thomas knew perfectly well neither of the children she had borne were his. She had not the idea that whilst she gestated, and nurtured these children, Thomas also knew all he needed to about her extra-marital affairs first with Harry Winterton, and then with the schoolteacher, George Avery. Thomas had not yet worked out who was responsible for Isabella's latest pregnancy, but he knew damn well it wasn't his child she was carrying.

Isabella shifted uncomfortably again and sighed because pregnancy was the unpleasant result of some more than pleasant couplings. True, she had had to seek company with her husband each time she suspected she had fallen, and thankfully, Thomas had had no objection to her amorous advances. She wondered why it was that she was unable to simply perform her wifely duties with her husband, and bear children that were actually his, rather than seek her sexual pleasures elsewhere and present her husband with the children of her lovers.

Her sister, Clara, gave her the answer on a brief, whirlwind visit south with her husband en-route to London, they stayed at Harmer House for two nights during which, Isabella confessed her erring to her sister, who peeled with laughter and patted Isabella's hand comfortingly.

'Darling girl, do you think all the children who inherit these estates from their so-called fathers were conceived within wedlock, and belong to the man married to their mother? Come, Isabella, forget that notion, and remember that you are not the only one who strays outside of your marriage. Thomas has numerous mistresses, as you well know. Do not be concerned at all that he will not claim your children. He has no option. It is the way of the world.'

***

'It's the way of the world, Madison, why are you so angry?' Juliet smiled at Madison's belligerent expression and watched her friend stomping around the robing room in righteous anger.

'But it makes a mockery of the trial, of my whole defence!' She cried, throwing down her wig and pouting petulantly.

'What, because your client has turned Queens? Oh, come on, it makes the whole thing easier, to be fair. Thomas Carvell is guilty as hell, and you and I both know it – he would have faced life, Madison, not just a minimum sentence here. It happens all the time and you know it.'

Madison sighed. Juliet was right, of course, defendants turned Queen's Evidence all the time, and Thomas Carvell was obviously no exception. It was a sort of "Get Out of Jail" card for defendant's whose backs were to the wall. Given Tommy Carvell's criminal record, and the seriousness of the charges which he was facing; the possibility of a life sentence for armed robberies, one of which had seen the actual discharging of bullets and the killing of a security guard was all too close for comfort. His decision to turn Queen's Evidence – to request to a prison officer that he wanted to speak to a senior police officer which basically meant in a very coded message, "I have information about my co-defendants that will implicate them in other unsolved crimes and in exchange for this information, I can get out of jail faster," was probably a canny move on Carvell's part. It wouldn't make him particularly popular with his co-defendants or other inmates of whichever prison he was sent to whilst serving a much shorter sentence than his various crimes usually warranted, but then, he wouldn't care once he was out and neither would Madison. The only thing which didn't sit right with Madison is the fact that someone else knew. Someone else knew that her client had done this and had told her. Her client had not.

Barristers usually get to know if their client had turned Queen's Evidence. Once their client had passed on the information to a senior police officer, the Judge presiding over the trial would be passed a note advising him of that fact. There would be a conference in Judges' chambers advising her of the fact, and the trail would continue as it would have without the defendant having basically "grassed" on the other defendants. The only difference would be in the length of the sentence once the defendant had been found guilty.

Madison allowed Juliet to soothe her ruffled feathers, but she was secretly filled with disquiet over the whole trial. Things had not been proceeding well for the defence. There was too much damning evidence against her client for her to even contemplate a "not guilty" verdict, and however many rabbits she tried to pull out of hats in order for the defence to secure a minimum sentence for Tommy Carvell, her conjuring abilities on this trial were weak. The anonymous, gruff voice on the other end of her private line in Chambers last night simply declaring, "Thomas Carvell has turned Queen's Evidence. You need to tell him to watch his back," had done nothing to alter her opinion that she should have returned the matter or wish that Simon Latymer had been available for it.

Sighing again, she tried to do what Juliet suggested and what she herself knew was the correct thing, indeed the only thing, she could do and that was carry on with the trial. Perry had once said to her that the whole court thing was like play acting, and Madison had laughed and disagreed. They had had a bit of a row about the whole thing. Now, pulling on her gown, and fixing the bands on her collar, with the knowledge that her client had turned in evidence which would potentially incriminate the other defendants and exonerate him to the tune of a significantly lenient sentence, Madison wished she had time to call her ex-husband and apologise for the argument.

She walked to the court room slowly, knowing now that her whole defence was farcical. She could get up and recite the alphabet backwards and her conduct of the case would not matter one iota. Her client had turned Queen's Evidence and in turn, had turned the case into nothing more than play acting with an unexpected ending. Except for Tommy Carvell, he would now get away with murder, literally; and be able to serve a ludicrous sentence for it. He'd be sitting at home enjoying tea with his family whilst his co-defendants served his time, too. There certainly was no honour amongst thieves in this trial, she thought as the Usher opened the solid wooden double doors to admit her to the court room.

***

For once, she was glad to be home. Judge Harrington, having better things to do than sit around a draughty old courtroom in central Manchester, had ended the day's proceedings early, at three, and Madison had collected a delighted Phoebe early from her after school club. Now they were both sitting in the tiny basement kitchen of the cottage drinking lemonade, after an unscheduled visit to the park and the swings across the bridge which separated the two halves of the village – Higher and Lower Winterton. Reaching for the revered, almost sacred bottle of *Watenshi* Gin, Madison felt no guilt in pouring a second hefty measure into the crystal tumbler despite the fact that the *Cambridge Distillery* only produced six bottles per batch and that she was currently knocking back one of the world's most exclusive gins. Hell, some lemonade, she grinned to herself, watching her small daughter drinking the non-alcoholic cloudy stuff which always made Madison think of 1950's Britain, for reasons that she couldn't explain.

'Bad man!' Phoebe announced, suddenly pushing away the lemonade and starting to cry.

Madison took a large slug of gin and sighed. She had promised herself that she would take more notice of her daughter's, what? Intuition? Or childish make-believe? Whatever it was, tonight Madison had no patience with Phoebe's petulance. She looked at the small bottom lip, stuck out in fear and defiance, and at the challenging expression on her daughter's three-year-old face and Madison had had enough.

'Bed!' She announced to her daughter as she scooped her up

in her arms and headed for the stairs.

With much protestation from the small, surprisingly strong arms and legs which scratched, and beat and kicked her as Madison carried her daughter upstairs, she eventually managed to undress the wriggling child and tuck her into the pink four poster bed with a peremptory kiss on the forehead and a firm, 'Goodnight, Phoebe!'

Madison switched on the night light and then closed the door, leaving it slightly ajar. Standing on the landing, she peered downstairs and shrugged. She really couldn't be bothered going back downstairs again. What for? She hated drinking alone and the only company she had was a truculent toddler. She decided to go to bed herself.

Pausing only to apply her eye-wateringly expensive cleansing balm, which she loved because she could simply smear it all over her face, wipe it off with a muslin cloth, and then apply lashings of moisturiser, Madison was stripped and in the big sleigh bed quickly, fed up with the day, half an ear listening for disturbances from across the landing. Nothing.

'Good,' said Madison, to herself, 'I need this.'

She leant across the bed to the nightstand and opened the drawer. Inside were several wands, vibrators, and other various sex toys. Madison opted for a vibrator, large, pink, and veined. She needed something to penetrate her tonight, as opposed to the wands and clitoral stimulation she usually enjoyed, tonight she wanted to fuck herself.

She lay back on the rather hard pillows, encased in their tartan pillow shams, threw the duvet off her still luxurious body, revealing the round, pale orbs with their pink, pert nipples; the thankfully flat stomach, and the shaven pussy; lips glistening with need. Madison groaned, and parted her legs, switching the vibrator on, smiling at the comforting buzz, anticipating the pleasure she could give herself.

Closing her eyes, she guided the tip of the vibrator over the slick wetness of her pussy, feeling the gentle vibrations, the insistence of pleasure and she groaned as she ran the toy in circular motions over her entire pussy, which swelled with each expert flick of her wrist and hand. Enjoying the delicious sensations of her self-love, Madison spread her legs wider and wriggled down further into her big, empty bed. How long it had been since she had had a man between her legs? The thought made her even more hungry and she moved the tip of the vibrator, placing it on her hard, tumescent clitoris. She groaned aloud as the hot bud flooded with pleasure, and the tremors of desire grew and grew, shooting from the tight hood towards her pussy in bolts of delight. Greedily, she thrust the vibrator inside of her and arched her back at the sheer delight of being filled. She imagined, as she pushed her sex toy further into her aching pussy, she imagined a man, his cock, thick and hot and hard, penetrating her, possessing her.

She ground herself against the pink toy, feeling the wetness gush from her inner lips till her thighs were soaked and her fingers slippery as she pushed the vibrator in, out; in, out; buzz, buzz, buzz. *Oh God,* she thought, stretching towards the sensation that was building inside of her, the want, the need, her pussy started to contract. Madison was shaking, her free hand clutching her breast, pinching her erect nipple as she crested on the wave of her orgasm, arching her back, wanting, needing the release.

The scream.

It pierced through the myriad of pleasure, ripped the quiet night air apart.

The scream.

Madison sat bolt upright in terror, all thoughts of pleasure and climax forgotten in every wretched sob. Throwing herself out of bed leaving the vibrator, still buzzing, abandoned on the floor as she flung herself towards the bedroom door, horrified as the screams of her child grew louder, more terrified, with every second.

Phoebe's bedroom was empty.

Madison stared around wildly, in disbelief at the abandoned bed, the absolute stillness of the room, broken only by the intermittent terrified screaming and the sudden loudness of Madison's own heart beating ferociously against her rib cage.

Phoebe! Where was Phoebe?

The screams were heart wrenching, the sound of true terror and they tore at Madison's pounding heart. Her wild eyes scanned the room and fell, disbelievingly at the sight of the window. The closed, casement window.

Oh, God!

Phoebe!

Madison bit back a scream. Her tiny, three-year old daughter, shaking visibly and screaming, screaming loudly, was harrowingly perched on a precariously narrow ledge beneath which there was a sheer drop down into the steep rockery, and beyond that, the river relentlessly cascading through the shattered night.

Fear pulsated through Madison's body like a piston and made her drip ice cold terror, mingled with sweat and the remnants of the sexual desire she had been enjoying only moments before. She ran towards the window shouting to Phoebe to stay still.

'Don't move, Phoebe! Don't breathe. Don't do anything, darling baby. Mommy is coming. I'll get you. Stay still!'

Through the inky darkness, the terrified child spotted her mother moving towards her, and her frightened sobbing ceased, replaced with a silence that enabled Madison to think, through the loud thumping of her own heart.

She twisted the old-fashioned casement catch on the window. In keeping with the authentication of the modern additions to the house, the double-glazed windows had been modelled on the original fitments, and instead of having a press and release catch as most modern windows have, this one in Phoebe's bedroom had one which had to be unlocked and twisted at the same time as being pulled inwards before the window would move outwards. Thankfully, the key was still in the lock.

Madison refused to think about how the window was locked and her daughter balanced on the ledge outside. She was almost sobbing herself as she fought with the stiff catch, twisting, and turning time and again in desperation; fear making her stupid and pushing when she should be turning and all the while, Phoebe was outside, with a vast drop of death beneath her, as she trembled and made little sounds of terror.

'Stay still, Phoebe!' Madison commanded, feeling the lock give slightly, as she turned the handle inwards, gratefully hearing it squeak, as if it had not been opened for years. She saw Phoebe start edging towards her.

'NO! Phoebe, baby! Stay still, I won't be able to open the window if you are in front of it. *Stay there!'*

Frantic with fear, Madison pushed the window with all her might and with a groan and a sigh, the window opened slowly, and she was able to fling her upper body outside and grab her sobbing child, pulling her inside, to safety.

Into her arms.

Phoebe was freezing. She wound herself around her mother's neck and nuzzled into her. Madison felt the small body shaking, convulsing with fear and she buried her face onto Phoebe's small, blonde, precious head and sobbed herself.

They stayed there for a long time, mother holding daughter silently, whilst the terror subsided and the stars in the clear night sky twinkled mockingly. All around, the malevolence curled its way through the cottage and the evil settled itself around them, outwitted tonight, but waiting for another opportunity.

FIFTEEN

Never one to miss an opportunity, Isabella's father was making the most of the *Industrial Revolution*. Along with several like-minded men, he had formed a consortium which proceeded to buy and build mills for spinning, weaving, and printing.

None of this made an impact on Isabella, except for the fact that the men, her father, her husband, Lord Peveril Winterton, Sir Robert Peel and Harry Winterton, often met at Harmer House. Tucked in between Ramsbottom and Holcombe, Isabella's home was the perfect meeting place, easily reached from either direction across the green-grey patchwork of fields and smallholdings which clung to steep precipices and then fell away dramatically to the somewhat barren and often inhospitable crevices of farmland. Despite Sir Robert being an exceedingly prominent politician, a subject in which Isabella had no interest, the consortium had little effect on her except for the need to be responsible for entertaining Harry Winterton, in addition to the other business associates of her husband.

Isabella was still beautiful, despite now being a mother to three children; the beautiful Belle, now four and living up to her name both in looks and in character; Georgina, an awkward child lacking Belle's beauty but an exceptionally clever little girl and of course, the heir, the son and the youngest child, William. Harry, looking at her now as she oversaw the serving of refreshments for the five gentlemen during yet another meeting, saw her beauty and that it had become something rather different to how he had remembered it. Whereas once, it had been robust, tempestuous even, a very evident beauty; childbirth and motherhood had taken away Isabella's edge and replaced it with a gentleness, a subtlety she had not had before. It was like viewing her through a fine, early morning mist.

She moved now, instructing the maids, ensuring the important male guests had everything they needed. Then, nodding to her husband, she withdrew, walking backwards behind the departing maids and closing the large double doors as she vacated the drawing room. As she stood between the doors, her astonishing azure eyes had met Harry's quizzical brown ones in one unguarded look of shared understanding and longing.

Harry couldn't concentrate. So far, during these meetings he had only the knowledge that this was Isabella's home, that she was somewhere, within its walls. He had not had to lay eyes on her before now, but now that he had seen her, felt her presence, and shared that one impassioned look, he knew that she was what had been missing from his life all these years. Apologising to his associates and pleading a headache, he had to excuse himself, eventually, from the drawing room.

She was waiting in the Great Hall, as though she knew he would come.

At first, speech was impossible, and they simply stared at each other across the years; across the memories of passion, excitement, disappointment and hurt. Their look built a bridge where once there had been a chasm between them.

Harry was the first to break the eye contact. He coughed, turned his head lest she see how his emotions filled his eyes, his mind. In that moment, he knew he wanted her again, and moreover, he knew that she wanted him, too.

'I must go, Lady Harmer,' he announced, 'I have a headache. I thank you for your hospitality, but I am returning to my cottage.'

At the mention of the cottage, the tiny stone terrace which had borne witness to their passion, Isabella flinched. It was almost physical, the longing she felt.

'As you wish, Lord Winterton. I trust you shall be feeling better shortly.'

'I shall spend a few days there, recuperating from this

beastly headache. It is a peaceful place, my cottage. I find it far more relaxing than Winterton Hall. Maybe that is why it's called Enchantment Cottage.'

And with a bow, he took his leave.

***

'Perry, I need to leave this fucking cottage!' Madison was on the phone to her ex-husband after spending the remains of the night clutching her daughter against her; both of them burrowed beneath the duvet within the safety of Madison's huge sleigh bed and outside, the lamp on the corner casting a comforting orange glow into the bedroom.

Her first call that morning was to Chambers, to let them know she was unable to appear, and she sought leave to be excused. Thomas Carvell could go to Hell! Someone, or something, Madison shivered at the thought, had tried to kill her daughter last night, and there was no way on this planet that she was going to spend another night here with her.

Then she called Perry, who was listening now to her Bostonian accent, which she had never lost, despite living in England for nearly twenty years.

'Madison. Stop! Are you saying that someone tried to kill Phoebe? Then call the police, Mads, it's not me you need, it's the local plod.'

Madison almost exploded with rage. 'Perry, you need to come, you need to fetch me and your daughter from this place! This isn't the only thing that's happened, and Phoebe is scared most of the time. Perry, help me on this. Please get here as soon as you can!'

Listening to his ex-wife yelling into the phone from a few hundred miles away, Perry sighed and reminded himself again why his former marriage had not worked. This was so typical of Madison, her selfishness, her demanding self-consumption, once again trying to overtake him. He shook his head sadly at the vanity which had driven a wedge between them as man and wife and which had eventually made her his ex-wife and made him a whole lot happier being without.

'Madison, I cannot just drop everything! I, too, do have a career. I have a job to do and other responsibilities. I'm sure you and Phoebe will be fine. If there is a problem, call the police or a priest!'

He disconnected the call angrily. Even now, she had the ability to make him doubt his own self-worth. He threw the phone down onto the bedside table, and turned his attention back to the naked, delicious delight of a woman who had been spread beneath him before Madison's call had distracted him. He delved joyfully back into the pleasures of her flesh which he had been just about to turn into a shaking, quivering disarray.

Madison stared in disbelief at the telephone she was clutching tightly in her hand, unable to quite comprehend that Perry had hung up on her and was leaving both her and their daughter in this dreadful predicament. Lifting her eyes from the phone, which she then threw back on the bed, she put her head in her hands. A few hundred miles away, her ex-husband threw himself back in his bed and returned himself to taking his new wife in his hands, wondering whether or not he should have told Madison about his second marriage.

Carefully surveying the bedroom, Madison became aware of the peculiar sensation of being watched. It was a feeling that made the hairs on her arms and the back of her neck stand on end. A feeling of unease, uncertainty. It made her voice just that little less firm, and surprisingly, her resolve to leave crumbled a little. Where would she go? How could she conduct a major criminal defence trial without the infrastructure of her home office, her files, her papers? How would the upset of yet another move affect Phoebe – thankfully recovered from last night by Madison's confirmation that her daughter had simply had a bad dream. Perhaps she was being silly. Perhaps there was a logical explanation after all. Phoebe was a curious child;

it wasn't beyond the realms of possibility that she had unhooked the bunting which had caught around her neck a few days ago. It was perfectly feasible that she could have opened the casement window and climbed outside but was reluctant to confess her naughtiness to her mother.

Madison glanced at Phoebe now, sitting on her mother's bed, still wearing her pink gingham check pyjamas, and totally absorbed in a game she was playing with two of her dolls. Madison was in her nightgown even at twenty past eight on a weekday morning. This is no good, she decided. The cottage was their home, at least until the new one was built. Squaring her shoulders, Madison decided that the best thing to do was for both mother and daughter to have a bath together, then dress and go out for the day, first stopping off at the garden centre across the bridge for a delicious breakfast and then exploring the surrounding countryside. A long, long day trip out – a reprieve from the cottage, a change of scenery for Phoebe, and then they would get back to the cottage thoroughly tired out and hopefully to a more restful night for both of them.

***

Isabella stared around the cottage delightedly, and almost clapped her hands at her sheer pleasure of being back inside Harry's dark, cosy terrace home. She twirled around inside the tiny living room, skirts flying and the rush of air the motion made, sent sparks flying up the chimney breast from the flames which danced in the hearth. Harry was not there, but he had thought about her. The fire had been lit, and there were blankets on the sofa as well as a tray of sweetmeats and a bottle of wine. Taking off her bonnet and setting it next to the tray on the oak table at the side of the fireplace, Isabella sank into the glorious comfort of the sofa, and popped a sweetmeat into her mouth.

When Harry finally stooped through the wooden entrance door, returning once more to his cottage rather than to the Big House because he felt that dinner wouldn't be nearly so entertaining at his manorial home, he thought what a pretty picture Isabella made. Reclining on the sofa, replete after an afternoon by the fire, nibbling sweetmeats and sipping wine; the fire had flushed her cheeks and as she turned and watched Harry enter the sitting room, her face grew warmer still and as Harry said to her later, in bed, she flushed with love.

Neither spoke. There were no words. Harry simply held out his hands to her and she gave hers to him, allowing him to pull her up from the sofa. He led her up the small staircase to the bedroom that contained so many of the memories which Isabella had tried to forget, in her belief that Harry had forgotten her.

As if he was able to read her mind, at last, he spoke.

'Never forgotten, Isabella. Suspended perhaps; maybe even pushed aside, but never forgotten.'

He traced the delicate lines which had appeared around Isabella's eyes and which spilled onto her cheek bones; his fingers leaving the gossamer touch of love as she lifted his hand from her face to her lips and she kissed his palm in a gesture so simple, so full of love and adoration, that Harry felt certain that if he had been able to tear his eyes from Isabella, he would have been able to see the love they felt surround them.

Feeling her lips on the palm of his hand, he felt a surge of desire rise within him, and he could no longer bear not to touch her. The wait had been too long, the exile of motherhood and circumstance too harsh and the dalliances he had had with others too futile. He needed her, he wanted her, and he was going to have her.

Isabella felt the need and responded with a desideratum of her own as she began to mirror his movements and undress him also. She felt his hands removing the layers of cloth, satin, and lace from her body and she shivered with excitement, fumbling over his buttons and fastenings until they were both naked, both wanting and needing what they had not had for so long.

Harry cast a critical eye over Isabella's ripened body; heavier breasted, thicker waisted through childbirth but still beautiful. Still desirable, he thought, still with curves which begged him to touch her, to enfold the rounder, fuller breasts into his hands, and then his mouth as he sucked on first one large and erect nipple, and then the other. Isabella threw back her head, abandoning herself to the pulling sensations which created little ripples from nipple to stomach; from stomach to the hub of her sex between her legs which she could feel growing wet in anticipation of Harry being inside her.

Falling into a tangle of love in Harry's big wooden bed, their bodies fused together easily, knowingly. Beneath her, he was surprised and then ignited afresh as she straddled him, as the softness of her thighs surrounded him, and he felt the heat and the wetness between them. Looking up at her, he could see the voluptuous, rounded breasts heaving with need, and his hands instinctively encased them. She groaned as she felt him take each nipple between forefinger and thumb and he teased them, and pulled and pinched and the actions, the very touch of him, made her shake and shudder.

Her hands took his large, long, and hard penis and guided it to the place between her legs where he could make her his. She held his engorged tip, circled it tantalisingly around the wetness of her outer lips, and slowly, oh so slowly, she lowered her aching and swollen womanhood onto him. Now it was his turn to groan, as he felt her surround him, her fanny grasped him and contracted around him as she impaled herself upon him.

All thought abandoned, as love took precedence long into the inky violet dusk. He moved within her as the ochre and amber trails of a blazing sunset bled into the velvety mauve of the evening sky and as his cries of triumph resounded in the air, the sun bowed down and stood aside so that a multitude of stars could light the way to their love.

SIXTEEN

Normally, Madison loved this moment. The moment when the jury walked back into the courtroom from their deliberations. The moment she knew when the foreman would deliver the verdict of the twelve men and women upon whom her client's immediate future depended.

She watched as the seven men and five women all walked in single file back to their seats. Jurors at this stage all wore the same nervous and serious expression on their faces, as they waited for the Clerk to address the Foreman, to ask him or her, "Have you reached a verdict upon which you are all agreed? Please answer yes or no." The charges would be read out and the Foreman would be asked, "Do you find the defendant guilty, or not guilty?". This would usually be Madison's moment.

Today, she saw all this happening, but Madison was not filled with her normal end-of-trial confidence or euphoria which she usually felt having delivered a confident, solid, defence and a searing closing statement. She would watch the jury filing back into court, and she would *know* she had cast the element of doubt of her clients' guilt in the minds of the jurors upon whom his or her liberty relied.

Adjusting her wig, she let out an audible sigh and leant back into the bench, head back and eyes closed. For the first time since she was a junior, she would not hear the verdict she wanted. She would not get the outcome her defence deserved. Her ever increasing catalogue of successfully defended cases had earned her a kudos she now took for granted. Her reputation made her popular and much in demand, yet she wished she had not accepted this case, because of course, Thomas Carvell would be found guilty. Not only was there the damning evidence against him, but the little matter of turning Queen's told of his guilt and made a mockery of Madison's defence. Thinking back to their first meeting, and his implied threat, *"I like the outside, Miss,"* coupled with the anonymous telephone call tipping her off about her client's actions, Madison realised she had always felt uneasy about this whole trial. Who else had known what Carvell was doing, and more importantly, *how* did they know and why were they contacting her? Should she have spoken to someone about the tip off? She knew it was too late now for a mis-trial ruling. Had someone got to Carvell? Or was this just a carefully constructed avoidance of justice by her client?

Adding to her worries, during her questioning of Thomas Carvell it had felt as though they were not on the same side. Almost as if they were pitting their wits against each other instead of working together to enable the casting of the doubt required. Of course, Madison reasoned, Carvell knew it didn't matter, now that he'd turned Queen's, but she wondered why he was trying to wrong foot her by giving the wrong answers to her questioning when he was in the witness stand. The whole thing was a joke, Madison decided as she sat upright, listening to the Clerk speaking to the jury Foreman.

'Have you reached a verdict upon which you are all agreed?'

It's irrelevant, Madison concluded. They would find him guilty. When you turned Queen's, it was usually because you knew you were going down for a long time, but you were exchanging information for a shorter stay. Carvell knew himself there was little chance of any other verdict, but the sentence would not fit the severity of the crime and that, in itself, was the real crime. Their verdict didn't matter, and neither did Madison's defence or the death of the security guard, killed, so the evidence said, by Carvell in the last of the armed robberies with which he had been charged along with his co-defendants. Thomas Carvell was, literally, going to get away with murder.

The "Guilty" verdicts were returned, one by one and at the end of the process, the courtroom fell into silent expectation as the Judge began sentencing. Carvell's co-defendants were dealt with first. Twenty-five years. Madison glanced at Carvell. He smirked back at her and Madison turned away, disgusted with herself and the legal system which allowed someone to escape with their life, having taken someone else's.

The next words which the courtroom should have heard were, "Life Imprisonment" for Thomas Harmer – Carvell. Instead Judge Harrington considered ten years an appropriate sentence. The Court erupted into a loud uproar. People stood, shouting at the bench. Tommy Carvell, in the dock, was standing up punching the air. Security personnel were advancing towards the bench and the public gallery. Madison's colleagues were looking around nervously at the fracas around them. The hushed murmurs were becoming angry cries.

Madison heard the sentence at same time as the sound of a whiplash crack, resounding through the disbelief and then, a split second later, shouts of confusion as Judge Harrington slumped forward onto his bench, his life bleeding out of him like an apology. She heard someone scream and she lay down on the floor. Everything was a blur, slow motion. Madison could not understand it, nor why Thomas Harmer – Carvell also crumpled to the floor, collapsing into himself as his life rushed out. Suddenly, as two security personnel reached her and bent down towards her stricken form, Madison realised who she had heard screaming as she felt the warmth and the stickiness of her blood, ebbing out of the gunshot wound in her chest. She tried to stem the flow, but it was too late. Amidst the sounds of the chaos, the alarms ringing, the court security officers shouting, the screams from the public gallery as they were shepherded out of harm's way, Madison realised she was dying and closed her eyes to shut out the scene before her. She saw a bright, blinding light, and she wondered who the man was telling her he was sorry.

***

Perry stood for a long time outside the cottage, looking around, seeing it for the first time, in reality. The last time he'd looked at the greyish brown sandstone frontage, he'd been looking at an estate agent's description; he'd not actually ever visited, he realised now. Peering up and down the little street, he saw the rows of terrace cottages on either side of a steep, uneven cobbled street. At one end there was a viaduct. He remembered having a conversation with Madison, about steam trains running through the village, she had loved that as she had the river, at the back of the cottage. The sound of the water rushing by broke into his silent thoughts and he glanced upwards, to the right where the street narrowed and became pedestrianised. Trees overhung the pathway, joining in the middle, their branches outstretched as if they were reaching to comfort each other. The quietness filled his ears, it was so different from Tufnell Park and the noise and the bustle and the smartness of the houses, large, gracious, and grand five and six bedroomed Victorian detached houses. A world, and a few million pounds away from this quaint two up, two down with its dated, wooden effect double glazing and the uneven stone steps leading down from the street into the tiny lobby.

He was going to have to go in.

Squaring his shoulders, Perry took faltering steps towards the front door. As he walked down the three stone steps, he shivered, feeling the thickness of the atmosphere, reaching out to him. He fished in the pocket of his trousers and pulled out the keys, inserting the mortice key into the lock and stepping over the threshold for the first time.

Inside, everything was still. A pall of death hung in the air, it made him shiver unwittingly. Looking at the room, it was exactly as she had described it. The bow fronted china cabinet against the half wood panelled wall on the left as he walked in; the oxblood leather Chesterfield sofa and chairs grouped together around the fire; a waxed pine bookcase groaned under the weight of tomes of legalese, case reports, court records. He smiled when he saw the volumes of *Butterworths*, as he remembered her pouring over them night after night, her glasses slipping to the end of her nose, the small crease in her forehead between her eyebrows as she concentrated on absorbing knowledge from the pages she was turning. Walking through the door into the small back room, which she had made her office, he leaned heavily on the staircase dowel, looking at the papers, the files, the folders, the living evidence of the law she had loved, and which had ultimately taken her from him more finally than their divorce ever could.

Did he want to go upstairs? The house seemed to hold its breath and once again, Perry found himself squaring his shoulders, breathing deeply as he put first one foot and then the other onto the stairs and found himself in the large, uneven shaped bedroom at the front of the house.

It was the smell which finally freed the grief he had held in check since he had received the phone call that made him not an ex-husband anymore, but a widower. He inhaled the intoxicating scent of her *Jolie Madame* perfume. It was the only one she ever wore, and it was one that described her so well, but which she would never be able to wear again. He started to cry.

"Madison!" He called her name into the thick silence.

How he had loved her, once. Where does it go, the love, when it dies?

He fingered her array of night creams, cleansers, and body lotions which sat on her dressing table. He picked up the bottle of perfume, but wasn't brave enough to take the stopper off, so he placed it back onto the glass topped counter and went to lay down on her bed.

She and he had never slept together in this bed. Madison had left the marital bed behind, as she had left their marriage. The glorious king size solid rosewood sleigh bed was not something he had shared with Madison. He kicked off his shoes, and got in, underneath the covers, hugging the duvet close. It smelt of her. A faint trace of the girl he had fallen in love with and the woman he had lost to life, and ultimately, now, to death.

He could not comprehend that Madison was dead. The word meant nothing in comparison to the vibrant, bossy, sexy, fun loving and absolute bitch that had been Madison. Theirs had been an eclectic relationship from the start; both swingers, both in love with the alternative lifestyle. They had come together in order to set each other free; and their lifestyle had given them the freedom they both craved. Picking up one of the pillows, he hugged it to his chest, remembering how she had felt, laid against him, limbs entwined, replete with love.

Smiling through his tears, he buried himself in the faint trace of her perfume, which he could smell lingering on the pillowcase, and he recalled one of their most sexual and erotic forays into the world of swinging; an experience they had both enjoyed, a high of true hedonism.

***

Madison smiled. She was wearing cherry red lipstick and a devilish expression along with an almost see-through chain link effect mesh mini dress. Her long, long suntanned legs were stretched out in front of her as she reclined on the velvet sofa. He touched her feet, encased in exceedingly high, very shiny pointed toe black leather stilettos and his fingers traced a line of desire up her calf, caressing her knee and then sliding between her inner thighs, working his way inside the tiny leather thong she was wearing. She was already deliciously wet. He looked up at her as she spread her legs wide for him.

Wanton.

That was how she looked at that moment, with her cloud of platinum blonde hair tumbling in waves around her face, and down her shoulders and her fingers guiding his inside her. Their eyes met quixotically as the door to the hard room at their favourite swinger's club opened.

Not missing a beat, Perry looked over Madison's head and nodded imperceptibly at the three men and one woman who had entered, all in various stages of undress – the vixen haired woman quite gloriously naked except for a pair of black *Louboutin's* with red ribbon ankle straps. No-one uttered a word, but they all knew what to do. The woman laid her lushly curvaceous body beside Madison's tight and tautly toned one and she immediately started to kiss her cherry red lips. Perry watched as he felt the gush of Madison's appetite wetting his fingers as they prodded and probed inside her pussy. The redhead's tongue slid inside Madison's mouth and licked her teeth. With his free hand, Perry fondled the redhead's breasts, which were bountiful, beautifully proportioned handfuls with hard, brown peaks standing to attention.

One of the three men spooned the redhead, sliding his hands between her thick thighs and parting them to reveal a large, dripping wet auburn-haired pussy which Perry bent to taste as the man behind her rammed his cock inside her anus. Of the other men, one had positioned himself on the other side of Madison, and he was sucking greedily on her breasts, which he squeezed together so he could feast on both her nipples at once. Madison's back arched with the sensation. Perry caught her look down at him, as he felt the third man walk around behind him, push himself up against Perry's backside, and then he felt the man's hands on his straining cock.

Perry moved slightly, and got between Madison and the redhead, whose muffled groans were becoming louder the faster she was anally fucked. He didn't want to fuck Madison, he could do that any day, he did want to kiss her though and watch as the man who had been sucking her breasts moved down to Madison's open legs. He pulled her towards him, and started to finger her clitoris, deep pink, engorged and swollen. Perry kissed his wife as he watched her wanking the man who was now holding her hips as he pushed his thick, hard cock deep inside her sopping wetness. Turning to the redhead, Perry pushed two, three fingers inside her and felt her contract against him. At the same time, his arse cheeks were being spread apart and he felt the head of a cock nudging the entrance to his anus. He groaned as he felt the cock edging inside, splitting him. But God, he wanted it. He pushed his arse back against the other man's cock, and felt it in deep, felt the man behind him reach down underneath and grab Perry's balls, squeezing them tight to the point Perry cried out. The redhead moved and her man withdrew his large cock, as she spread herself over Madison's face and Madison took that hairy, wet pussy into her mouth as Perry took her man's cock in his.

Long into the night they fucked, sucked, caressed, spanked, punished each other, swapping consistently – Madison at one point was being fucked by two of the men in a spit roast as he and the other man fucked the red head; all four men watched the redhead fuck Madison with a large rotating head vibrator. It was a night when Madison's inhibitions – and his own – parted company with themselves and left the two of them to enjoy what was on offer with no moral or judgemental attitudes to prevent the seeking and the finding of sheer, abandoned pleasure.

***

Perry awakened suddenly, realising his hand was down his trousers, masturbating his cock, and he was still hugging the pillow upon which the traces of his dead wife reminded him that he should not really be doing this. He needed to go home and explain to his daughter why her mommy was not coming home.

Upon learning of Madison's demise, Perry had taken his daughter to London. It was not easy. Phoebe was confused, and uncooperative. She did not behave well for Annalise, Perry's new wife and the atmosphere at the large, detached house in Tufnell Park, was deteriorating rapidly. His mother, who had moved into the granny flat when Madison had finally, thankfully, left, had suggested bringing Phoebe back to the cottage for a while. They could sort things out, and it would enable Phoebe to be somewhere familiar for a while, where she could remember her mother. Perry was going to drive back to London, to fetch his daughter and his mother to the cottage. It was a good idea, Perry thought, to allow Phoebe to say goodbye to her mommy. Annalise did not agree and was staying in London, she told him, after telling Perry his daughter needed stability, not sentiment, and London was a far better place for the little girl to be - right now, rather than an old cottage she was afraid of, stuck in the middle of nowhere. Perry had disagreed. His mother, walking into the midst of her son's and his new wife's first argument, knew what must be done.

His cock went limp as he thought of these things, and he stood up, feeling his shame and sorrow overwhelm him. Oh, how he needed Madison now. He tore the pillowcase from the pillow, burrowed his head into it before folding it neatly, so that it was small enough to put in his pocket. He could take the traces of his dead ex-wife with him, whilst he went to collect their daughter from his new wife.

Placing the pillow neatly back on the bed, he glanced around at Madison's bedroom, wondering where the sudden rush of cold air had come from. Checking there were no open windows, he went downstairs, grabbed his jacket which he had thrown over the back of the sofa, picked up his car keys and closed the front door quietly as the sound of another man's laughter drifted through the centuries. The cottage wept silently, as if it knew that yet again, it would shortly be empty and that love had, once more, died because of it.

SEVENTEEN

The cottage was empty, just as Thomas had known it would be. He sat upon Tudor, who turned his head and whickered softly at his master. Thomas looked at the stone exterior with interest and mild contempt. Did they think he was stupid? Did they think he would not know? Isabella, abandoning her brats, and visiting her sister in Scotland, and at the same time as Harry Winterton was curiously also in Scotland, supposedly visiting cotton mills in Lanarkshire that he wished the consortium to buy.

Tudor danced restlessly, tossing the bit about in his mouth as he shook his head and stamped his hooves; Thomas, gathering the reins, pushed the chestnut into a trot, and with one last look at the cottage, which glared back broodingly at him, he turned onto the track which led him past the Winterton's cotton mill and towards home and his plans.

***

'Have you made any plans, Perry?' His mother asked him, gently, as she sat in the living room of Madison's cottage with a subdued and bewildered Phoebe sitting on her lap.

Perry, equally bewildered, looked up from his reverie at the sound of his mother's voice. He shook his head.

'Mother, plans? For Gods' sake, I can hardly put one foot in front of the other!'

'Nasty lady!' Phoebe suddenly lunged herself at her father, flinging herself onto his knee and burying her head into his chest. Perry scooped his daughter closer to him; feeling the frail little form pressed against him broke his heart afresh. He tried to imagination what it would be like to be three years old and have your mother die. Phoebe would not know the finality of death; she would not be able yet to comprehend that her mother was never going to come home. He hugged his tiny daughter closer.

'The funeral, Peregrine,' his mother said now. 'And Madison's parents, her family in America. Have you told them? You need to get this settled, so that you and darling Annalise can get on with your lives.' Francesca Clarke had not liked Madison.

Perry sighed and kissed the top of his daughter's head. 'I'm not going to talk about it now, Mother,' and he gesticulated to Phoebe, who was falling asleep at last, cuddled into the safety of his arms.

Francesca nodded, accepting Perry's argument, and then she stood up, and took Phoebe from him.

'I'll put her to bed.'

She left him leaning forward, elbows on his knees with his head in his hands as if he were trying to shield himself from the memory of that telephone call across the Atlantic Ocean. The one which had woken Madison's parents from their sleep, in Boston, to discover that their daughter was dead and then, the call, which came from her brother, Tate. Perry had listened to the gulping, heart rending sobs of loss and disbelief.

'My heart is aching with pain,' Tate had whispered, and Perry's own heart understood as he listened to his brother-in-law crying for the sister gunned down in a courtroom by an assailant still at large, for a motive still unclear.

He was still sitting with his head in his hands when Francesca returned to the living room. He hadn't noticed his mother return, it was only when he felt her nudge his hand with a glass containing a generous finger or two of whisky that he looked up at her, wordlessly. After all, what is there to say to someone when the person who you really want to talk to is dead?

***

She was dead and he was glad. She was dead and Isabella was going to suffer. He smiled, but it was not a pleasant expression. Closing the door of the bedroom Belle occupied on the nursery floor, he walked towards the back stairs. He did not want to attract the attention of any passing servants on the main staircase, who may still be snuffing out the lights or dampening down the fires in the floors below. His whole body was suffused by an intoxicating blend of euphoria, excitement, and something else. He stood on the half landing, surprised to acknowledge that the third emotion, the one he had not expected, was sorrow.

Belle had been a pretty little thing. A rosy cheeked, plump little poppet with eyes the colour of the ocean and strawberry blonde curls that so obviously had not been inherited from him. She had been graced with a beguiling innocence, perhaps it was childhood that dispensed it. Maybe her mother had once had it before she'd turned into the harlot he had married. It did not matter, because now he'd not only saved Belle from following in her mother's footsteps, but he had also ensured that her mother's pleasure in her lover, that man – his supposed friend - would be killed, just as he had killed the daughter who had been born as a result of their disgraceful and distasteful liaison.

He went into his bedroom and closed the door quietly, before entering his dressing room and jangling the butler bell to summon his valet. Thus, he would be safely otherwise occupied at a time when it would be likely little Belle's body would be discovered by the nursery maid, going into each of the children's rooms in turn, checking on them all before she went to bed herself.

A short time later, he was standing in his nightshirt, whilst his man folded and put away clothes, and poured water from the pewter jug into a china bowl on the washstand, when the scream came. A sound of sheer terror and disbelief. He knew Belle had been found, lifeless, in bed with her toys and her pillows and her mother's licentiousness around her.

***

The scream was the sound of sheer terror, and it made Perry sit bolt upright in the bed he had never shared with Madison, where her memory kept him company in the velvety darkness of his sleeplessness. On and on it went, piercing into his very soul. He heard shouting, sobbing and he fumbled for his pyjama bottoms, cursing himself for sleeping naked. He wasted precious time scrambling around, trying to push impatient legs into un-cooperative pyjama trousers. He rushed across the landing into the smaller room at the back of the house, which was Phoebe's bedroom.

He took in the nightmarish scene before him. His mother, gasping, crying, bent over his daughter as she lay lifelessly in her pink four poster bed. His mother screamed again, this time she was saying something to him – he was rooted to the spot in a disbelieving terror – his mind struggled to understand – Francesca screamed louder.

'An ambulance, Perry. Call an ambulance!'

It took him a few moments to snap out of the stupor of fear as he saw his mother tip Phoebe's head backwards, one hand on her forehead, the other underneath her chin. He watched in morbid fascination as his mother placed her mouth over his daughter's and then, instinct kicked in, and he rushed from the room as Francesca tried to remember what she had been taught all those years ago, when she was a volunteer for St John Ambulance.

She had attended a demonstration in resuscitating a child – five rescue breaths into the child's mouth – checking for movement of the chest – then – *come on*, Francesca willed herself to remember! *That's it!* Place the heel of the hand in the centre of the chest, in line with the child's nipples – thirty compressions. *What was the song?* Francesca's mind refused to work! *Come on! Got it! Nellie the elephant!* She sang *Nellie the Elephant* to get the correct rhythm. *Count in your head, Francesca,* she thought desperately, and then began thirty compressions before another two rescue breaths into Phoebe's tiny, rosebud mouth. After all, she reasoned, if she didn't, they would know, wouldn't they?

She heard Perry screaming for an ambulance, stumbling over the address, unfamiliar with the postcode, not remembering his phone number for the dispatcher on the other end of his frantic emergency call. Francesca stopped pushing firmly on the unmoving, fragile looking chest of her only granddaughter. She still sang *Nellie the Elephant* at the top of her voice, staring at the stillness of Phoebe's chest. The child had wanted her mother, she thought, with satisfaction, smiling at the man who stood watching from the corner of the room.

Perry was pacing the floor – in the front bedroom, onto the landing – Francesca could hear him gasping, and yelling with the fear. Crying, shouting, Perry ran down the stairs to the front door, wrenching it open and leaping up the steps outside into the street, searching for the sound of the sirens.

Help me, please God, help me!

As his eyes adjusted to the darkness and he peered into the night, there was a resounding crash. He spun around on his heels in time to see the heavy wooden front door slam shut. Running back to the house, he turned the door handle, round and round, over again and pushed with all his might on the door. It did not move, it was locked.

This could not be happening. It could not be happening! He heard his mother, still singing *Nelly the Elephant*, and in the vague distance he could hear a siren. His eyes fell on the plant pot. Heavy bottomed, filled with Madison's summer blooms, he picked it up and with superhuman strength, he threw it at the double-glazed window. The pane shattered but did not break. Letting out a frustrated roar, he picked up the plant pot from where it had fallen on the doorstep and threw it again and again. He heard a screech of tyres, neighbour's voices, shouting, blurred with sleep, wondering at the commotion.

'The door slammed!' Perry yelled at the green clad paramedics. 'My keys are inside, my daughter...'

Another siren sounded and the police arrived, took over. Within minutes they were in the house and Perry ran back inside his nightmare.

Francesca, sobbing now, had started to press Phoebe's chest again, half screaming *Nelly the Elephant.* She looked up as the paramedics filled the room, one knelt down on the other side of Phoebe's limp little body, and quietly took over.

Standing up, Francesca fell into her son's arms.

'She's not breathing, Perry.'

Minutes felt like hours as mother and son clung to one another, and they both clung to hope. Perry never realised what it was his mother was hoping for.

Amidst the chaos, no-one noticed the sudden and distinct drop in the temperature; no-one noticed the rush of cold air spinning like a vortex around the bedroom and no-one heard the sound of manic, gleeful laughter, which faded gradually as Phoebe died. Francesca, relieved, held onto her son and comforted him as his world fell further apart.

***

When a child dies, suddenly and unexpectedly in the night, the immediate suspicion is that the parents, or caregivers are the ones responsible. Perry and his mother discovered this in the immediate, harrowing aftermath of the paramedic shaking his head and quietly speaking to his colleague.

'She's gone, it's twenty-three twenty-seven, for the record.'

Perry realised afterwards this was Phoebe's time of death, as the second paramedic turned to him, and to Francesca and they heard the words no-one wants to hear in the midst of a medical emergency involving a loved one.

'I'm so sorry.'

Francesca collapsed in Perry's arms and the paramedic had to attend her out of a faint.

Leaning against the wall of the landing, Perry looked up and was surprised to see a woman in a long blue dress on the stairs, shaking her head sorrowfully; her arms held out in distress. He was about to say something to her, when she disappeared, and his attention was taken by a man in a dark suit walking up the stairs, walking through the exact spot where the woman had been standing not two seconds ago.

The man in the dark suit did not seem to notice that the woman had even been there as he introduced himself as Detective Inspector Astley. Perry looked at him blankly whilst the police officer told him what would happen next. Phoebe was being taken to the Emergency Unit of the local hospital, where a paediatrician needed to "take a look at her" to try and establish what had happened. In order to help, the detective was going to drive Perry and his mother to the hospital where Phoebe was being taken, and they could talk there once more was known. Gently, the man asked Perry to get himself and Francesca dressed, so that they could go with Phoebe to hospital. He would be downstairs while they did this and the paramedics would stay with Phoebe, until they were ready to leave.

Ashen faced, both Perry and his mother managed to get themselves ready and eventually a sad, small procession left the cottage whilst inside, a woman in a blue dress wept for another daughter, lost years before in a house not far from here, whose fate had been inextricably tied to the cottage forever.

EIGHTEEN

A sad consequence of Belle's death was delivered to Harry Winterton in the form of a note from her mother.

"Dearest Harry,

I will always love you, my darling, but I must never see you again. Belle is dead. My beautiful baby girl, my firstborn, my Arabella Henrietta Eliza. I cannot comprehend resuming our relationship, I fear the depths of my grief for my child supersede any other emotion at present. I cannot love you, Harry. I cannot love anyone, anymore, because of my love for Belle, who is now dead.

Eliza is my grandmother's name. I hope you realise why Belle was given the name Henrietta, I suspect we may have touched on the delicacy of the subject whilst we took our sojourn in Scotland, our very last time, Henry.

I do not tell you this lightly, perhaps it is wrong of me to want you to bear the grief also, but I do so want you to know what Belle meant to me and now, she means the same to you.

Goodbye,

Isabella."

The death of the daughter who he'd never been allowed to know until it was too late, hit Harry hard. Crumbling the note between his fingers, he flung it into the fire. His relationship with her mother was now also dead, along with the child their love had created and for the first time in his life, Harry understood the finality of death, and loss.

His mother proved to be a surprising ally. When news of the note, and Belle's death filtered through Winterton Hall, and Harry's roar of grief and disbelief had resounded through the corridors, filling the nooks and crannies with his sorrow, his mother had found him, sobbing, in the library. She'd sat opposite him, in a leather Chesterfield wing chair that was exactly the same as the one which sat in the corner by the fireplace at Enchantment Cottage. She has sat silently, listening to her only son's heart breaking and falling in jagged pieces onto the oak parquet flooring and then, after a small lifetime, she had reached out and patted her son's forearm. A woman not given to physical displays of affection, this gesture from his mother made him raise his red, sorrow laden eyes.

Lady Winterton looked at her son, her hand still gently laid on his forearm.

'Your elder brother died when he was two, Henry. He died of measles. I was expecting you at the time. For a while, I didn't love you, how could I when Robert was dead? I have not been a very demonstrative mother because I blamed myself and I know you will do the same. We all had the same suspicion, Henry, that Arabella Harmer was your child. I understand some of the grief. I do not berate you for your actions, as I now have stopped berating myself for dealing with Robert's death in the way I did. You must not blame yourself, Henry, for not acting on that suspicion and you must not blame yourself for her death. To lose a child is a dreadful experience because nature does not prepare us to outlive our children. I never told you of Robert's existence, Henry, simply because I did not want you to have to live in his shadow all your life. I tell you of him now, because you need to know that you,' she hesitated, 'you and Lady Harmer, will survive.'

She withdrew her hand, and looked at her son's grief ravaged, shocked face.

'I will say no more. We will not speak of Robert again; but I know you will survive Henry, because I did.'

With a last, unguarded glance of shared understanding and pain, she turned, and Harry heard the rustle of taffeta as she swept out of the library without looking back.

***

Without looking back, Perry stumbled up the steep steps

which lead from the cottage onto the cobbled main street and he threw the keys to Gavin, the unfortunate estate agent to whom this sad, sinister little cottage kept returning to be sold, along with its grief and its sorrowful story.

Gavin caught the keys and stood helplessly as his bosses' best friend walked quickly and heavily towards the blue *Porsche Carrera*. He watched Perry, whom he had once considered something of a knob, with his Etonian schoolboy mannerisms and his loud, braying, upper class accent. Gavin watched him get into the car and drive away without a backward glance, and felt a new, all-consuming respect for the older man he had never really liked.

He had been in the office on the day Perry had walked in and quietly asked to speak to Marcus, Gavin's boss. Laraine, who was Gavin's colleague had told Perry that Marcus was out, and Perry had said fine, he would wait. He'd taken a seat next to Gavin's desk and he had just sat there, staring vacantly into space with big, fat, quiet tears flowing freely down his ruddy complexioned cheeks. Several times he had been asked if he were alright, which he clearly wasn't and, in the end, Gavin told Laraine to go and make a cup of tea, simply to stop her talking to Perry, who he could see was sitting there with his heart breaking around him. Gavin could almost hear the invisible pieces hitting the floor in despair and sorrow.

When Marcus had finally turned up, Perry had stood up and simply said, 'She's dead, Marcus.'

Laraine, the daft cow had gasped and said, 'I knew something was wrong!'

Gavin had wanted to punch her to shut her up.

Marcus had looked at Perry and said, 'I know, I'm so sorry, Perry. We all loved Madison.'

Perry had shaken his head and sort of crumbled. Then he had whispered, 'Phoebe, too.'

His sorrow had unleashed itself, there and then, in the full view of the busy estate agency office. He had roared with pain, such an unbearable sound; true, loud, raw grief bursting, uncontained into the stunned silence.

Marcus has simply patted Perry's arm and turned the sign on the front door to "Closed". Then he had taken hold of his friend, and half walked with him, half carried him into the private meeting room at the back of the office.

Gavin and Laraine didn't really know what to do, so Gavin had told Laraine to go home, and that he would stay to answer the phones. He apologised to the clients he had had to ask to leave, and with the closed sign still on the door, Gavin had worked the rest of the afternoon - running the office single-handed, whilst listening to the sound of the older man's grief pour itself out behind the closed blue door. For the rest of his life, grief was always painted the same colour as that door for Gavin. Much later when Marcus opened the blue door, he pulled Perry out, holding his hand.

Marcus said, 'Thank you, Gavin. You're welcome to come with Perry and I to get rip-roaringly, disgustingly drunk!'

Nodding, Gavin took hold of Perry's other arm, and the three went across the road to the pub, to do exactly that.

The next day when both he and Marcus were sat at their respective desks, gripping their heads as they swallowed paracetamol and bacon sandwiches, Gavin had learnt that Madison was Perry's ex-wife, and the lawyer who had been shot in the city centre courtroom earlier that week. Realising that not only had he suffered the loss of his wife, but Perry's three-year-old daughter had also died at the little cottage that they were now going to try to sell, Gavin shuddered, and felt even more new respect for Peregrine Clarke.

Gavin sighed as he recalled the events of the last few days. Such a sad story to add to the cottage's history – he had sold the cottage previously to the lady author who had fell down the stairs to the kitchen and died. There were so many deaths linked to the cottage, three in the last two years and he knew from village records which dated back to the early nineteenth century, when the cottage was first built, there had been at least two other owners who had died in the cottage. Gavin's knowledge of the cottage told him that the man who had built it, Henry Winterton, had been found hanged there, and his son Jasper, a toddler, had fallen out of the rear bedroom window. It was always going to be difficult to sell, this little cottage with tragedy binding its stones together.

Reluctantly, he straightened his shoulders, and stepped down the stone steps which Perry had recently walked up. Opening the front door, he went in.

The air inside the cottage smelt of sadness and venom. There was a heaviness to the atmosphere, and it made Gavin nervous. He wanted to turn around and run but of course, he had to prepare new sales details, and take an inventory, because the cottage was unoccupied. That was why he was surprised, when he walked upstairs, to find a woman in a blue dress sitting in the smaller bedroom. To be honest, his imagination had been running riot all the while he had been measuring up and dictating his sales details so surprised was an understatement. Gavin actually let out a small yelp of fear, which made the woman in the blue dress look up at him. She smiled, and Gavin felt the hairs on the back of his neck begin to prickle.

'Hello, who are you? Perry never mentioned anyone was in the cottage?' Gavin asked, swallowing his fear, trying to take control.

'I am always here. I knew you would come again.'

Her blue dress rustled as she moved; languid, liquid movements. She mesmerised him, as he stood looking at her hair, which was the colour of foxes and her eyes, deep blue eyes – the colour of oceans or the brightest sky on a summer's day. Staring at her, he found himself unable to tear his own brown eyes away.

By now, she had drifted into the larger, front bedroom and was sitting, settling herself on the bed, leaning against the headboard and Gavin's cock was growing hard. He placed his phone and his papers on the top of the chest of drawers in the corner by the window, as if he knew what would happen next.

'Come to me,' she beckoned to him as she stood up, the dress tumbled down to the floor and lay at her bare feet like a pool of desire waiting for him to step into. She was naked. Her body was a ripe, velvety peach. Voluptuous, full breasts awaited his eager mouth; the curve of her hips made his hands snake over them and her thighs pressed against his groin in an urgency of want.

His mouth ate her nipples eagerly, and she threw her head back in a paroxysm of pleasure as the glorious tugging sensation flooded through her. She felt his fingers probing between her wet thighs and she parted them in order for him to seek out the hub of her desire, as she felt his growing manhood strain against the trousers which kept her from enjoying his flesh.

She stepped back and they both fell onto the huge, polished wooden sleigh bed, Gavin undressing lightning fast as she lay on her back and parted her legs, abandoned and wanton. His cock was huge, and hard and ready. He settled himself in between her open thighs and he felt her arch her back as she thrust her pussy towards him. Catching hold of the generous hips, he held her still as he plunged his cock into her, and she let out a gasp, then a groan of pleasure, of fulfilment. Gavin's thrusts bore hard into her as he felt her fingernails gouge into the flesh on his back. He took hold of the backs of her thighs, shifted her position so that he could penetrate her more deeply. Her breath was coming in short, sharp gasps and her juices flowed like nectar spilling out of an overripe flower.

Something caught Gavin's eye. On the floor by the legs of the headboard was a large, pink vibrator. Reaching down, he picked it up, flicked the switch and it buzzed to life. The woman looked at him in puzzlement, but he ignored her questioning gaze and moved the vibrator over her clitoris as he pumped his cock into her.

Her groans became cries of astonished pleasure. The pink thing was sending tiny tremors, frissons of delight between her legs, her bud – her clitoris became engorged with pleasure and hardened with each ecstatic pressure Gavin applied. She felt her release gathering beneath the sensation of his thrusts and the buzz, buzz, buzz of the thing; she became still, rigid beneath him. He knew she was near orgasm and he thrust and thrust again, faster, harder as the waves took hold and a torrent flooded over his cock. He groaned and spurted inside her as her fanny tightened and released, tightened, and released until he had emptied himself into her.

She lay still, and smiled, making a noise like a very satisfied little fox cub. Gavin groaned as his orgasm subsided. She stroked his hair, his face and kissed his cheek. He slept in her arms.

***

He awoke on the bed, fully dressed, with his hand down his trousers wrapped around his cock. He felt bewildered – what had happened? Where was she? It took him a few minutes to recall, and when he did, he realised, it must have been a dream. There was no-one there, there had never been anyone there, except his fevered imagination and a horny man who missed having a girlfriend and needed to have sex. It wasn't until he got home and had a shower that he noticed the scratches on his back. The marks left of a woman in a blue dress.

NINETEEN

Isabella threw the peacock blue dress onto the wooden chest which stood at the bottom of her bed. She let out an exasperated sigh. It was too small, the dress. Which meant that soon, the evidence of her pregnancy would potentially be visible to others. She'd done well so far; she was entering the fifth month of gestation and had managed to keep secret her nurturing of this child, who she knew beyond doubt, would be her last child. Harry's child. Another child who would be borne of her, conceived in such passionate abandon with the only man Isabella had ever loved. Oh, there had been affairs – sex, fun, hedonism in her very humdrum existence as the wife of a man she did not love but to whom she was chained, by a marriage more akin to a business transaction. Yes, there had been affairs but there had only ever been love with Harry.

This child that kicked her belly, and kept her awake at night with heartburn and cramps; how was she going to give birth to this child without her husband knowing? She would eventually have to tell Thomas, and he was not a stupid man. He'd know that she and he had not lain together and then he would know that the child she was carrying was not a child he had created. Isabella wondered what would happen at that point, what would become of her, and for that matter, her remaining living children – Georgina and William. It was a situation she did not think about too very often.

Sighing, she shook herself out of her reverie and went to the closet to select one of the gowns she had worn when she was expecting Belle. The dress she selected was the colour of buttercups, one of her favourite flowers. She remembered sitting in the woodland, which formed part of the Harmer House Estate, with the children and a nursery maid had sat making daisy and buttercup chains with Belle and Georgina while Isabella had sat nursing William. A happy day, one which she would never have again.

She had taken to dressing alone, for fear that her pregnancy would show, but now she could not fasten the buttercup dress without help and she called for her most trusted maid to assist her. Jeanie was a stout, pragmatic woman who had been in Isabella's mother's employ before Isabella had married Thomas, which she hoped would secure the servant's loyalty, should it ever be tested.

Jeanie was quick and capable and helped Isabella into the dress, and then brushed out the younger woman's auburn curls until they shone like beaten copper.

'You should go to your sister, my lady.' Jeanie said, patting Isabella's shoulder as she replaced the silver hairbrush onto the dressing table where Isabella was sat, on a stool staring at the looking glass in its mahogany frame. Her reflection caught the eye of Jeanie as she said this, and Isabella turned around on the stool to face her maid.

'Whatever do you mean, Jeanie, pray tell?'

Jeanie bobbed her head subserviently.

'I apologise, Madam. I only thought that you seemed a little dispirited. Perhaps it is the extra weight you are carrying, in addition to your loss. It cannot be easy to be here at this time.'

Isabella nodded slowly, beginning to understand the coded message in her maid's conversation.

'Memories are the hardest things to forget, Jeanie. I see her in every room in this house and it is more difficult every day, my health.'

Her maid looked at her squarely in the eyes. Isabella took a deep breath.

'Do you know, Jeanie?'

'I know that in the coming months, being here will not be possible, Madam. You should go to Lady Clara; take the other children to your parents. Scotland will be safer for your health.'

It was a guarded conversation, both lady and servant knew it; full of secrets and innuendos, yet each of them understood the other perfectly.

'And when I come back?' Isabella asked.

'Lady Clara will be able to keep hold of anything which you would be unable to bring to this house, Madam, and Lady Clara would, at last, be blessed with a child.'

***

'Clara is with child, Thomas,' Isabella announced to her husband a few nights later, over dinner. 'She needs me to be there and I wish to attend her. I shall make the arrangements and take Georgina and William to stay with my parents, subject to your approval.'

She held her breath as Thomas picked up the heavy damask napkin from his knee, and dabbed at his mouth, brushing off non-existent crumbs from his moustache. He seemed at least to be considering her request.

'When is the child due?'

'October, I believe, Thomas.'

Another long silence and then, Thomas spoke again. 'I need you back for the opening meet of the season, Isabella. We meet on the first Saturday in November, so I shall need you here at least a week beforehand so that you can oversee the arrangements.'

Isabella let out a sigh of relief and bowed her head in acquiescence.

'When do you leave?'

Isabella had already agreed with Clara that she should arrive in two weeks' time and for the first time in her life, Isabella thanked the technological and industrial revolution for the appearance of the telegraph in her life, which had enabled her to contact her sister in Edinburgh. She told Thomas now of the arrangement and he nodded curtly before excusing himself from the dinner table without a further word.

***

As he made his way back to the dining table and the men, who were sharing port and cigars, Harry listened with half an ear to his mother and her friends, who had withdrawn to the drawing room, and were exchanging idle gossip and tickle tackle. Upon hearing that Isabella's sister, Clara had given birth to a baby boy, Harry turned on his heels and left, without uttering another word.

His father was apoplectic with rage at his only son abandoning the dinner party whose guest of honour was Sir Robert Peel, but Harry simply did not care; his only care was Isabella and the baby, whom he knew without a doubt did not belong to Clara. Poor misshapen Clara, whose riding accident as a child caused her to not only walk with a slight limp, due to the hip injury, but whose insides had also been damaged to the point of her parents being told that their eldest daughter would never have children. It was not common knowledge; so far as Harry was aware, only Clara's husband, her parents and Isabella knew of this. It had been Isabella, of course, who had told Harry.

Harry just hoped that she'd never told her husband.

***

'Her husband wants her to go back,' Clara said, raising her eyes from the telegram she had received and looking to her own husband, who raised his eyebrows in surprise.

'Clara, she has only recently given birth in the last few days, surely he will understand?'

Clara sighed, and realised that she was going to have to tell Angus the truth about the reason why Isabella had come to

Lochinvar, their glorious seaside home which nestled between the centre of Edinburgh and Portobello.

When she had done so, her husband stood up, placed his head in his hands and let out a roar of frustrated disbelief.

'Clara. Clara, I cannot for a moment comprehend that you think she will be able to get away with this. It is outrageous, and as for the baby remaining in our care – Clara –*when* exactly where you going to tell me this? I cannot believe what I am hearing. No, Clara, this is not going to happen. It is simply not going to happen. I will not have this – dishonour – coming to my house. Make the arrangements for her and the child to return home.'

'Angus! Thomas, Lord Harmer does not even know Isabella was pregnant! How can she turn up with a baby?'

Her husband looked at her for a long time and simply said, 'Oh, Clara', before leaving the room.

Clara sighed heavily and went to break the news to Isabella that she was going to have to go home.

***

Home.

It did not feel like home, thought Isabella, who looked pale and wan as she stepped from the carriage and stared at Harmer House, which glared back malevolently. She shuddered suddenly, then went inside.

Thomas, watching from an upper floor window, smiled unpleasantly, and wondered fleetingly what she had done with the baby before he moved away from the window and went to greet his wife.

***

Some two hundred miles away, Jasper David Henry Harmer slept peacefully, whilst all around him, chaos and tragedy laid the path he would tread for the rest of his life.

***

Later that night, whilst Jasper slept, Isabella was awakened by her husband entering her bedroom with a purposeful demeanour.

Isabella sat up in bed, trying to shake the sleep out of her mind, and focus on what Thomas wanted. He stood patiently at the side of the bed, fully clothed despite the late hour.

'Thomas!' Isabella gasped, in a voice full of sleep. 'What is it? Is it the children?'

'No, Isabella. It is not the children. Why on earth would I be worried about your children? I am more worried about my wife, who has been away for several months, and has not deigned to even kiss her husband.'

Isabella, more alert now, looked at him. Thomas's expression was guileless and that, in itself, made Isabella nervous.

'It is late for a kiss, sir,' she told him, 'and I am very tired.'

This alone was true. Isabella had only recently given birth; Jasper had been a difficult baby to deliver- a breach – and she had laboured long and lost a lot of blood. She had not regained her full strength, and the journey home, at her husband's command and her sister's apology for asking her to leave, had been arduous and harrowing. She was still bleeding intermittently from the birth, and this made her feel faint all the time. The coach she was travelling in had had to stop several times for her to vomit and the vomiting had made her even more lightheaded. She wished Thomas would go.

'Well, I am tired, too, Isabella. I am tired of having a wife who is either never here or when she is here ignores me for much of the time. So, I have come now to ensure that you cannot ignore me tonight. I want you, Isabella, and I shall have you, whether or not you are tired.'

Thomas started to undress, and Isabella started to feel very afraid. It had been a long time since her and Thomas had lain together – you could not call it making love – there was no love between them; Thomas was fulfilling a need and Isabella was fulfilling a duty. This night, though, it was different, Thomas's need was outweighing or ignoring the boundaries of his wife's duty, and whether or not she wanted Thomas's sexual attention, she was going to get it.

Naked now, Thomas got into bed beside Isabella and ordered her to take off her nightgown. She took a long time to do this, being careful to hide away the long knickerbockers containing the pads which disguised the bleeding. Her body had still not returned to its pre-pregnancy state; her breasts were large and sore, filled with undrunk milk as they were, and her stomach was jelly like, with a paunch of baby weight around her middle. Her body disgusted her in this state, but yet Thomas, who could have a choice of beautiful mistresses with appealing, lean, and slender bodies, chose Isabella's pregnancy scarred, unattractive one.

She winced when he grabbed her breasts, and he squeezed them hard, leaving finger marks in her tender flesh and bite marks on the nipples as he grazed them cruelly with his teeth. He had never been a thoughtful lover, and Isabella had never been attracted enough to him to be aroused by him. What they did in bed previously had been bearable; this was not, and Isabella cried out as Thomas asserted himself over her.

It was as if he was punishing her for the baby, thought Isabella, although she was certain that he had not known, that he had not guessed. She lay beneath her husband now and suffered for his ardour – or his hatred, she could not work out which. He grasped her roughly, straddled her and forced her to take his large, red engorged cock in her unwilling mouth, pushing it in, commanding her to suck. She could not breath, with his cock in her mouth and the weight of him on her chest. When he finally pulled out of her, she was gasping and crying for air.

He slapped her face, hissing at her to be quiet, not to wake the servants with her cries. She bit her bottom lip as she felt his hand roaming over her body; scratching, smacking, pinching. This was not love – this was not even sex, she knew. This was anger and venom and hatred. He forced her plump thighs apart now, his knees held her open as his fingers sought the secret place which Harry had kissed and entered with such love. Now Thomas was slapping her fanny and rubbing her clitoris frantically and roughly. He thrust his cock in and Isabella screamed with the pain. She felt Thomas's hand sting her cheek again, and he put one hand over her mouth to quiet her and with the other, he kept on pinching her breasts, her nipples, until she was sure that they bled.

He took delight in turning her over and pushing her face into the pillows, again it was hard to breathe, she struggled against the sensation that she was losing consciousness. She tried to close her legs so Thomas could not penetrate her anymore, but Isabella had no strength against him, and again and again he forced her open and forced his cock into her. He took her from behind in her fanny, and then, degradingly, and acutely painfully, he thrust into her anus and she struggled feebly against him to no avail.

Her horror and shame finally stilled her. She stopped resisting and simply let him do to her what he wanted. She let him pump his cock into her backside; she let him pull out and back into her vagina; she let him pull her hair, smack her bottom, pinch her tender flesh anywhere he wanted. She just wanted it to be over. She lay beneath him like a rag doll as he pushed her onto her back once more, and in a final act of degradation, he spurted his juice all over her face, and it mingled with the tears that escaped, at last.

He stood up and looked at the mess Isabella had become. He saw that she was bleeding down below. He did not care. He despised her.

'You're bleeding, Isabella. Was I too rough? Not what you

are used to?' He smirked and the expression was soon replaced by one of utter distaste. 'Clean the bed up, my lady, before that blood stains.'

The sound of the door closing behind her husband was one of the last sounds that Isabella heard, as she lay quietly, bleeding to death in the milky light of an early morning winter sunrise. She tried to move, several times, but found that her arms no longer possessed the strength to raise her body off the bed. She felt woozy, and the room kept spinning. She felt as though she was falling several times and she tried to grip hold of the bedclothes so afraid was she of actually falling. Her hands had disappeared. She could not feel them, and everything kept going black, which frightened her. She tried to cry out, call for help but although she opened her mouth, she could make no sound. She was wet and cold, as the blood seeped out of her and soaked into the bed, which Thomas would later burn.

Suddenly, the door to the bedroom opened, and Isabella could see it was very bright in the corridor. They must be lighting the lamps. The brightness made her feel less afraid. It was one of the things she feared, dying in the dark. Was she dying? She was weak, unable now to move, and she could not stop the room from spinning. She nearly fell again, as the swooping sensation returned. She wished it would stop, when suddenly, Belle was there. Her tiny daughter took hold of her hand, and Isabella went with her, into the light.

FELICITY

TWENTY

It was perfect. Absolutely perfect. So perfect, in fact that she wanted to do a little dance, right there in the living room in front of the rather dishy estate agent chap, who was pacing up and down on the scuffed wooden floor and who looked rather nervous. Maybe kissing him on the cheek when she had met him a few moments ago wasn't the "done" thing in this tiny little village in northern England. She had lived in France for the last three years, studying Fine Art at the *Sorbonne* and everyone kissed everyone in France, so she hadn't really thought it odd.

Stop thinking about kissing estate agents! Concentrate on the cottage, you silly girl, she thought. Tearing her mind from the estate agent, she turned her attention back to the living room – wooden floors, a stone wall with a huge stone fireplace, a woodburning stove, and beamed ceiling. Okay, so the beams were not original, but they were sympathetic with the house and the age of the property. She could live with unoriginal beams. Through the door on the left of the far wall, there was a long, narrow rectangular room with two staircases, one leading upstairs to the bedrooms, and one leading downstairs, presumably to the kitchen as it wasn't on this floor. Clattering down the steps, she nearly overbalanced on the wooden stairs, they were so steep. She clutched hold of the banister rail and managed to get down into the kitchen without mishap, which was more than could be said of the woman who lay in a crumpled heap at the bottom of the stairs with her head at a peculiar angle to the rest of her body. The kitchen was adequate. An "L" shaped collection of waxed pine units and tiled working surfaces at one end, with two tiny windows overlooking the garden. At the other end of the room, there was a huge black fridge freezer, a small pine table and three mismatched chairs.

She took one last look around, noting the peeling paint and the slight bulging of the plaster above one of the windows, and then she went up the two flights of stairs to the bedrooms. There were two, the larger at the front, overlooking the cobbled street and a tiny rear one, with the girl standing on the window ledge outside. The bathroom was lovely – a quirky mixture of tradition and modern – she loved the roll top bath with the ball and claw feet; very romantic, she thought, but totally impractical, which was why there was also a power shower built into the corner opposite the bathroom door. She opened the bathroom window and peered down into the garden, which backed onto a river and was shrouded by trees. Looking to the left, she could just make out the railway arches, and right at that moment she heard an impatient hoot and then a burgundy and cream steam train trundled past. What a fabulous sight to be able to see at the end of your street, she thought. A piece of living history.

Shutting the window, she returned downstairs to find the dishy looking estate agent sitting on the wall at the front of the house, next to the three stone steps that led down to the front door. She could sense his unease about the house and didn't have to be told twice that he wasn't very keen on the place. She stepped outside onto the flagged pathway – there were no pavements just a private pathway which led from the bottom of the hill past the seven little cottages on this side of the street. The sun was shining, and all around there was a quiet stillness, no traffic noise, no passers - by, no screaming children who had just been dismissed from school and who made a nuisance of themselves as they walked home. It was perfect.

As she appeared out of the doorway, the estate agent stood up and smiled at her. He had a nice smile, it got rid of the nervous expression on his face, and it reached his eyes, which she liked. People who only smiled with their mouth were not to be trusted.

'All done?'

He smiled as he spoke, and when she nodded, he moved passed her to lock up the house. He smelt deliciously of *Joop*, her favourite smell on a man besides bare, naked skin. He locked the door and looked at her expectantly.

She realised that he was waiting for some sort of response from her regarding the viewing and she smiled at him.

'I like it,' she told him, returning his smile, 'but I'm not ready to put any figures together yet, I'd like my Aunt to see it first before I make any offer.'

He nodded. 'That's fine, just let me know when you want to see it again and I'll come and sit outside while you do the viewing.' He handed her his business card, eager to secure interest in the property.

'You don't like the cottage very much, do you,' she consulted the business card, 'Gavin? May I call you Gavin? I'm Felicity Keating. Fliss.'

Gavin smiled that estate agent smile again, the one Fliss was drawn to. 'I'm afraid I don't like it, no. I should be less prejudiced about it, I know, but sometimes you get a feeling about certain houses.' He shrugged. 'Or maybe I'm just being silly.'

Fliss smiled and Gavin noticed how it lit up her whole face. It was an attractive face, surrounded by a cloud of dark, wavy hair. Her eyes were almond shaped and so dark brown that they were almost black. Even, straight white teeth smiled from sensuous full red lips the colour of ripened cherries, which complimented her slightly dusky, olive toned skin. He became conscious that he was hardening in his trousers, so he coughed and looked away.

'You're not being silly, Gavin,' replied Fliss, the smile still dancing on her mouth. 'Houses have atmospheres, formed from their history, I suppose, but she did not mean you any harm.'

Gavin looked puzzled. 'Who didn't mean any harm? I'm

sorry, I'm not with you.'

'The woman in the blue dress.' Fliss replied, as she leapt up the steps and headed towards her quirky little red and black Mini before Gavin could reply.

***

An air of anticipation hung over the sad little cottage. The dark shadows scuttled away from the corners and the agony and pain which had embedded itself in the emptiness began to recede as the hope, which he thought had abandoned him when she had gone, returned once more to light up his lonely vigil.

***

In the year of Our Lord, sixteen hundred and sixty-five, bubonic plague came to the tiny and extremely pretty village of Eyam, which nestled in the glorious countryside of the Hope Valley in Derbyshire. It arrived in a parcel of contaminated cloth to the house of the village tailor, one unfortunate George Vickars, who upon receiving the parcel of damp cloth from London, hung it out to dry in front of his cosy fire. Thus, he unwittingly released the plague infested fleas which would eventually, over some fourteen months, decimate the population of the village, killing some two hundred and sixty people.

The villagers of Eyam, in an act of brave unselfishness, isolated themselves and cut the village off from the rest of the county; in an effort to contain the disease and stop it spreading to outlying and neighbouring villages. Food was donated freely to the village by the *Duke of Devonshire*, who lived nearby at *Chatsworth House*. It was left at pick up points on the outskirts of the village to prevent anyone entering the village, and returning home accompanied by an unwelcome and dangerous guest.

Cornelia Blackwell-Keating was a direct descendant of one of the plague survivors, and she supposed this was the reason why the tiny cottage she had bought on Church Street appealed so much. This was the very row of cottages now known as the "Plague Cottages", where poor George hung his cloth and thence caused the demise of nearly three hundred of his neighbours. Cornelia saw many of George's neighbours from time to time as she went about her daily business as a clairvoyant and medium, which often dredged up a laugh at Cornelia's expense considering she was definitely larger than a medium.

In fact, Felicity Keating's Aunt Cornelia was larger not just than a medium, but larger than life. She had been described as "flamboyant" on more than one occasion, which Cornelia had denied, saying it didn't quite match up to her life of glorious excesses and enjoyment. She often said she was either a weeble or a beach ball, having the physical attributes of one, and the ability to bounce back from life's knocks of the other. It had been in dealing with one of those knocks she had discovered that she was a medium – a clairvoyant, a spiritualist – call it what you will, but when Cornelia's son, her only child – had died suddenly and unexpectedly, Cornelia kept on seeing him. Frightened at first that she was going crazy with grief, she had contacted an old friend who had a degree in paranormal psychology, and he had suggested that perhaps Cornelia was a medium, or a psychic. In fact, the friend had made something of a study out of Cornelia, and as a result of that study, Cornelia's psychic ability had developed significantly. Now Cornelia Blackwell-Keating was a world renowned Forensic Psychic Medium, helping and assisting police forces world-wide in criminal investigations. Flamboyant she may be, but she was also a leading authority in mediumship, and this enabled her to recognise Felicity's gift as soon as it became apparent, when her niece was a small child.

As a result of their shared gifts, Cornelia and Fliss had grown remarkably close, and over the years when Fliss was growing up, Cornelia had quietly slipped into the role of matriarch to the little girl, whose relationship with her natural parents was uncomfortable at best, and downright volatile the rest of the time.

These past events were the reason why it was Cornelia, and not Fliss's parents, who was helping finance the purchase of the small cottage in Winterton, which Fliss had excitedly telephoned her about that weekend. It was what had prompted Cornelia – never what you would call a reliable driver – to get into her aged Volkswagen Beetle and drive the thirty odd miles to meet her niece outside the cottage which she was so keen about potentially purchasing.

It was a pretty setting, in a very dour, northern way – the prettiness was not subtle; the railway arches and the river, which both cut through the village like scars, told of a more austere prettiness. The hills and valleys did not peak and trough gently across the landscape here like the rolling folds of Derbyshire. Here, they were stark, hard, and work worn. Cornelia sensed deprivation, hardship, and penance within the solid stone facades of the mean little houses cuddled together on the fringes of the tough cobbled streets. Standards and values had been fought for here, she sensed. Of course, Winterton had been a strict Methodist stronghold, the influences could be seen all around; the Methodist Chapel, the infant school bearing the name of a prominent long dead minister. In the early nineteenth century, the public house had started selling ale, causing a huge rift between the villagers and the family to whom they were indebted. Harry Winterton's father and grandfather had never set foot in the village again, although Harry had, in fact, built this little cottage which Cornelia was standing outside now.

Cornelia could sense people and sadness, and then she would see them. Generally, the dead interfered when she wanted to do something for the living, and as she wanted to concentrate on the viewing and Fliss, she asked her spirit guide to shield her from any sightings whilst she was with Fliss.

She spotted her beloved niece now, pulling up in her little mini. Fliss got out and waved to her Aunt, who could sense her delight and excitement. At the same moment, a large black car appeared around the corner and parked behind Fliss's car. The young man who got out greeted her with a kiss on the cheek and Fliss laughed. They walked together down the lane opposite the cottage to meet Cornelia, who smiled and waved back, thinking that if what she had seen for Fliss's future was the direction her niece took, then she had a happy future ahead of her.

Fliss drew level with her Aunt and hugged and kissed her before introducing Gavin.

'Gavin doesn't like the cottage, Corny, so we can have the keys, he said, and look around on our own.'

Cornelia looked from Gavin over to the little cottage, standing stoutly on the rise of the hill shrouded in virulence with watchful eyes following them, keeping tabs and she understood the estate agent's reluctance to step over the threshold. Maybe her niece's inexperience and untrained perceptive skills meant that she could not feel as much of the past; of the history reaching out to her with its story. Cornelia could feel it, and as always, it intrigued her as much as it frightened her slightly. Never one to be beaten by history and a couple of centuries, she straightened her tubby little frame and went inside.

TWENTY-ONE

She hardly ever drank, but after the events of the day, Cornelia's first action upon returning to her tiny plague cottage had been to walk directly to the sideboard, reach inside its cupboard where she kept her meagre alcoholic stock, select an exceptionally good whisky, and pour a hefty measure with hands that shook slightly. She was going to put the bottle back in the cupboard, but on reflection, she shrugged and took the bottle with her to the dining table, where she perched herself on one of the oak spindle-back chairs and took a huge gulp of the amber liquid. It burnt a trail down her throat and made her cough for a long time, but she eventually recovered enough to take a second slug before placing the glass onto the table, and then she placed the palms of her hands against the cool, solid surface.

She took a deep breath, visualised a protective barrier of light around her and exhaling, she recalled what she had felt when she had stepped over the threshold of Fliss's cottage – oh, she would buy it, Cornelia was certain beyond doubt of that – what she was uncertain of was her niece's ability to cope with it. The only thing that would help her would probably be her inexperience, as she would not be receptive to much of the activity Cornelia had felt.

The venom had hit her like a head on collision as soon as she had walked through the tiny lobby – a vortex of negative emotion, loathing, hatred, all spinning towards her, like a dervish. Fliss had neither seen nor felt the putrescent atmosphere. Instead, she had taken Cornelia on a whirlwind tour of the tiny house, pulling her from room to room with a childlike excitement and anticipation. Cornelia had resisted rushing, trying to connect with the souls in the house. She felt there were many; that the house had seen so much tragedy that it seemed impossible the solid stone walls had not crumbled under the weight of its tears.

Resisting her niece's impatience, Cornelia had brushed her hands aside and shook her head, telling Fliss that she needed to walk through the house more slowly, that she needed to imbibe the atmosphere, make sense of what Fliss thought might be a house containing an "interesting" past.

Interesting it certainly was, thought Cornelia now, unscrewing the bottle and uncharacteristically pouring herself a second generous whisky. But at what point did interesting become dangerous, and how could Cornelia warn her favourite niece without frightening her?

***

Clara was frightened. She had to admit it, although she did not know why. She shifted uneasily in one of the guest bedrooms at Harmer House and picked up her fan from the bedside table so that she could cool down her flushed face. She and Angus were 'down South', as her Scottish husband called anywhere beyond Edinburgh, for Isabella's funeral, and even the thought of her sister being dead frightened Clara beyond comprehension.

Her hip, which always seemed to ache whenever she was upset, caused her to fidget restlessly and she started to cry. Big, fat, sad tears of loss and something else, which she hardly admitted to herself – shame. Shame, when she recalled the look of absolute fear and horror on her sister's face, the day Clara had told Isabella that Angus would not agree to their subterfuge and she must return home.

She felt her husband's hand now, creep across the bed and settle on her stomach. Painfully, because her hip was hurting badly, almost as badly as her heart; painfully, she shuffled closer to the solid and comforting bulk of her husband's warm body and she felt him gather her into his arms and then him kiss her on the top of her head.

'You are not the only one who feels responsible, Clara.'

Angus's voice drifted towards her in the darkness.

She said nothing, only moved closer to him, as he continued, 'I didn't want her at Lochinvar. I was angry and upset at you both and with your disregard for our honour. You know as well as I do that had I been complicit, whilst my pride and morals may have been damaged, your sister might still be alive.'

Angus was a man of few words and, Clara knew, even fewer deep feelings such as those he had just expressed and whilst those words might contain a grain of truth in them, there was no blame. There was no blame for Isabella's death so far as Angus was concerned. She reached out to him, a small token of love and understanding, which he took gratefully without another word.

Clara lifted her face towards her husband, and kissed him very slowly, for a long time. She wanted him to feel her love, feel her own remorse, and guilt and sadness. Angus may have wanted Isabella to return here to Harmer, but if she, Clara, had not agreed to Isabella's crazy idea in the first place, maybe her sister would have found another way to deal with her pregnancy and then the baby who was the result of that pregnancy would not be motherless and secreted away with foster parents.

She returned out of her thoughts to the delicious sensation of her husband's fingers, tracing a delightful pathway up her aching thigh to find her warm wetness. Silently, she willed him to explore further, to make the ache of her bones and muscles disappear, to be replaced by another, far more pleasant aching between her legs.

Clara moaned softly and Angus moved closer, carefully positioning himself so that he did not hurt her hip and thigh. He was aware of her great deal of pain, which was the reason that they made love so infrequently. The lack did not worry Angus; his life on the estate was a busy one, and Clara was a good wife. He had no need, as Thomas Harmer had done, to seek out mistresses for his sexual satisfaction. What Clara had to offer, when she offered it, was enough for Angus.

She offered it now, shifting her weight and her painful leg, so that she was spread apart beneath him. As Clara had never had a child, she had a magnificent body apart from the misshapen hip which one tended to not notice when the rest of her nakedness was on show. Angus now removed her lace nightgown and revealed that splendid nakedness in the soft darkness of the bedchamber. Long, firm legs, a tiny, deliciously curvaceous waist and then the swell of her stupendous breasts. Clara was fair haired, and her breasts creamy white, with delectable pink nipples; they were large breasts, firm and malleable. They didn't droop or sag when Angus placed his workmanlike hands over them, but they swelled beneath his touch and grew even more bountiful; the nipples standing up clamouring for his attention.

He took one tumid nipple into his mouth and Clara let out a stifled moan of absolute pleasure as his tongue rolled around the hard bud and then his mouth pulled her into him and the steady, rhythmic sucking shot bolts of pleasure through her body. She shuddered in the sheer delight of the touch of her man. Her hands roamed his thick, muscular torso and her nails raked his work and weather toughened skin. She loved his body not just physically as now, but unreservedly, absolutely. A love in excess of the physical pleasure, Clara loved Angus's soul.

Now the physical joy of him was hers to give to and take from, and her hands traced that joy down to the cleft of his bottom and it was his turn to let out a moan of abandon as he felt her fingers slip between his cheeks, seek out his anus and gently slipped inside and work up and down. Up and down as his large cock penetrated her wetness and his movements synchronised with the movement of her fingers.

Arching her back, she threw her head back against the pillows and revelled in the power she felt between her legs. His cock, growing, hardening, lengthening inside her as her juices drowned him and their thighs were soaked with their pleasure.

As they gave to and took from each other time and again, he came at her over and over and she lay with reckless passion in his arms; her legs wrapped around him, her body contracting with the slippery, wonderful sensations he evoked in her.

Later, quietened, sated, and replenished by the wine Angus had slipped out of bed fetched from the drawing room, they lay together in the large four poster bed. They gazed at the pool of silver blue moonlight, which leaked through the grand, arched window from the ocean of inky blackness that formed the night sky. Silently, each of them thought of Isabella, searching for her memory in the vastness of forever, crowded with the moon and the stars and the universe that was hers to keep for eternity. The stars seemed to whisper her name. Isabella.

***

Isabella.

The name whispered into Fliss's dream, as she tossed and turned restlessly in her narrow bed, pushed up against the wall of the tiny bedroom in her rented flat above an Indian takeaway in Clapham Old Town, where she had settled briefly upon her return from France in the mistaken belief that being closer physically to her parents would bring them closer emotionally. It hadn't, and that was one of the reasons she was fleeing north, to put enough distance between them so that she would not be mistaken again.

Isabella.

This time, the urgent whisper made Fliss wake up, sit up in bed. Suddenly alert, shaking off sleep which grabbed the corners of her mind, she found herself listening intently for the connection to the voice again. Clearing her mind, she called her guide, and sat, surrounded by white light, and reaching out to whoever might be listening.

Suddenly, inextricably, Fliss was overwhelmed by a feeling of utter and complete desolation. Her very soul felt melancholy and she was choking in a grief that didn't belong to her, but called out, cried to her piteously. Fliss wanted to weep. How could one word contain so much pain?

Isabella.

The word's jagged edges, dripping with sorrow, cut through her thoughts like the edge of Excalibur. She shivered involuntarily, and suddenly could not breathe. Her neck suddenly felt as though it was being squeezed tightly, she could feel something wrapping around it. Clutching frantically at her throat, she felt the roughness of the rope. She felt heavy; her breath came in short gasps and she was now clawing desperately at the noose around her neck. Terrified, she felt as though she was suspended, and she could feel her legs kicking out, trying to reach the chair; the chair that had been placed beneath the beam in the back bedroom of her cottage. She tried to scream, felt herself slipping out of consciousness; her ears were ringing.

The ringing would not go away, it was loud and reminded her of a telephone. With a shocking suddenness, her body thumped against her bed as if she had been released and dropped from a great height. Winded, Fliss was gasping for breath and rubbing her throat, which was aching, although the rope had gone. Noting it was growing light outside, she realised it was her mobile phone she could hear, ringing on and on determinedly. She flung herself towards her nightstand, and grabbed the phone, still gasping for breath as the call connected.

'FLISS! FELICITY!!'

It was Cornelia's voice, harsh, urgent; pinging down the line, piercing through what was left of the night and of Fliss's dreams.

'I'm here, Cornelia. What's wrong?'

'You tell me, Felicity!' Cornelia's voice was sharp with worry. 'What have you been trying to do?'

Fliss managed a wan smile. Of course, Cornelia would

know.

'I had a dream. I wanted to find out more, so I tried to summon him. I heard him call her name. His voice was full of pain.'

'Isabella,' said Cornelia.

'Isabella.' Fliss repeated, not surprised at all that Cornelia already knew. Cornelia was, of course, far more experienced than she was in these sorts of matters. 'Who else?'

'Felicity, there is so much activity in that cottage, you *must not* try to visit it in your dreams. You *must not* summon anybody. There are others there, in the ether; that I do know. There is too much for you to cope with, right now.'

There was a silence, and Fliss got the distinct impression Cornelia wasn't telling her everything she knew. Cornelia's voice was breaking through her ruminations.

'Do not summon anyone else, Fliss. Do you hear me? Alone, you are too raw, too naïve.'

Once Cornelia had rung off, leaving Fliss strict instructions about grounding, cleansing, and keeping her nose out of the afterlife, at least until she was in the cottage and Cornelia was nearer to hand, Fliss looked at her phone. It was half past five. Too early to get up, too late to go back to sleep.

Fliss sighed, unsettled by the events of the night. How she missed Gael. Now, uneasy, restless, and alone; with no-one to turn over and hold or persuade to awaken, she missed him. Whereas, in France, he had been there. He'd been there in the tiny studio apartment on the *Rue Oberkampf*, an easy walk to the *Sorbonne,* and close enough to the *Place De La Republique* to enjoy the bars and the cafés. The apartment's crowning glory, tiny patio doors with a little Juliet balcony overlooking a delightful green space, they left open and let in the heady breath of a Paris morning whilst they made love. Her restlessness would have propelled her into Gael's arms, and he would have known what to do to ease her mood. Only now, Gael was in France, and she was here in this dreadful rented flat, and she was not eased. Not yet.

Her hands moved over her hot, naked body. Her breasts felt pliant under her touch, and her nipples hardened at the insistence of her fingers, circling each in turn until she could not stand the rush of wet desire which she felt between her legs. She let her legs fall apart, and her left hand found a familiar route to her clitoris which she knew was already tumid, waiting, needing the touch of her fingers. She took the hot bud between finger and thumb and pumped it, feeling the sweet sensation of a growing orgasm spreading through her body. She pushed two, three fingers of her right hand into her sopping and delightfully responsive pussy, which contracted as she continued her delightful coaxing of herself to a squirming, glorious release.

Quietened, sated with the intensity of her orgasm, Fliss did not notice the woman with the broken neck sitting on the dressing table stool watching her intently. The same woman Fliss had seen earlier, laid on the floor of the cottage.

TWENTY-TWO

The cottage was hers! At last!

It had taken until early September for all the paperwork to be sorted, for Cornelia to set up the trust which would purchase it, and for Fliss to arrange for all the decorating and alterations to be done, all the old furniture removed and her own things to replace that which she was donating to charity. The one thing she did keep, however, was the oxblood leather wing chair, which stood in the corner by the stone fireplace. She has thrown a cream fleece blanket over it and filled it with cushions to make it hers, but for reasons she didn't understand, she had to keep it. Several times, whilst she was at the cottage during the summer, meeting builders, agents, decorators and changing her mind every second day, before giving the go ahead for any work; several times, she had had a vision of a tall, dark haired man; handsome, sensuous looking with dark eyes filled with longing. Whenever she had seen him, he had been sitting in that wing chair, which may have been the reason she had kept it.

Cornelia helped her move in. On the day, with the sale having been formally completed, Gavin met the two women outside. They watched in some dread as the large removal lorry struggled down the hill towards the cottage, lumbering dangerously from side to side and with the driver presumably cursing the narrow and winding lane, which was the only way into the village.

'Your keys, Miss Keating,' Gavin said, laughing with the pleasure of seeing her as he drew level with Fliss and her Aunt, and he brandished a set of house keys which he pulled from his pocket.

She snatched the keys from him and laughed along with him, accepting the bottle of champagne that he had proffered.

'We should drink it now, while it's still cold,' she said,

smiling at him. 'I just wish I could remember which box my glassware is in!'

He smiled back. 'The perils of moving. I'm driving anyway, but maybe another time?'

Fliss pushed back her dark hair and, clutching her keys and champagne, she reached up to Gavin and gave him a kiss.

'Definitely maybe.'

'Good luck with the move!'

Gavin grinned and headed back to his car, while Fliss ran towards the cottage, eager to take ownership. He watched her skip down the three stone steps that led to the solid wooden front door – unable to be changed during the renovations because the house is located within a conservation area. She struggled a bit with the newly cut keys, jiggling them about in the lock before he saw her open the door, and step inside.

***

He stepped inside and stood in the little vestibule he'd built, waiting for the memories to hit him. Sure enough, they came one by one, beating him about the head and his solar plexus. He started to cry, and the weight of his tears embedded itself into the stone walls; sorrow spanning centuries as he remembered the only woman he had ever loved.

He watched as the memory of her dancing in the living room waltzed before his eyes; he saw her clapping her hands in delight at wine and sweetmeats; he felt her kisses melting upon his lips as their passion overtook them. They had sunk down into the thick, overfilled feather mattress on the big bed in the bedroom which had borne witness to their love, and to the creation of their children.

Jasper. The son he had never seen and the son he would never know. His only son, the outcome of his only love. Now he stood in the little stone cottage, which he had built for business, but which had been the source of his greatest pleasure and he grieved for the son he could not have in life, and the daughter he had lost to death.

He found that he was brave enough to walk through the house, his footsteps echoing on the wooden floors as he stepped through his memories and through time. He watched silently as the woman with the dark hair, who looked so like the woman he had loved, ran ahead of him, and peered delightedly into each room. He saw her stop stock still on the landing and look around unhappily as if she sensed his intentions. She shook her head and turned away, ran back down the stairs.

Yet he knew he would not, could not stop. The story had already been told, and his time within it was over. He picked up the length of rope that lay in the corner of the landing and took it into the smaller bedroom at the back of the cottage. The chair was there, as he knew it would be and, knowing also this was what he had to do, he climbed up onto it. With great care, he fastened the rope around the end of one of the ceiling beams. Satisfied, he tested his handiwork, and knew it would suffice for what he needed it to do.

The end was already noosed. All he had to do was slip his head through it, and he would slip into eternity, where he would be able to be with Isabella. He took one last look around the bedroom before gathering his courage. There was nothing else to do except to push the chair away from underneath his feet, and then, in a little while, Harry's life without Isabella would be over.

***

Both Fliss and Cornelia were glad when the day was over. Thankfully, Fliss had found some wine glasses and because Gavin's champagne wasn't quite cold enough, she had acquired some Malbec from the local shop, which she was now pouring whilst Cornelia arranged a selection of cold meats, cheese, and crackers onto a couple of side plates. Both women were tired out and neither could face the prospect of cooking or rather, working out how Fliss's brand new oven worked.

Wobbling with exhaustion, they both climbed the steep, almost perpendicular kitchen stairs up to the room that had been previously an office but which Fliss had turned into a dining room. Yes, it was going to be annoying having to carry meals upstairs from the kitchen, but Fliss did not enjoy eating in the kitchen.

Aunt and niece plonked themselves onto the hideously expensive *Danetti* dining chairs and both heaved a sigh of relief as they picked up their wine glasses and toasted themselves for a job well done. Fliss sipped her wine watchfully, as Cornelia selected some *Lord of The Hundreds* cheese and watched her niece.

'Fliss, don't. Leave it for tonight, darling girl. In fact, leave it for a while. You need to settle, to get used to the house before you start delving into its history.'

'And the visions, Cornelia? How do I stop them? The little girl on the window ledge? The man in the wing chair, crying? The woman with the broken neck in the kitchen? I've changed the kitchen completely, but she's still lying at the bottom of the stairs every time I go down there. Tell me how to stop that!'

Fliss took a huge gulp of Malbec and stared at her Aunt questioningly.

Cornelia sighed. 'They are there, stuck in the ether, Felicity. They don't come and go to order because they are telling their story, they are stuck in the loop as it were. Changing the layout of the kitchen wouldn't help because you can't change history. You can ground yourself; you can meditate, and you can repeat a mantra that you say out loud and you tell your spirits to leave you alone, that you cannot speak to them right now and don't want to see them.'

Fliss looked sceptical.

'It does work, Felicity,' Cornelia told her, 'You need to practice it more often. Right now, you are like the blank pages of an open book.'

Fliss sighed. 'I feel as if I'm going mad.'

Cornelia patted her hand. 'Well, you're not, dear. Any more than I was when my dear brother and sister -in -law tried to have me sectioned and incarcerated in the local looney bin when I first revealed that I had visions and heard voices. As they say baby, look at me now!'

She did a little victory dance around the dining table, wobbling her considerable girth back and forth. Fliss managed a smile.

'There have been some interesting studies done about psychosis and psychics, you know,' Cornelia told her niece, as she sat down and poured herself another glass of wine. 'One by a psychologist and psychiatrist called Albert Powers at Yale University. You should read it. He and Phillip Corlett took a group of psychics and a group of schizophrenics and examined them to evaluate whether their social context affected their outlook on their experiences.'

'You mean if you think you are going mad, then you probably are!' Fliss cried, indignantly and glared at her Aunt.

Cornelia shook her head. 'Not at all, but how the participant viewed his or herself was interesting. Most schizophrenics, for example, view their voices, and their visual hallucinations as a negative, whereas the psychics affirmed their experiences as good and positive. It's all down to perception.'

Fliss smiled. 'Well, forgive me if I don't rush up to the next person I see and say, "Hey, I'm a psychic medium!" They'd think I was crazy, and maybe they would be right!'

Cornelia put down her wine glass and stood up.

'As the next person you see is probably going to be me, I would simply agree with you and say, "Snap!" Come on, darling, time for bed. You look all in. This moving lark is hard work.'

***

Lady Winterton put her head in her hands. It was hard work trying to sort through Henry's things. She sat down on the bed and simply wept until there were no more tears for her to shed. Both her sons; both dead, one a long time dead and the other recently buried in the grounds of the private chapel at the back of the house. She had not wanted Henry buried there, she had wanted him to be buried in the village churchyard, where Isabella Harmer lay, because at last, too late, she understood the relationship between Isabella and her son had been love and she had wanted them to be together in death; as they could never have been in life.

She picked up a riding coat of Henry's and as she held it up to her face to try to inhale a trace of her son, a bundle of papers fell out of the inner pocket. They were tied with a ribbon. Her hands shook as she unfastened the pretty bow, knowing without reading them that they were love letters. Love letters from Isabella to Harry. Only his parents ever called him Henry – he had been Harry to his sisters, his friends, and obviously, to his lover. She unfolded the last letter, the one on the top of the pile.

It was difficult to read, when tears blinded your vision, but she read, again and again, until the words of the woman who had loved her son were imprinted in her memory and the resolve to make what in effect was Isabella's last wish come true was imprinted in her heart.

'My darling Harry,

We have a son! A little boy, whom I have called Jasper. He shall remain with Clara and I shall have to return to society back in Lancashire without him. How I wish things could be different, and I could be returning home to you, with our child, to live as we wished, in love, in our little Enchantment Cottage, forever. We both know this cannot be, and I fear that shortly, your family will insist on your marrying some most respectable and suitable young girl who will provide an heir to the Winterton estates. Poor Jasper will never fill that role, we both know, but he shall be happy and prosperous with Clara and dear, stolid Angus. They will bring him up as their own, and he shall be a Scottish gentleman, instead of an English Lord. Oh Harry, my darling. I shall miss him all my days, as I miss you.

Your Isabella.'

Henry's mother put down the letter, and a vision of her son appeared before her eyes, at the dinner party they were holding at Winterton Hall for Sir Robert Peel – there had been some gossip about Clara, Isabella's sister giving birth to a baby boy, and Henry had stormed out of the gathering. He'd known then, and the letter that she was holding now; the letter had arrived only a few days after Isabella's death. Leonora imagined the woman, still in childbed, writing to her lost love to tell him about his lost son, the one they could never call their own. She sighed. How hard it must have been for Henry, to find out Jasper was his, to lose him for the sake of propriety; for the child to be hidden away in the wilderness of Scotland, and then, to hear of Isabella's death. Finally, Leonora understood the reason why her son had ended his life.

There were other letters, too. Lady Winterton sorted through them, letters telling of such love, such delight in each other. Letters which confirmed Belle Harmer had, indeed, been Henry's little girl. That made her begin to cry again; anguish filled her sad soul, remembering her christening, and Henry's discomfort at being there. Had he known then? Had he known, when Belle had died, that she had been his? Her heart ached for her son. How wretched that knowledge must have been for him, the death of a child he had never known. In effect, he had lost her twice. Poor Harry. Poor Belle. She carried on selecting random letters, her hands lovingly caressing the fading parchments, touching the words which had touched her son's heart and his soul. The curt note, telling him she must not see him, when she knew she was with child. The joyous reawakening of their affair. The words on the pages spoke of real, true love between two people who had everything to gain and instead, had lost what little they were able to cling onto for such a short, sad time.

Lady Winterton sighed and wiped her eyes again with her lace handkerchief and then, suddenly, unmistakeably, wonderfully, Henry was suddenly there, standing in front of her. Was he a thought, a memory, or a ghost? She reached out, but as quickly as he had arrived, he vanished. A wisp. A trace of the past that decided Jasper David Henry's future.

Whatever it took, Henry's son – the heir to the Winterton Estate – was not going to be brought up in Scotland by Clara and her Scottish "gentleman". Lady Winterton tutted, as if the prospect of Scotland's male population being gentlemen in any way was ridiculous. Standing up, she swept the letters into her arms and departed to her private chamber, until she was composed enough to go and speak to her husband about finding their grandson.

***

Cornelia lay awake, looking at the man dangling from the noose which was attached to the beam above her head in the small bedroom overlooking the river. The rush of the water was very calming, although Cornelia was not afraid of the vision she saw. She'd never been afraid, there was nothing to be afraid of. Ghosts did not hurt you, they were just visions, of the past; and more often than not, there was always a rational explanation for their death. You slipped on the stairs, fell, and broke your neck; you got shot in a courtroom defending a man whose ancestor long ago had his heart broken by his wife, who had betrayed him; your child died because your ex-husband's mother didn't want her son burdened with bringing up a child alone. The spirits were simply here, playing out their story. They did not cause the pain and the death surrounding this sad, stone cottage; they simply endured their own pain, repeatedly, hauntingly for the rest of time.

Looking at Harry's contorted face, eyes bulging, blood trickling out of his blue tinged lips, his body swinging gently from the rope he had placed around his neck out of grief for a woman who had died at the hands of the husband she had carelessly disregarded, Cornelia sighed. Such a sad story, she hoped that her niece would be able to cope with her psychic abilities, as the tale was repeated, night after night and as Harry and Isabella searched for each other in the afterlife. In the morning, she must sit Fliss down, and tell her all that she knew, so that Fliss could sympathise and tune in to the sadness without becoming obsessed by it.

In the event, the next day, Cornelia never saw her niece again. Fliss had woken early, disturbed by sightings, she had explained in a hastily written note to her Aunt, she had gone into Ramsbottom, where she had heard there was an excellent farmer's market. She would get them both something delicious for breakfast and, also, stock up on some provisions. Cornelia smiled, and put the note on the bedside table, heaving herself out of the small, narrow bed – dreadfully uncomfortable for someone of her age and shape – when her mobile phone rang. Answering the call, she realised she would not be able to stay for breakfast. Her professional services were required, and she was going to have to drive to Devon. Washing and dressing quickly, Cornelia did the same as Fliss, and left a note, as she had noticed her niece's mobile phone had been left on charge, on the kitchen counter.

Fliss and Cornelia missed each other by about ten minutes; Fliss arriving home just as Cornelia was joining the traffic on the busy motorway, heading for an even busier motorway on her journey southward. They never saw each other again following what police believed to be Cornelia suffering a massive stroke at the wheel, and her little Volkswagen Beetle crashing into the central reservation, killing Cornelia instantly.

TWENTY-THREE

'She was killed instantly,' Fliss sobbed, clutching hold of Gavin's hand and her sanity, after she had heard the news of Cornelia's death, which she had felt before the dreadful knock on the door of the cottage.

She had just arrived home, that lovely word – home! Cornelia's note was propped up on the kitchen counter, by her biscuit jar. Her Aunt had left the lid off and Fliss had smiled, imagining Cornelia's indignation at missing out on a delicious breakfast. The note told of the unscheduled journey to Devon, and to expect another visit when Cornelia was on her way back to Derbyshire. Reading this, Fliss smiled, imagining the little Beetle, tootling down the motorway, and her Aunt sweating profusely because she was not a person who enjoyed driving and the experience of motorway driving always flustered her. It was then, imaging Cornelia sweating, that Fliss had heard the blare of horns; she screamed, and a dreadful sense of foreboding had passed through her body. When she had calmed down, she unpacked the breakfast delicacies which she had bought in Ramsbottom a few hours ago. Smoked bacon, duck eggs, strawberries dipped in chocolate, fresh French bread, crumbly cheese. She put them methodically into her new, stainless-steel refrigerator along with the other provisions, all the while waiting for the inevitable. And then it came. She was expecting it. The dreadful knock on the door.

The officers had been lovely. There had been two, one male and a female. The male officer had been the one to tell her the news and the female officer, who ridiculously looked around Fliss's age, had sat holding her hand as her world fell apart. Asked by one officer if there was someone Fliss would like them to call, Fliss realised that she knew no-one here except Gavin, the estate agent, and it was his details she gave to the female officer. It was Gavin whose hand she was holding as she sobbed for the loss of her Aunt, the only relative she really genuinely cared for and who had reciprocated Fliss's feelings. Now, she had no-one. Things had ended with Gael when she had returned from France, and her uneasy relationship with her parents never really picked up where it had left off before she went to study in France. There was no-one Fliss could have called, except the estate agent who had sold her the cottage, who had bought her champagne yesterday and who had asked her if they would be able to drink it together, in future.

Gavin had arrived, flustered, but concerned enough to put his fear of the cottage aside in order to be with Fliss when she needed him. Anyway, he'd thought, as he made his way down the three stone steps that led to the cottage from the steep hillside on which it was perched, it was stupid for a grown man of thirty-one to be afraid of a bloody house, for God's sake! A male police officer, who had offered his condolences in a grave voice, led him into the rear room, which Gavin remembered from the previous occupant, had been used as an office, but was now a very trendy looking dining room. The wooden half panelling on the walls had been painted a soft cream, and above that a very pale pink which complemented the dark grey table and six mismatched chairs which added a hint of quirkiness to the whole décor scheme. The large vertical radiator had been taken down, replaced by a two-column cast iron radiator placed under the window and a small, expensive looking Welsh dresser painted grey to match the dining table, had been placed where the old radiator had taken up so much space.

Why was he even thinking of these things, Gavin chastised himself when he saw Fliss, sitting clutching hold of a female police officer's hand; Fliss's face ravaged with grief, her whole demeanour broken. What he could not feel was the sudden change in the atmosphere which made Fliss cry out. The temperature dropped and the air grew thick with hatred. She shivered and started to cry again. Gavin strode in and sat next to her, on the opposite side to the police officer and she had simply fallen into his arms, both needing and wanting him to hold her. The other man in the room, who none of the small sad group could see, did not. He did not want them re-united and he was going to make them both pay.

Gavin sat for an awfully long time, just kissing the top of Fliss's dark head, flecked with auburn and copper which glinted in the early morning sunshine like gold. He smelt her shampoo and knew that for the rest of his life he would never be able to smell *Oribe* shampoo without thinking of death and the moment he had fallen in love with Felicity Keating, as he held her in his arms.

***

'I cannot think of Henry's death and not think of having his child in my arms.'

Lady Winterton looked solemnly at her husband, who winced at their son's name. Six months on from his son's death, he still flinched with pain whenever Harry's name was mentioned. Peveril looked up at his wife, from eyes laden with the loss he felt more acutely every day. However, he straightened up from his slumped position in his armchair and met his wife's stare with a determined look.

'You do not know for certain that the child is Harry's, Leonora. Do not interfere, I forbid it.'

Lady Winterton held her stare and her husband was the one to look away first.

'Of course, that child is Henry's. I shall show you the letters which Isabella wrote to Henry. The last one, Peveril – the last one is so heart breaking. In it, she tells Henry of Jasper. The child is Henry's, Peveril. As was Belle, if you ask me, and she's dead now, too. I don't want anything to happen to Jasper.'

Her lips quivered at the thought of another tragedy involving her son. She continued shakily. 'Someone is seeking vengeance for what Henry did – for Henry loving Isabella. Now they are both dead, and so is one of their children. We must protect Jasper.'

'I forbid it.' Lord Winterton repeated and turned away from his wife.

'That child is your heir, Peveril.'

She let that sink in and turned on her heels, leaving her husband alone in the library, which overlooked the courtyard where her son and Isabella had kissed for the first time.

***

Fliss had just kissed Gavin properly for the first time; gently, suggestively, on the lips. The touch of her mouth on his had made his knees literally go weak, and his body swoop and dive as if he were falling. Now he knew why people referred to "falling in love", because you did, quite literally, feel that way.

The policeman and woman had left, after they'd delivered the news to Fliss that Cornelia's ex-husband was going to formally identify her. They gave Fliss details of where Cornelia would be, which hospital they had taken her to, so that Fliss could visit her if she needed to. It was not as if Cornelia had died. No-one had referred to her as "deceased" and there had been no talk of a body or a mortuary. It made Fliss feel better, she was not ready to think of Cornelia being dead. They'd left Fliss alone in the dining room, and Gavin had shown the two officers out, shaking their hands at the door, thanking them for their sensitivity at this sad time.

When he'd closed the door, and turned back towards the dining room, Fliss was rummaging in the cupboard of the Welsh dresser, two glasses in her hand. Extracting a bottle of *Glenfiddich*, which even Gavin could tell looked expensive, she waved the bottle and glasses at him and beckoned to the living room, where she sat down on the *Eichholtz* shell shaped sofa and poured out two generous measures of twenty-one-year-old, ten-thousand-pound vintage whisky. Handing one glass to Gavin, she saluted the leather chesterfield wing chair in the corner and said loudly,

'To Cornelia.'

Gavin raised his glass, and looked slightly more warily, towards the corner.

'And Harry and Isabella, too.' She added and waited.

There was a resounding crash from somewhere above them. Gavin jumped and slopped whisky onto the wooden floor. Fliss hadn't moved a muscle, as if she were expecting something to happen. Very calmly, whilst above them sounded as though someone was destroying the house and its contents, she took a large swallow of whisky then spoke, again addressing the wing chair in the corner.

'Ah! That has you riled, hasn't it, Sir?'

More loud banging, it sounded as if the very walls were being knocked down by unseen forces. Gavin was petrified. Fliss took his hand.

'It's alright, he can't hurt you. After all, he's been dead for over a hundred years!'

'Stop it, Felicity!'

This was Cornelia's voice. Gavin had spoken to her several times, of course, and he knew it was hers. It couldn't be her! She, after all, was dead! He could not be hearing this. He couldn't. He took a large mouthful of whisky from a hand that shook as it held the crystal glass.

'You are not strong enough yet. Leave him be.' Cornelia's voice again, filtering across the room.

The banging stopped suddenly, and Gavin flung himself upstairs to see what was damaged.

'Gavin,' shouted Fliss. 'It's alright, nothing is broken, they're just noises. They will stop now that I've stopped, and Cornelia is here. She will hold him for me.'

Gavin appeared at the foot of the stairs; Fliss was right.

Upstairs, nothing was disturbed. There was nothing broken, or moved, that could account for the noises they had heard.

'I knew there was something weird about this house,' he said, wiping his brow. 'I've sold it three times now, and somehow it always ends up empty and back on the market again.'

Fliss smiled and put down her glass. She got up and walked towards him and kissed him very gently, very seductively on the lips. They were standing by the stairs, and that was where Gavin knew for certain he had fallen in love with Felicity Keating. In a strange sad cottage, which he hated, he was introduced to love for the first time in his life. Fliss smiled as if she knew what he was thinking and she led him upstairs to her bedroom; As he hesitated on the bottom stair, he was sure that he felt a push, a hand in the small of his back encouraging him to follow her, to take what was being offered. He climbed the stairs without another hesitation and when he walked into the bedroom, Fliss was already undressed, laid on her bed in her glorious nakedness. He was hard instantly.

Her long, dark hair billowed around her shoulders, caressing her bare, naked creamy skin. The curves of her shoulders, her arms, led his eyes to her heaving breasts – not large, but pert, beautifully formed orbs upon which sat dark nipples, begging to be sucked, to have his tongue circle around the expectant peaks until she cried out for him. She wanted him to take each one in his mouth and feast on it as if he was satisfying himself from a famine. Her breasts sat atop the soft curve leading to her waist; then her flat, almost concave stomach; her rounded hips, and a protruding mound where he noticed a tiny slash of pubic hair, auburn, not dark, hair disappearing into the cleft of her womanhood. She lay now, one hand caressing her own breast, and the other resting upon her pussy. She spread her legs as he impatiently tore at his shirt buttons and fumbled with the belt and the zip on his trousers. Sensuously, she raised the hand that had been resting on her pussy, put two fingers in her mouth and then returned them, wet with saliva to her pussy, which he could see now. Open, wanting, swelling, needing.

His cock was huge, the head straining against his foreskin, pre-cum oozing from the tip. He tried to calm down – he did not want to explode before he had even been inside her! He lay down on top of her, felt her heat, felt her need, her desire, and he kissed her delicious plump russet lips greedily, hungrily and she returned those kisses with a determined, almost angry desire. She bit his lip between her greedy, hungry kisses and then ate his mouth with a passioned appetite as he ran his hands through her glossy dark hair, entangled by longing. His thighs pushed hers further apart and he did not hesitate, he did not indulge in foreplay, he did not want to kiss that delicious labia or suck on her hard, swollen clit – he plunged his cock inside her and thrust himself as hard and as far as he could inside her, whilst she cried out, screamed with the need to have him fuck her as roughly, hurting her, pummelling her.

He grabbed her wrists, pinned them above her head as he thrust, pumped, fucked her. He bit her neck, her breasts; her nipples he feasted on biting and sucking as he felt her legs wrap around his waist and her hips arch towards him, willing him in harder, faster, roughly.

'Hurt me,' she begged in between gasps of delight. 'Fucking hurt me, Gavin, give it to me hard and fast. Don't stop. Don't fucking stop!'

Their lovemaking was almost like fighting – both at their limits – Gavin releasing his pent-up fear at the sounds and the events at the cottage and his fear transmitted itself by the way in which he pounded Fliss's body, almost not caring if he hurt her. She didn't care if he hurt her. She wanted hard, fast fucking and she was going to get it. Beneath him she stretched her body around him, arousing him with her mouth on his, biting his lips, his neck, fighting him for the use of her arms, so she could scratch his back, like *she* had scratched his back. Her legs were wrapped around him and she arched her back, wanting him deeper, wanting it to hurt. Wanting Gavin made her forget Cornelia was dead.

She was reaching now, for that feeling, growing desperation for the release that the magnificent white heat of orgasm would give her. His thrusts grew short, stabbing, deep. He was groaning and telling her he was going to come. She gasped, called for him to wait while she raised her hips to him, and they ground their bodies together. Suddenly, she was climbing; climbing high and her pussy and her clit felt as though they were pumping, and she was contracting. Throwing her head back and abandoning all thought, Fliss tipped over into the abyss of ecstasy and then she was falling as he exploded within her, until they grew quiet together.

After a long while, Gavin looked down on her, at her face, her breasts, and her body which was still shaking, still a tremoring mass of nerve endings of pleasure.

'To Cornelia,' he grinned and kissed Fliss's nose.

She smiled back at him.

'To Cornelia.' She replied.

TWENTY-FOUR

She smiled back at him. Leonora Winterton's mood was dangerous.

Angus David Stewart took out the handkerchief from his breast pocket and mopped his brow. One of the consequences of Clara's sister, Isabella, coming to live with them whilst she'd given birth which he had not anticipated after Isabella's untimely and unfortunate death, was having an interview with Lady Leonora Winterton; the mother of the man with whom Isabella had conducted an affair over a substantial period of time. Clara had never told Angus the name of the man involved with Isabella and here he was, having to deal with Lady Winterton turning up and demanding to see her grandson. She was not aware Jasper had been given to a foster family. Angus sensed Lady Winterton was going to be a little displeased when she was informed of this, and of whose orders had caused Jasper to be sent away from the Stewarts and a comfortable upbringing.

Angus was sweating profusely. He wished that Clara were home, but she was not. Having had a great shock following her sister's death, in a slightly ironic twist of fate which Angus did not fail to acknowledge; whilst Lady Winterton of Winterton Village was standing here in his study, Clara was spending a week or two at her parent's home, which was approximately fifteen minutes ride away from Winterton Hall.

Lady Winterton was still looking at him with her steely eyes and Angus mopped his brow again, discomforted under her gaze.

'Well, Sir? The baby. Let me see the baby.'

He opted for feigning ignorance. 'Baby? What baby?'

Lady Winterton leaned over his mahogany desk and placed

her face within inches of his.

'Do not dally with me, Angus, Lord Stewart of whatever God-forsaken little hole in this uncivilised country you inhabit. You and I both know that poor wretched sister-in-law of yours gave birth to a baby boy and that the child is a Winterton. Henry was his father's heir, and this child will be his; therefore, I am going to take him back where he rightfully belongs.'

She moved away and sat down opposite Angus, who was still sweating. She grabbed hold of the bell which sat on his desk and rang it once or twice to summon a servant.

'We shall take some refreshments, Angus, whilst you refresh your memory.'

Angus gave up. Instructing the servant who had answered the bell to bring tea and savouries, he sighed and reached into the drawer of his desk, pulling out a piece of paper upon which was written a name and address.

'We did not keep the child, Leonora. How could we? Clara and I have been childless for the whole of our marriage. People would have talked. They would have known. I – we made arrangements for the baby to be fostered.'

He handed her the paper. Leonora looked at it, then folded it up and put it into her carpet bag.

'Should that child be harmed in any way, Angus, then rest assured, people will talk a lot more. They will talk of how an English woman, a certain Lady Winterton, came to see you and how she arranged to have you killed. Should that child be in poor health or being treated cruelly by the foster family you placed him with, you will begin to wish you had not thought so greatly of your reputation, but more of my grandson's well-being.'

Angus paled visibly, in no doubt of Leonora's abilities to see to his demise. Satisfied with her handiwork, Lady Winterton relaxed, sat back in her chair and asked Angus how he was feeling.

***

Fliss was feeling dreadful. Alone, sad and confused. She hadn't seen Gavin since they had ended up in bed together and being honest with herself, she wasn't sure she wanted to. Not because she didn't like him, or because she hadn't been grateful to him that awful day, when she had found out Cornelia had died, but because she felt ashamed of herself. She'd taken him to bed with her. No, lured would be a better way to describe how she'd kissed him and then ran wantonly up the stairs, throwing her clothes off and arranging her naked self on the bed with her legs open asking him to fuck her. How could she? How could she have done that when she was supposed to be grieving for her Aunt, the person she felt closest to in the whole world? And grieving she was, without a doubt. This wretched feeling of being alone; this melancholy emptiness and longing for what once was could not be anything else other than the grief felt by someone who had loved another unequivocally and absolutely.

She wasn't sleeping well. The atmosphere in the cottage had changed. There was an unease oozing from the stonework, the building seemed to be lurking like an unpleasant stranger waiting to pounce on an unsuspecting victim. Fliss felt it and felt threatened by it. Quite often, she found herself not breathing; shoulders hunched as if she was waiting for something, anticipating some evil. Lately, when she walked into her bedroom, or the lounge, she would get the most peculiar sensation that someone had just walked past her, on their way out. More and more often, she found herself calling her spirit guide to offer her protection, and to still the visions, the sounds; the most upsetting of which was the sound of the chair, hitting the floor in the small bedroom, after it had been kicked away from underneath the body which swung from the beam and made it squeak.

And today, today would be awful, because it was Cornelia's

funeral. She felt ill equipped to attend, being exhausted, heart sore and infinitely sad. She was delivering a eulogy at the service, in the small church where so many of the plague victims had been laid to rest in the little village where Cornelia had lived, tucked quietly on the edge of the Peak District. It was an hour's drive from her cottage, and she wished now that she had taken her mother's advice and travelled up the night before; a suggestion Fliss had turned down simply because it had been her mother who had suggested it.

Now she stood in front of the mirror on the landing, balanced on a small pile of books – she had forgotten to buy hooks to hang it on when she had pounced on it in the antique shop in Ramsbottom. She stood there looking at her reflection soberly clad in a clinging, designer black wrap dress, and her rather excessive, but her favourite, *Jimmy Choo* shoes. Sighing, close to tears, she grabbed the black clutch bag and shoved her keys, her eulogy notes for her speech, her mobile phone and her credit cards inside before snapping it shut.

'Very nice. I'd lose the jewellery. You're going to a funeral, not a girl's night out.'

Madison.

The name came to her like a breath of cold air, stealing through the house. Madison, whose daughter was standing on the window ledge outside, screaming for Mommy. So many ghosts.

Fliss sighed but removed the crystal necklace in deference to the older woman, who had died about a year and a half ago in a courtroom shooting. At least she was friendly.

'That's better. You can do this, honey.'

Madison's deep, Bostonian accent with traces of high-end London was reassuring.

'Thank you.'

Briefly, Fliss caught a glimpse of her – a tall, blonde woman, impeccably dressed in a black suit and white shirt, except for the blood seeping out of a shotgun wound in her chest. She gave Fliss a thumbs up sign and then, Fliss felt a rush of cold air and Madison was gone.

***

'She is not gone.'

Shaking with nerves, Fliss stood at the lectern in the small parish church of Eyam and looked at the upturned faces of the mourners mingled with those of the long dead who had all turned out to either welcome Cornelia to eternity or bid goodbye to her time on earth.

'She is not gone,' Fliss repeated, her voice a little stronger, 'because we do not "go" but rather we use death as a stepping-stone to eternal life within the spiritual world, which sits alongside the one in which we exist now and which we endure day to day. This is what Cornelia believed, and she should have known because, as you know – or at least many of you know – Cornelia was – is – a psychic. A medium; a spiritualist. Call it what you will, but Cornelia could see what most of us fail to look for and that is the connection with that spiritual world, the one which sits next to us until we are ready to pass into it.'

'Cornelia's own son "died" many years ago, yet Cornelia was able to see him whenever he chose to contact her, and she was comforted by this. Her psychic abilities were sought after and scoffed, in equal measure, but I recall with absolute clarity the comfort her abilities gave to the bereaved, the lost, the lonely. They came to her in the hope of reaching someone sitting next to them in the spiritual world and lost, until Cornelia was able to re-unite the living with the dead.'

'Larger than life, at size twenty-two,' Fliss smiled, remembering her Aunt dancing around her dining room. There was a small collective laughter at her remark. Suddenly, she felt her Aunt's hand slip into hers and the church filled with light, despite the greyness of the day. Fliss continued.

'Larger than life, I think her gregariousness, her openness and her willingness to accept the things that many of us would dismiss as out of hand were just some of the qualities that helped her ability to connect with those who sit next to us.

'Cornelia helped me to develop my psychic abilities and although raw and undisciplined, I can see the people who try to make the connection with you, who sit next to you daily and walk with you through your dreams each night.' Fliss looked from person to person – and ticked them off mentally, looking at each in turn.

'I can see Jeffrey,' she said quietly, to the woman wearing pink lipstick.

'I can see Elizabeth.' She said this to the man with the shock of white hair, and finally, she almost whispered, 'I can see the twins.'

Her voice was a gentle caress to the couple who sat holding hands with tears running down their faces. Fliss could sense their children were buried in this churchyard, but she could see them. A boy and a girl of about seven, playing together in the aisle of the church, glancing over at their parents, and giggling every so often at the antics of a small dog.

'And Benjy is here, too.'

Fliss smiled at the man and watched the woman collapse into her husband's arms, crying with the knowledge that her children hadn't died. They had just left her for a while. Her husband held her whilst she dried her eyes, looking frantically around her. The girl came to sit beside her mother and the church grew lighter again. The little girl waved to Fliss, who smiled, and continued to talk about Cornelia.

'So, yes, for those of you who called my Aunt "mad" because of her abilities to see what you refuse to; I, too, am mad, because Cornelia helped me to develop my sensory perceptions and for this, I thank her. Yes, I say thank you, because I can see beyond; and if you can see beyond, then you realise that what is waiting for us is much better than what we already have. And, of course, our loved ones will be waiting for us also. Thank you, Cornelia, I know you are waiting for me.'

Fliss felt the small pressure on her hand as she stepped down from the lectern and she smiled at the weeping couple smiled a thank you through their tears. The boy came to join the family group and the dog wagged his tail and sat at the end of the pew. Fliss turned away and stumbled down the aisle, trying to find her seat again, blinded by tears. Suddenly a hand took her arm, and she almost yelled out in fright, but as she looked up, she simply gasped and fell into Gael's waiting arms.

***

Holding the baby in her arms, Leonora Winterton smiled at her husband and watched some of the great weight of grief fall away from his shoulders, enabling him to stand a little taller as he gazed down at his grandson. Henry's death had diminished Peveril, his sadness at the loss of his son seeming to shrink him both in stature and in personality. The once vibrant, overbearing Lord of the Manor had become a shadow of his former self, taken to dressing each day and simply sitting in either his bedchamber or the library, staring into space, refusing food and society. In Leonora's opinion, the loss of his son had taken much more away from her husband. She hoped his grandson would help return some of those things.

Now, staring down at the fuzzy, dark hair of the child in her arms, who looked up at her with Henry's eyes, Leonora kissed the baby's forehead gently and knew that her husband was slowly coming back from the depths of despair to which he had retreated.

***

So, they had found that repulsive brat and brought it back with them, bestowing upon it a future which he, Thomas, did not want it to have. Its very existence riled him and hurt him to the core and now the thing was going to be brought up in the lap of luxury and declared an heir to the Winterton's considerable fortunes which included the mills, businesses, the farm estates and of course, money. Was it the child's father's inheritance that had made him so attractive to that wretched slut of a woman Thomas has foolishly agreed to marry, and even more foolishly, fallen in love with? He let out a roar of anguish, of pain so great that it made him sound inhuman. He slammed the door of his study shut and roared again, the noise of a wounded animal. He slumped on the desk, burying his face into his enfolded arms.

Why could she not have simply loved him back, instead of taking the love she should have reserved for her husband and giving it to another man who had no right to such a prize? He recalled with venomous bitterness the times she had rejected his amorous advances; when she had flinched from his touch, turned away from his kisses, turned her back on his affections. He'd tried to tell her once, what she meant to him. He tried to explain why he sought relief from others for the physical aspect of his being, which he found so difficult to temper into actions suited to her, his lawful wife, and a lady.

She had looked at him with such distaste that he had had to turn away from her as she had said, so condescendingly, whilst looking at him as if he were dirt,

'But Thomas, my *Lord* Harmer, surely a man who is a true *gentleman* does not experience such ungentlemanly feelings of ardour?'

Thomas did not know how to respond to her cutting remark, and she had left the room, leaving her revulsion behind to mock him.

Of course, he knew why she despised him. Isabella's father, and Harry Winterton's father had both inherited their titles and were peers to boot. They had been born gentlemen, it had not been bestowed on them through the mere ownership of a few acres of land which they called a Manor, so Thomas's father had become Lord of the Manor. The Mountbatten's and the

Winterton's held their titles through rank and privilege; Thomas was a gentleman only in name, not heredity. In his eyes, this diminished him in Isabella's. This, he reasoned, was why he was rejected by her in bed and why he had to seek the pleasures of the flesh elsewhere. Lady Harmer, nee Lady Isabella Mountbatten, daughter of a Duke who was related to the Queen, had married Thomas Harmer, Lord of Holcombe, a manorial title only and it was clear to Thomas that she preferred the privilege of Harry Winterton's birth right. It was something Thomas Harmer never forgot.

TWENTY-FIVE

Fliss lay back in bed and wondered how she could've forgotten. Forgotten the feeling of raw sex; the sensation of soreness between her legs; the feeling of her body having been ravaged; the redness of her bottom cheeks and the bite marks - what Gael called love letters, written into her skin by his teeth.

She sighed and stretched, the sigh sounded like the purr of a sleepy kitten and the stretch was one of complete and utter satisfaction; of spent passion; of sex so good that the memory would sustain her for weeks to come, while the bruises and the bite marks faded.

Gael had gone, of course. He was an animal that did not like to stay in someone else's lair. Fliss was used to him, and found she did not mind, anymore. She had minded once upon a time, and that had been partly why she and he had never been "a couple" when she lived in France. She had wanted more than he was prepared to offer, and eventually, Gael had stopped offering. Fliss then decided to turn down the job offered to her by the *Modus* Art Gallery, opting to return "home" although living near her parents had been a mistake and then she had fled to Cornelia. Which was why Gael had turned up in the parish church at Eyam yesterday, at Cornelia's funeral.

Fliss let the dark cloud of Cornelia's death wash over her, and fade away temporarily, as she remembered the feeling of him, of Gael, enveloping her as she shook and cried in his arms in the church. They had sat together and somehow got through the remainder of the service, sang hymns, said prayers, and offered condolences to the rest of the mourners at Cornelia's graveside. They'd walked back to Cornelia's cottage, the little plague house; crowded today with the dead, and the mourners who stood around politely, drinking the remains of the alcohol which had lived in the cupboard by the fireplace, and picking at a finger buffet prepared by neighbours. They had helped

Cornelia's ex-husband, Uncle Jack, who Fliss did not like simply because he was her father's brother, and because he had moved into the cottage, temporarily, he said, despite Cornelia's will not even having been read.

Gael had sensed how utterly wretched and exhausted Fliss was, he had watched her move between mourners, offering each a little comforting word whilst she tried to avoid either of her parents and Jack who had callously, Fliss thought, been accompanied by his second wife, a woman half the size of Cornelia, not just in her physical appearance but in personality, too. Gael had moved towards Fliss when he knew she had had enough. Gently, but firmly, he removed the cup of tea she held in her hand as she tried to make small talk with two strangers who had been asking her how it felt to be a psychic.

'Exhausting,' interrupted Gael, before Fliss could answer, 'and now, we take our leave. It is time, Felicity.'

He refused to allow her to bid farewell to Jack and her other relatives; to discuss the arrangements for the reading of Cornelia's will or a million and one other things which Gael knew would upset Fliss anew. He took her by the elbow and firmly led her outside to her car, instructing her to drive. When Gael was in this mood, you obeyed him. Fliss drove.

It was quite late when they arrived back at the cottage, which was skulking balefully in the velvety twilight, at odds with the beauty of its surroundings. The rancour reached out and twisted itself around Gael and Fliss as they made their way down the stone steps and Fliss opened the door.

'Ignore it,' she told Gael. 'Your nervousness feeds it.'

Gael nodded and he allowed Fliss to draw him close to her, and he watched her close her eyes, saw the look of fierce concentration on her face but did not understand it. As if she had read his mind, she said, 'I'm protecting you, too. We have a circle of protection now, and outside "influences" cannot touch us.'

'Ah. *Bien*. So, I am able to touch you'.

He moved towards the stairs and pulled Fliss towards them. He had always been an aggressive lover; Gael was not a romantic man. He did not believe in love and roses and when Fliss had expressed a desire for both, making it clear to him that she was falling in love with him, he had withdrawn. She had tried for a while to make it work, she had subjugated and allowed him to lead her into the weird world he called a "lifestyle", of swinging, clubbing, sharing him and each other. It was one Fliss could not inhabit with him. Their parting had been swift, and painful, and had eventually hastened her return to the UK; eschewing the bohemian, arty future she has wanted in France. Gone were the job in the *Modus*, the apartment she had planned in Plassy, when she realised that falling in love with Gael was the one thing that caused him to fall out of love with their situation, their "understanding", he called it, although Fliss didn't understand at all.

Now, she knew what did work with Gael – and she was revelling in the sensation. She had gone upstairs with him, allowed him to lead her, to undress her with exquisite, infinite slowness. Unzipping the dress an inch, then his fingers had roamed up her stocking clad legs, tantalisingly coming to rest at her pussy – not touching – feeling her heat and her arousal inflame as he then returned to the zip. She had wanted to touch him, to kiss him but she knew she must not. She wriggled under his touch and he had commanded her to be still. When she could not because her arousal was too great, too overwhelming, he had simply unfastened his necktie – his eyes not leaving hers for a second – and he had grabbed her wrists firmly and bound them behind her back once he had removed her dress entirely.

She sat on the edge of the bed, hungry, wanting. Gael had stood up, considering her, mentally noting her heaving naked breasts, with large areolas and erect nipples. He ignored her and told her to stay there. Then he went to fetch cognac, glasses, ice, matches and candles. Still, he ignored her and by now she could feel her heart beating in her chest with excitement; she could feel her musky honey wetness soaking through her thin panties and her thighs become slippery with her need. He poured himself a brandy, took a sip and then, considering, he dipped his hand into the ice bucket, and she watched as he held the ice cube, bringing it to her breast. The white cold heat as he pressed it against her nipple made her cry out, made her nipple contract and her juices flow as he made large, icy circles around her areola. He moved from right breast to left before popping the remainder of the cube into the brandy he had poured. He took a large mouthful, and then took one of her breasts in his mouth; the warm amber liquid poured over her shivering skin and the sensation of warmth against her cold nipple was deliciously erotic.

Satisfied of her ardour, he grabbed her ankles, and swung her legs onto the bed, and then maddeningly, slowly, removed her panties. He made her open her legs and commanded her to be still. He picked up the glass and took a sip of brandy. Her breasts heaved. The pent-up feeling of need and desire pierced her between her legs and as he watched her, he could see a damp patch forming on the duvet cover.

'Candles.' Gael announced, raising his eyebrows.

Fliss's eyes widened and she breathed heavily through her nostrils. He lit two candles. One he placed in the candle holder on the windowsill. The other, he carried over to the bed. He dipped into the ice bucket again and this time the ice cube was placed between her two breasts, and he traced an ice-cold trail of desire down her chest, her belly, and as he covered each quivering inch, he leant forward, and dripped hot wax in its wake. The pain, heightened by desire, made her cry out and he tutted. The candle he held over her naked, exposed pussy and she shivered, waiting for the pain. Instead, Gael blew the candle out, put the ice cube he was still holding in his mouth and put his mouth to Fliss's dripping pussy.

She let out a low moan in response Gael's hand snaked up to her breast and pinching her nipple; warning her not to make a sound. She bit her lip to stop herself crying out at the delicious sensation of his tongue, lapping at her clitoris, long slow circular motions, around her engorged, hard little nub. There was blood on her lip now; she could taste it, as Gael used the tip of his tongue to seek out her innermost core of desire, penetrating each nerve ending hidden within the delicate and sensitive folds of her clitoris. She started to shake as his mouth moved to her inner thigh and he kissed and bit and sucked, writing those love letters, and pushing her further towards her orgasm. As he returned his tongue to her pussy, lapping at first her outer lips, then her inner lips and gently penetrating the swollen entrance, Fliss could bear it no more and she had to cry out, she had to cry his name in an agony of wanting, of sexual need.

Her cry angered him – Gael liked to be obeyed. His hand fastened around her throat and the cries of his name stilled on her lips as his grip became tighter. She choked a little and made a whimpering sound, which brought a smile to his lips.

'I know what will quieten you, *ma petite fille.'*

With his next movement he released her throat, she coughed, and he was over her, pulling her up so that she was sitting up and he was straddling her, kneeling so that his cock was just at the right height for her to be able to take him in her mouth and suck his enormous, thick cock. He took hold of handfuls of her luxuriant dark tresses, so that she could not move her head and as her hands were still tied behind her back, she was powerless and unable to disobey.

He pushed his cock towards her, the pre cum oozing from the tip, like a teardrop ready to fall and she opened her mouth obediently.

'*Tres bien, ma petite fille*. Enjoy. And make sure I do.' Gael commanded, pulling cruelly on her hair, making her wince, as she began to suck on his manhood.

She knew what he would want – she felt him ease the hold

on her hair, so that she could move the way he wanted – up and down his cock first, wetting the long length of it with her saliva, then she ran her tongue over the head, lapping up his pre cum and then tucking her tongue underneath the rim and circling the underside of his engorged cock head. She did this for a while, all the time knowing it was pleasing him as she felt the little shudders and tremors of enjoyment. Then she took the length in her mouth again, as far as she could take in, she took and she sucked hard, rhythmically until she felt his cock begin to throb with pleasure, with the blood pumping into it as his arousal grew.

Slackening her mouth, she let the saliva dribble down his shaft, and used her tongue to lap it up, delving downwards underneath so that she could wet his balls with her tongue. He liked her to take each ball in her mouth and suck each one, and she made sure she did everything she knew would bring him pleasure, before returning to the head of his cock and sucking first on just the head, and then pushing her mouth down on him. Further and further down until the tip of his cock was touching the back of her throat. He pulled her hair tightly, wound her curls around his hands like a ribbon and then pulled back, pulling his cock out of her mouth.

Mouth open, Fliss gazed up at Gael, her master, her man, her lover, her exploiter. He yanked her hair, and the force was enough to make her fall backwards, and then he was on top of her and his powerful thighs were pushing her legs apart. One hand in her hair, another at her throat, he forced his huge cock inside her tight, hot, and extremely wet pussy. He felt her contract around him, delightfully tight, contracting over and over again as her orgasm grew with each thrust.

The pressure on her throat was dizzying and time and again, Fliss felt near to passing out – saw the room spin and felt the blackness on the edges of her mind and each time, there would be a tiny release and a hard thrust of his cock, deep inside her. With each thrust she raised her hips, wanting, needing to take more, to have that cock penetrate her as deeply as he could.

They were both sweating now, their sweat mingling with their desire for each other, with that need to each reach their climax and explode in a frenzy of white, hot pleasure. Grunting now, Gael was almost feral – his hands were now holding her thighs wide apart as she grazed herself against him – her clit was being rubbed by his pubic bone as his pushed and pushed inside her. Now she felt it, that shiver, then the stilling as his cock pumped inside her. She groaned and pushed against him, felt one of his thumbs on her clit, rubbing and rubbing until the explosion took her and she cried out in the agony of ecstasy.

Fliss found that her hand had strayed to her clitoris once again, as she remembered the feeling, the subliminal feel of Gael's body on hers. She smiled, stretched again, and brought herself to a swift and very satisfying orgasm as she relived the previous night in her mind's eye. That such pleasure could be derived from the great sadness she had experienced in Cornelia's funeral was one of the great paradoxes of her life; one that she never forgot.

***

Thomas had forgotten about George Avery, until God reminded him of the other man's existence. Standing in the local parish church, with William and Georgina, he looked over at the tall, sallow skinned schoolteacher, singing hymns with the gusto and fervour of the truly devoted, and Thomas felt a little sick. So truly devoted to God, yet capable of bedding another man's wife and fathering a child by the woman who had been Thomas's wife, George Avery was nothing but a hypocrite. Thomas looked at that child now, Georgina, who was sallow and plain; she had not inherited Isabella's beauty. The girl's olive complexion was not one shared with either himself or her mother, and where Georgina's sister, Belle, had been fair, and plumply pretty, Georgina was thin, almost scrawny, and nondescript. In other words, thought Thomas, she looked exactly like her father. It was quite perverse, therefore, that he did not despise Georgina. He was almost fond of her, sensing in her a mutual feeling of not being good enough. No, he did not despise Georgina. But he despised George Avery and he would make certain that George Avery knew it.

TWENTY-SIX

'I knew it!'

Fliss stood up, glancing at the leather wing chair that sat in the corner of the living room by the fireplace.

She'd inherited the chair; it had been in the cottage when she had moved in and according to Gavin, whom she still saw occasionally and with whom she enjoyed a relationship that didn't really know that it was a relationship, the owner before Fliss had inherited it too. The occupant of the chair got up and disappeared through the wall which separated the lounge from the dining room. Fliss shrugged, and turned to Cornelia, perched on the rattan bubble swing seat in the opposite corner – a place she would not have been able to sit in, in life, as she was too large. Fliss smiled at the sight, and not for the first time since her Aunt's untimely death, Fliss thanked her lucky stars that she had inherited Cornelia's gift of psychic ability which enabled her to talk to her Aunt and bridge the gap between life and death.

Cornelia spoke to her now, nodding to the space vacated by the man in the chair.

'Does your knowledge have anything to do with him?'

Fliss nodded.

'It's not Harry – or Henry, or Hal, as I think he is also known. I am so glad it's not him, because this means Harry is not responsible for the malevolence I can sometimes feel.'

There was a crash from upstairs and as Cornelia went to investigate, Harry suddenly appeared before them, a handsome, dark haired man, with a moustache and holding a rope in his hands.

'I only love Isabella.' He told her sadly, before heading

towards the stairs and disappearing upwards.

Fliss followed him to the foot of the stairs, watched him go into the spare bedroom at the back of the house. A few minutes later, she heard scraping – the chair on the wooden floorboards, and then the chair being pushed over. The sad loop of death, being played over and over again.

When she went back into the living room, Cornelia had gone. Fliss could not feel her. She sighed, missing the solid, everyday presence of her Aunt was one of the things she could not get used to. There were so many questions Fliss needed Cornelia to answer.

She had been researching the history of the cottage, simply because there was such a lot of paranormal activity that she was not able to sleep some nights. She was not afraid, as such, for she knew that the dead could do no harm, but they could become noisy, and disruptive. Some nights, Fliss needed nerves of steel to withstand the knowledge that in the bedroom across the landing, a man was hanging from the ceiling. Night after night, he kicked away the chair and she heard it fall to the floor; a sad clattering of the end of someone's life. She knew Isabella had been here, although she had not lived here and Fliss did not know why or how Isabella was connected with Harry.

***

The doorbell chimed, breaking into Fliss's thoughts. She pulled open the front door to find Gavin, brandishing two enormous coffee cups and a paper bag, all bearing the name of her favourite coffee shop emporium. Fliss knew the bag would contain her favourite raspberry and almond square. She smiled and he followed her in, both of them making their way into the dining room. Fliss could not abide eating anywhere other than at the dining table, even if it were just a packet of crisps. She fetched two side plates from the dresser. She couldn't bear eating from a paper bag, either.

Gavin glanced at the laptop, and some notepaper filled with

Fliss's immaculate handwriting, which she had set to one side so that they could sit at the table to eat their impromptu snack.

'Busy?' He raised an eyebrow as he took a sip of cappuccino.

Fliss, munching heavily on the gooey traybake, nodded and when she had finished chewing and swallowed, she replied.

'Yes, as a matter of fact. I'm researching the history of the house. I thought it might help me understand more about what is going on here; the energy, you know, paranormally.'

She glanced upstairs, but all was still and quiet. Gavin could hear the birds, tweeting gaily outside the window of the dining room, which was at a level with the treetops. Further below, the river rushed by, making its usual impatient sigh as the water flowed over the rocks and stones, delaying its progress towards the open countryside beyond.

Turning his attention to Fliss again, Gavin grinned, 'Ask away. I am an estate agent, you know!'

She smiled, 'Yes, but it wasn't an Energy Performance Certificate of the type you lot produce that I want to know about. Mine is a different type of energy.'

'Then perhaps I might be able to help you in my capacity of once being a Winterton.' Gavin gave a little mock bow and smiled. When he noticed the shocked look on Fliss's face, his smiled disappeared.

'You mean to tell me that you are *related* to the Winterton who owned this cottage? To Harry Winterton?' Fliss expostulated, glaring at Gavin, who looked discomfited, and well he might, she thought, angrily.

There was an obligatory crash from upstairs, which both of them ignored.

'But your name is Burrows. Gavin Burrows, it said on your business card. I've still got it, somewhere, in case I ever sell this place.' Fliss looked confused.

Gavin smiled.

'Well, thank you, Miss Keating, in advance of the proposed instruction; and in answer to your unspoken question, the surname was my mum's fault. She married twice. I was just a nipper when my dad died, but I know when she married my stepdad and got pregnant with their first child, she didn't want me to have a different name from my siblings, so they changed it by deed poll from Winterton to Burrows. Voila!'

Fliss had to smile at Gavin's use of the French word. It reminded her of Gael. She shook her head reproachfully at Gavin.

'Gavin, knowing what has gone on in this place, about the ghosts and sightings plus the fact that I'm a psychic, did you not think that little snippet of information just *might* have been significant to me? To what was going on in the cottage?'

Gavin looked crestfallen.

'I thought you might have known, without me saying as you can see and feel things we can't.'

Fliss shook her head. 'It doesn't work like that, Gavin, even I have to refer to the history books, or be *told* things!'

He supposed it might have been wrong of him not to tell Fliss and he was just about to say so when they were both distracted by the front door slamming. They both watched in terrified fascination as an extremely angry man, wearing breeches and a velvet riding coat strode into the cottage, shaking his fist.

'I'll make you pay for this, Avery,' he shouted, before disappearing into thin air. 'I will make you pay for this for all eternity!'

It was the man who sat in the corner, in Fliss's leather wing chair.

***

'Oh, come now, Sir!' George Avery laughed in Thomas's face. 'All eternity? Pray, Sir, what have I done to deserve such a punishment?'

Thomas was shocked at the audacity of the man, a nondescript, sinewy looking creature, who taught at the local school for the unfortunate of society. George Avery supported the education of these ragged, dirty faced urchins, who were destined for a life no better than what they deserved, working in one of the mills owned by the Winterton's or the consortium to which Thomas himself belonged. He wondered what Isabella had found attractive about him. George Avery, studying the man in front of him who was shaking with rage and righteous indignation, supplied Thomas with his answer.

'I am not a rich man, Sir, and nor am I the most physically attractive in comparison to many,' he nodded to Thomas, who was tall, with thick, wavy dark hair, set atop an attractive moustached face with very piercing blue eyes. His body was muscular. Thomas, despite his tendency to sulkiness and his querulous nature, was not a lazy man and he expended a great deal of energy on his estate, riding and sometimes working side by side with his men, on the land. His thick set body made George Avery look puny.

'But what I give to my lovers – Isabella Harmer being one of them,' Avery continued, watching Thomas's face grow almost puce with rage. 'What I give to my lovers, Sir, is consideration. My time. My adoration. My understanding. I do not think for one minute that I am physically attractive to them, but I make myself attractive in my treatment of them.'

'Your attitude, Sir, I find repellent,' spat Thomas, 'and as for you even turning up here, of all the places. A decent man would have turned down my invitation.'

George Avery looked around and studied the living room of the cottage with great care.

'It always did give me quite a thrill, you know, to have

Isabella here – where she had been with her other lover. Although, forgive me - Lord Harmer, I believe? Forgive me if I do not understand quite why you are able to invite me here, and more to the point, why you did invite me here?' He waved his hand about the cottage.

Thomas smiled, 'It is mine now, Avery, and I am entitled to invite who I like here. And I chose you, first.'

'I wondered what the Winterton's would do with it,' mused George. 'After all, it was so much Harry's, wasn't it? He brought all his women here, I believe. Although Isabella was the first, of course. I used to hear them, and I must admit, their lovemaking filled me with a certain frisson. It made Isabella most attractive to me. Which, of course, she learnt, eventually.'

***

'You will learn, eventually.'

George, of course, was well versed in punishment, and cruelty. He was, after all, a schoolteacher, and a Methodist schoolteacher at that; his methods of applying discipline could well have been brought into question, had anyone been interested enough in the plight of the unfortunate children whom he taught.

Isabella had not been interested and, of course, had not known that George Avery, despite his solicitousness and his public façade of polite deference was, in fact, a sexual deviant. She knew now, naked, humiliated, and exposed. He had her laid on the bed – Harry's bed, in Harry's cottage, which Isabella had a key to – and he had her tied to the bedposts, spread-eagled and slightly afraid. Her breasts heaved in fear of what he was going to do to her and at the same time as the fear enveloped her, she was wet and waiting and she wanted – oh! She wanted whatever George Avery was going to do to her.

He was unfastening the leather belt which held up his rather shiny and seedy looking tweed trousers. His very manner was threatening, and Isabella found that the threat and the fear made her want whatever he was going to give her. Unable to move, straining against the cords with which he had bound her, she felt her fanny contract with the need to be hurt, to be punished for whatever wrongdoing George Avery perceived of her. The belt dangled threateningly in his hands and her eyes grew wide and staring, as she awaited the first, delicious crack of leather against her delicate skin.

It made a snapping sound against the delicate flesh of her breasts, and her nipples stood erect, stinging from the blow. He drew the leather slowly back and forth along the welt, making Isabella wince and groan with fear and longing. The next application of the belt was between her legs and that did make her cry out with the sheer pleasurable pain. She had not believed that pain could be so beautifully sensual. It made her shake all over with desire for the man administering it. She gasped and said, "please", not knowing if it was a request to stop or whether she was begging for more.

'She kept begging for more, Lord Harmer,' George smirked as he regaled Isabella's wantonness to the other man, who stood before him growing angry and apoplectic with rage as Avery intended.

'She was laid spread-eagled before me, wet with the need for me to take her. She kept coming back for more, such was her pleasure. Did she pleasure you in this way, Sir?'

Avery's look was triumphant. Thomas's anger could be contained no longer. The more powerful of the two men, he lashed out and struck Avery with his left fist, and as he did so, his right hand swooped inside his riding jacket and he pulled forth a gun. The noise of the gun's exchange as Thomas pulled the trigger and shot George Avery in the head, surprised both men. It was Avery's last thought. Thomas staggered backwards, the pistol having misfired, ending his life and his time in this world in a cacophony of anger and hatred that followed him into the next.

***

'Do me a favour, Fliss. If you ever sell this cottage, give the instruction to someone else, please.' Gavin was the first to speak after they had both watched the angry apparition stride through the living room and simply disappear into thin air.

'You saw him too?'

Fliss was fascinated at the small scene which had just been played out before their eyes. Gavin nodded.

'I probably should have told you before, about my suspicions that the house was haunted. I've felt the atmosphere – change, and of course, I knew Perry and the Cooper-Clarkes. Madison and her little girl, Penelope, or something. They are both dead now.'

'Phoebe,' Fliss corrected, looking at the little girl with the bruises on her chest, dressed in a thin cotton nightgown. She looked as though she were sitting on thin air and then Fliss realised that the layout of the room would have been different when she and her mother lived here, and Phoebe was actually sitting where her mother Madison's desk and chair would have been. Fliss smiled. Phoebe looked up and disappeared. Gavin had not seen her.

'Yeah, Phoebe. I also saw the woman.' Gavin said in a confessional tone.

'Madison? Phoebe's mother? I have seen her, too.' Fliss told him.

Gavin shook his head.

'No, not Madison. Another woman. Gorgeous. Red hair, the colour of a fox.'

Isabella!

They both looked at one another and each knew neither of them had spoken the name, that it had drifted towards them through the centuries, spoken by the man who had loved her most.

TWENTY-SEVEN

Leonora stood looking sadly at the cottage and knew that whatever they did with it now, following Lord Harmer's death, the family would never sell or rent it again. She knew that whatever tragedy had taken place within its walls, including her own son's suicide, the cottage was going to stay part of the Winterton estates, of Jasper's inheritance. She'd never been inside the tiny stone house and wondered now if she should; if it might bring her closer to Henry, who had chosen to end his life there. Had he been sparing the family – or had he chosen the cottage because it was his link with Isabella? Was that why he had wanted to die there, because he had experienced love, and perhaps, life, there?

It was a pretty little cottage, Henry had called it Enchantment Cottage, Leonora had learnt. It stood on the crest of a hill, at a junction where three lanes met each other and across the bridge, over the river there was the mill, within easy walking distance. Neighbouring cottages were rented out to the mill workers, but this one was where Henry fled to; this one was where he had known true love, of that Leonora was certain.

She looked down now at the child pulling on her hand, an auburn haired, dark eyed three-year-old boy. Was it really that long since Henry had gone, and Isabella, too? Leonora sighed. Death and time were two things from which there were no escape and one led, eventually to the other, except in the cases of Jasper's parents, for whom time had moved a little faster and death taken them a little sooner.

Pulling herself out of her reverie, she smiled at her grandson.

'Shall we go in, Jasper? To the little house? Your Grandmama would like to see inside.' Leonora looked down at the child and briefly, saw her own son, Henry, again, reflected back at her through her grandson's eyes.

Jasper nodded, thrilled at the chance of an adventure, somewhere new. Life was rather boring sometimes at Winterton House with dull old Jeanie and the nursery maids, and Grandmama and Grandpa, who were as old as time itself. Life was not fun for Jasper and the chance to explore a new place, and maybe play there, was not one he was going to turn down. He nodded to his Grandmama again, and she seemed to gather herself up to full height and hold her breath for a while.

'Come, Jasper,' she said now to the little boy, 'let us go in and see the cottage that your father built. One day, like everything, it will be yours!'

Obediently, Jasper followed his grandmama down the three stone steps to the front door of the little house. She had to struggle a while to turn the key; the lock was old, and unwieldly, having not been opened for so long, but eventually the lock groaned and his grandmama was able to push the door open. She stepped back, to let her grandson inside first.

Letting Jasper run on ahead, Leonora entered the cottage along with her mixed feelings about being there in the first place. She walked into the cosy looking living room, with its stone wall, and open fireplace. There were the remnants of a long-ago fire still in the hearth, ashes of a love affair. Had Henry and Isabella sat in front of the fire together, watching flames dancing whilst they loved each other in the firelight? Leonora, whilst finding the thought of their physical act of love distasteful, felt comforted somehow that Henry had, at least, experienced love during his lifetime. She knew without doubt that Isabella Harmer had loved her son and she was grateful for the knowledge.

She walked slowly across the wooden floor, through the doorway which led into a sort of passageway – hardly a room. Dust bunnies startled and skittered across the floor as Leonora's footsteps tapped sadly across the stale and neglected smelling room. Jasper was standing by the kitchen stairs and Leonora shook her head. The stairs were very steep, and it felt cold and unwelcoming down there. She suddenly understood the term "below stairs" and made up her mind to make sure their kitchens and outer rooms, used solely by the servants, were improved, made more bearable.

Retracing her footsteps, she took hold of Jasper's hand and they went upstairs.

The front bedroom overlooked the hill, and Leonora could see the farmhouse at the top. To the right, building work had begun on a row of terrace houses, opposite the new railway station that connected the village to several main towns, which were now thriving as a result. Henry had always been a champion of progress; he had steered the family's fortune away from farming and the estate work and persuaded his father and his business colleagues to invest in the industrial revolution. Despite his father's reservations, which Henry had fought vigorously, he had been proved right and the family had benefitted enormously. How Leonora wished Henry had lived to see all this, and to hear his father's pride and praise for the innovation Henry had supported.

Leonora turned from the window and Jasper pulled away from her hand, he was beginning to get bored. She let him toddle into the rear bedroom, the smaller of the two, and hoped he'd be amused for a while looking out of the window at the trains which went past fairly frequently. He always got excited when they sounded their whistle and the steam hissed from the engine as the train gathered speed. How amazing was modern technology, she thought, Henry was right in everything he did.

She sat on the big feather bed, laden with pillows and soft cushions. A couple of woollen blankets were strewn carelessly at the foot of the bed, as if they had just been pushed to one side in the midst of passionate love making.

'I did love her so, Mother.'

The voice seemed to fill the room, out of nowhere. Leonora sat upright, her hand at her throat as she stared around wildly.

It wasn't just a voice she had heard. It was Henry's voice! Here, in this room, Henry was here!

She called his name, 'Henry!'

Her voice broke, 'Henry, my darling son. Where are you?'

She spun around wildly, and her ears strained into the silence filling the room, only broken by the distant rumbling of a train. Her eyes scoured the dimness which surrounded her. She thought for a brief, unnerving minute that she saw a shape; the outline of a man's body, but she could not be certain that it was not merely the suggestion of her own grief-stricken mind.

'Henry.'

She said his name once more, quietly savouring the opportunity to have the word slip from her tongue as she glanced about her, wishing desperately to see the shape again. Then she remembered Jasper.

'Henry! Your son!' Leonora looked around her. 'You must come and see him, he's in the other bedroom, Henry. You can meet Jasper!'

The air seemed to hang expectantly, and a strange excitement filled the space around her as Leonora held her breath. The rumble of the train grew louder.

'Jasper'

Without a doubt, it was Henry's voice. Tears streamed from Leonora's eyes, making small rivulets in her heavily powdered face. She moved in a haze of joy to the landing towards the smaller bedroom.

'Come and see him, Henry,' she said, addressing the air where she thought she had seen the outline of her son. 'Come and watch Jasper play.'

Leonora flew into the other bedroom. The atmosphere hit her like a solid wall of evil; rancorous, and bitter tasting. She gasped, in horrified fear, as if she knew that something dreadful was about to happen. She tried to reach him, but she could not. Whatever it was in that room held her with unseen hands and she quailed as she heard the whistling of the approaching steam train get louder and louder until it filled her ears as her terror filled the room. The rumble of the engine, the scream of horror, the clattering noise of the lock mechanism on the window, which suddenly snapped open and the horrific sight of her only grandson tumbling out of the upper floor window. The hiss of the steam train told her it had stopped.

***

Fliss groaned, raised her aching, sleep deprived body up onto her left elbow and reaching across the bed to the bedside cabinet, she picked up her mobile phone. Not yet five in the morning. She let out a groan. This needed to stop now. The paranormal activity, which she had sensed during the very first viewing of the cottage several months ago, was now reaching a level which was affecting her everyday life to such an extent, it was making her ill. She put down the phone and snapped on the bedside lamp, easing herself upright, feeling all the aches and pains of a restless night. Sighing, she got out of bed carefully and made her way slowly down to the kitchen, two floors below, to make a hot drink to take back to bed with her.

She was aware of scenes being repeatedly played before her eyes, which she kept averted from the rear bedroom, so she could not see Harry Winterton hanging from the ceiling beam or his son, Jasper falling from the window. She tried to avoid George Avery and Thomas Harmer fighting in doorway of the lounge, but she couldn't avoid noticing Phoebe sitting in the dining room. On her way down the kitchen stairs, as usual, she felt the brush of taffeta as if someone were walking past her. She stepped over Vera, the woman who had broken her neck in a fall and who lay on the kitchen floor.

Once downstairs, Fliss sat at the small round dining table by the door with Madison, while she waited for the milk she was heating to boil. She got up to add some cinnamon to the frothing liquid, and turning around, she looked out of the tiny kitchen window, watching the daybreak, and wondering what to do.

There were too many spirits, Fliss thought sadly, too much tragedy in this tiny house. She wished Cornelia or her spirit guide, Waya, a Cherokee Indian whose name meant "wolf", would appear, but she knew they would not. The house was experiencing too much activity for them to add to it.

Pouring the hot milk and cinnamon mixture from the pan into her favourite mug, Fliss decided she couldn't be bothered to climb the two flights of stairs back to bed, so she took the mug back to the table and grabbed a fleece blanket from the cupboard under the stairs. Wrapping the comforting, warm folds of the blanket around her shoulders, she sat at the table with Madison, and Vera, who had uncharacteristically got up from the floor, as if sensing that Fliss was more troubled in life, than she was in death.

'This is the pits, you know,' Madison waved a manicured, bloodstained hand around the kitchen and pointed up the stairs. '*They* shouldn't be here anymore than we should. You need to get rid of us ghosts.'

Fliss smiled at the thought of being told to get rid of ghosts by a ghost.

'Spirits. There's no such thing as ghosts.' Vera corrected, trying to straighten her neck unsuccessfully. 'I look like Quasimodo!'

'At least you're clean!' Madison groaned, looking distastefully at the blood stains on her hands and her clothes.

Fliss wondered if this were the beginning of how she would eventually be sectioned under the Mental Health Act and thus removed to a suitable hospital for treatment. She appeared to be sitting at her kitchen table, talking to the spirits of two dead women. Both of whom had owned the cottage before her, and who had both died suddenly and prematurely. Maybe she was next, she wondered, and the hairs on the back of her neck stood up.

'Hold a séance. Get rid of us.' Madison advised.

'She's right. You look like I did when I was going through this.' Vera told Fliss, who put her head in her hands.

When she awoke later, it was light. A pale amber glow was flickering through the venetian blinds and the birds were singing to each other as the dawn broke, heralding another fresh start. Fliss lifted her head up off her arms, took a mouthful of milk and pulled a face. It was cold. Had she really sat here and had a conversation with two dead women, who had suggested holding a séance at the house, or was she just another basket case, as most psychics were often described?

She got up, made a fresh drink - coffee, this time to waken her up - and took it to the living room to drink. She called to Waya for protection, and when she walked into the living room, all was peaceful; she could begin to sort out the mess in her head and put some thought to the suggestion of the séance.

'It's not a séance that you need,' said Gavin, later, when she met him for yet another coffee in *Grind and Tamp*, her favourite little café in Ramsbottom.

They were seated at the corner table by the window and Fliss was poured over a delightfully strong and aromatic single origin speciality coffee. The friendly café owner, Adrian, had just brought their Sourdough toast over with a smile and a wink and Gavin was helping himself to peanut butter.

'No, you don't need a séance, Fliss, it sounds like you need a flaming exorcism!'

'I would do it if I thought it would help them, Gavin, but as a psychic I can't help thinking that there is a reason for them still walking this earth. I think there is a mystery to be solved.'

She looked at him from beneath her dark fringe and suddenly, he had the strangest feeling that underneath Fliss's look, a pair of cerulean eyes were also staring back at him. The eyes belonging to the woman with the blue dress and the red hair.

TWENTY-EIGHT

Fliss smiled at Father Maguire in amusement. 'I don't know why,' she grinned, 'but I didn't expect you to have red hair.'

He grinned. 'Well, it makes a change from people expecting me to speak like a leprechaun and be dressed in a black frockcoat, carrying a crucifix and a bible.'

'I'm disappointed now, Father. I thought they were the tools of your trade.'

Father Colm Maguire appraised the attractive young woman standing in the doorway, wearing a smile which he knew hid a gamut of emotions. Early thirties, he'd say, with masses of cloudy dark hair, eyes that reflected the depth of her soul and a curved bow of a mouth with sultry lips that spoke of trouble without uttering a word. Not for the first time in his working life, Colm Maguire wondered at the sanity of his decision to marry the church and devote his life to God.

'Ah, to be sure, Miss Keating, to be sure,' he replied, in an exaggerated Irish accent. 'Oi left dem in de car along wid de twelve disciples. Shall Oi be goin' to get them or will we wait for Jesus and de Holy Ghost to arrive?'

Fliss burst out laughing and stood aside, inviting the priest into the cottage. He stepped into the doorway and he felt it immediately. The house seemed to recoil at his presence and the air thickened with a hatred so palpable, he could almost taste it. Fliss's smile died on her lips as she watched the priest's reactions.

'You can feel it?' She asked, closing the front door.

It was all he could do to not turn around, wrench the door open again and run up the hill in the opposite direction.

'*Pater noster, que es in coelis,*' he muttered, and his hand automatically reached into the pocket of his tweed jacket to finger the rosary beads that went everywhere with him. *'Pater noster que es in coelis, santificatur noem tuum...'*

'Is it that bad, Father, that you feel the need to summon the Lord?'

Fliss looked at him steadily, her dark eyes fixed upon him as she waited for his reaction. She beckoned him to sit down and he shook his head, indicating without words that he wished to walk around the house.

He was still uttering the Lord's Prayer, she noticed as she followed him into the dining room; he glanced briefly at the corner where Fliss often saw Phoebe playing and a small smile played upon his lips. He reached the kitchen stairs.

'Holy Mother of God!'

'You can see her?' Fliss asked.

Father Maguire turned around to face Fliss.

'I wonder how you can bear to spend a night here.'

It was a statement rather than a question and Fliss remained silent, beginning to wonder the same thing herself. Suddenly, she felt Cornelia's hand in hers. The dining room filled with light. The priest heaved a sigh of relief and made himself walk up the stairs, heavily, slowly.

The house held its breath.

At the top of the stairs the landing broke into two, like a "T" junction, the bathroom behind the stairs and the two bedrooms on either side. The sadness reached out from the bedroom on the left at the back of the house and Father Maguire had no need to go in to see the wretched sight of Harry Winterton hanging from the ceiling or the child falling from the window. He turned and went into the bedroom at the front of the house. Fliss's room.

He didn't really need to go in there, but he went anyway,

curious to know more about the woman who had summoned him to this tragic little cottage in the heart of a village bearing the name of the long-ago family to whom it owed so much and whom it resented in equal measure. The exploitation of its inhabitants who worked in the mill, or on the estate, was not easily forgotten by those upon whose labours the Winterton family had grown incredibly rich.

Fliss had expensive, and eclectic taste, he noted as he took in the top-quality bedroom furnishings, and the well-known designer brands of cosmetics and make-up which sat atop of the dressing table opposite the window. She had obviously been in a rush to get ready for his visit this morning, he thought, seeing the stopper on the perfume bottle laid on its side and the spillage of fine face powder dribbled carelessly on the tabletop. The untidiness was out of variance with the rest of the house.

This room had, at least, seen great love, he knew. Its balm eased him, and he was strengthened by the tendrils of passion he could feel stretching out and wrapping themselves around his soul. He took a deep breath, tried to ignore the flimsy, very sensuous looking, ruby red negligee which hung on the back of the bedroom door and he returned downstairs to find Fliss sitting on the sofa, with a tray bearing a cafetière of coffee, two mugs and a plate of biscuits.

'You're honoured,' she smiled. 'I won't normally eat anywhere except the dining room or at the kitchen table. However, this is a special occasion!'

She busied herself with the making of rather excellent coffee and handed him a mug of the steaming liquid.

'Being a man of the cloth does bring with it some special dispensations,' he declared, happily, 'although I must say, Miss Keating, I do rather admire you, being able to live here at all. You sense that there is a lot of – activity?'

He chose the word very carefully and took a sip of his coffee.

Fliss smiled, appreciating the choice of words. 'So, you do

believe that there is cause for an exorcism?'

The cottage seemed to recoil; the atmosphere dripped with venom.

It was Father Maguire's turn to smile. 'I fear they don't fancy the idea.'

Fliss didn't need to ask who *they* were, but she was impressed with the fact the priest had picked up the dip in the atmosphere, the sudden switch from a bubbling undercurrent to a raging torrent of hatred.

'Well, I do, Father Maguire. I fancy it very much and I should like to have this happen as soon as possible.'

'Then I am going to disappoint you, Miss Keating, I have a certain procedure which I must follow in order to perform a major exorcism. Believe it or not, the Catholic Church has a protocol for this sort of thing, and it means unfortunately perhaps, for you, that there is going to be a slight delay in the actual ritual being carried out. I must obtain permission from the Bishop in order to perform a solemn – or major exorcism, such as I feel is needed here. I will also need at least one other priest here; it is unwise for an exorcism to be carried out in solitude.'

Fliss sighed in resignation.

'I suppose it was rather stupid of me to think that you were just going to reach into your pocket, pull out a bottle of Holy Water and sprinkle it around the place, asking everyone who's haunting it to leave.'

She smiled, wanly.

'Haunting is quite a strong word, Miss Keating, for a psychic.'

The priest raised his eyebrows and looked across at Fliss, studying the tired smile and the small lines of worry etched on the bridge of her nose, between her eyes.

Fliss gasped. 'You know? How?'

Father Maguire smiled as he stood up, looking at his watch to check he was not running late to his next appointment.

'I suppose it comes from the whole "being an exorcist" thing, Miss Keating. Although I prefer to think of myself as a Deliverance Driver, as I'm afraid the film sensationalised us somewhat. We do, however, tend to pick up some psychic abilities of our own due to the nature of what we do, I suspect.'

It was Fliss's turn to smile.

'Deliverance Driver! I like it, Father Maguire, and thank you for your time. I shall wait to hear from you once you have spoken to the Bishop.'

They shook hands and the priest took his leave. He took large, long gulps of the fresh country air once he was outside the cottage, as if he were purging himself of the thick unpleasantness that permeated the atmosphere inside the building. Walking towards his car, which he had had to park at the bottom of the hill underneath the railway arches, he wondered if he was up to the task ahead.

***

Phillip Harmer stood taking large, long gulps of fresh country air. He was standing outside the cottage where his brother had died in somewhat puzzling circumstances. Thomas had apparently been shot, as had the schoolteacher who had taught in the school, which used to be further up the hill. Phillip had learned from the locals that the school had shut down and the building was now a Mechanics Institute. It was also from local gossip Phillip had learned of the affairs Thomas's wife, Isabella, had conducted from the cottage; affairs which Phillip thought may well have had a connection with the gunfight that had added to the cottage's death toll.

He sighed heavily. Staring at the cottage which had taken his only living relative from him, he felt very alone. Whilst they had not been close in life, it had been a comfort to Phillip to know he had a brother. It was to Thomas, and Harmer House that Phillip returned on the rare occasions he was allowed an exeat from school. Thomas was ten years his senior and their parents having died long before either Thomas married, or Phillip grew up, meant most of Phillip's life was spent in the confines of his boarding school.

Their childhood relationship had always been blighted by the resentment Phillip felt about being the younger son, the one who would not inherit. Despite his expensive education he was always jealous of Thomas having been educated at Winchester, being the elder son, the important son. Phillip's resentment of his elder brother was only marginally assuaged by Thomas's death. By dying, his brother had left one male heir – William, aged just ten. He was now the new Lord Harmer and his Uncle Phillip had been left his guardian and therefore it came about that Phillip also became guardian of the Harmer Estate. Phillip smiled at the little terrace cottage, which may have inadvertently brought about the death of his brother, but which also had given Phillip a new lease of life.

***

Gavin smiled at Fliss.

'I bet once this is over, you'll feel like the cottage has a new lease of life!'

They were standing outside the cottage, having just been for a walk and Fliss was trying to find the keys, rummaging in the amazing number of pockets the manufacturers seemed to be able to sew into one of their waterproof jackets. Eventually finding them in an inside breast pocket, she brandished them at Gavin with a flourish, opened the door of the cottage and waited on the threshold.

Gavin looked at her questioningly.

'I'm waiting to see what mood is inside,' she told him. 'The atmosphere has been very unpleasant since Father Maguire was here.'

Fliss stepped tentatively into the tiny vestibule and began unlacing her walking shoes. The inner glass panelled door leading into the living room was open, but as she straightened up and peered inside, for once, the atmosphere was benign. Heaving a sigh of relief, Fliss went in and Gavin followed.

'I'll make us some cheese on toast for supper, in a moment,' said Fliss, 'I'll just retrieve this message on the answerphone.'

Gavin nodded. He, too, felt that the atmosphere in the cottage was bearable, almost welcoming. He sat down on the shell shaped sofa, which he hated but it was either that or the leather winged chair in the corner and after Fliss telling him that she'd seen a man sitting on there and then walking straight through the wall opposite, Gavin decided that an uncomfortable sofa was preferable to a haunted chair. He watched Fliss now, pacing up and down, listening to the message left on the telephone's answering service; he loved the way she bit her bottom lip when she was concentrating. In fact, Gavin was beginning to think he loved everything about her.

She put down the telephone and beamed at him. 'They're coming next Tuesday – Father Maguire and his colleague, to perform the – ceremony.'

She somehow did not want to say the word exorcism. Was fear, making her avoid it?

There was a bang from upstairs. They knew. The atmosphere began to thicken.

***

'But surely you knew?' David Trevethan looked in astonishment at him.

Phillip Harmer was sitting with David, Thomas's solicitor and his accountant, Charles Buckley in the Drawing room at Harmer House. It overlooked the paddock, where Phillip's niece, Georgina, was riding her pony, a glorious fifteen hand thoroughbred called Madame, and Phillip reflected what an expensive picture they painted – rider and horse; an expense which his late brother could obviously not afford, if the information he had just received from Thomas's men was accurate. The estate was basically bankrupt, it owed more than it produced and several of its so-called assets were mortgaged to the point of foreclosure as monthly repayments were not actually being repaid. Georgina and her pony were an expense which the estate could not sustain. Phillip laughed – it dawned on him that the solicitor and the accountant fell into this category, too; and in bringing him this news, they'd brought about the removal of their services from his employ.

Of course, he hadn't known. If he had, would he have been so eager to accept the responsibilities of running this considerable estate, together with the guardianship of Thomas's two children, with little or no money to enable him to live the life he had anticipated such a position would bring him? At least he knew the answer to that conundrum – it would have been a resounding *no*.

He looked once more at Georgina, now dismounting whilst one of the grooms held her pony. She was walking down the mounting block, an elegant black gloved hand holding her riding whip and her hat, looking every inch the picture of wealth and privilege. Well, thought Phillip, the privilege of wealth was not one that they had, it seemed. He smiled at the irony and returned to the two men, sitting waiting for his thoughts.

'Well, gentlemen,' he said, looking at them quizzically. 'What shall I do? Besides bringing your services to an end. After all, should you not have warned my brother many, many months ago of the situation he was getting himself into?'

Both men bristled, affronted that their professional expertise was being brought into question, but more worried about the prospect of unpaid fees.

Charles, studying the accounts yearbooks, looked back at

Phillip thoughtfully.

'The debts are mainly owed to the Winterton family. Thomas seems to have borrowed rather heavily against his shares in the mill consortiums. As they are neighbours, perhaps you could come to some arrangement over land; it's still a valuable asset, Phillip.'

David smiled. 'Or here's food for thought - you could marry Amelia Winterton.'

TWENTY-NINE

'Marry me? Whatever for?'

Gavin looked at Fliss from his position on his knee. His being rather a traditionalist, Gavin had wanted to do this properly and that evening, he'd gathered his courage and thrown it down on the floor in front of her, where he was kneeling now, rather painfully. Fliss's answer was not encouraging.

'Do get up, Gavin. The Maître d' is looking rather worried.'

Reluctantly, Gavin got up and sat himself down again at the table where they were having dinner at *Al Bosco*. The restaurant was their current favourite, on account of it being within walking distance of the cottage, so neither of them needed to drive and they could enjoy a nice bottle of wine with their meal. Gavin stared at the three quarters empty bottle of Malbec. Maybe he was drunk, and that was what had propelled him onto his knees suddenly.

'I must admit, proposing on one knee is a bit painful and I didn't quite get the reaction I was looking for.' Gavin sighed. 'I do love you, Fliss. You know?'

Fliss looked at him, sitting forlornly now, crumbling a piece of bread between his forefinger and thumb. He returned her look, and Fliss gasped. For a split second, the features of Harry Winterton juxtaposed themselves over Gavin's face. For that brief moment, she was staring at Harry's dark eyes, and not Gavin's hazel ones; it was Harry's dark, slightly longish hair framing his face, not Gavin's short, spikey cut and she distinctly heard Harry's voice say, 'I do love you, Isabella.'

She grasped her napkin and held onto it tightly, until Gavin became just Gavin again and she heard herself say to him, in a voice that didn't really sound like her own, but may have been the voice of another women, drifting through time. The one with red hair and piercing blue eyes, the one called Isabella.

'I do know. And I love you, too.'

***

'Love? You don't love him, Felicity.' Gael had never called her Fliss, he didn't agree with nicknames or pet names. 'You don't love him, and I shall prove it.'

There was a click from the other end of the line and Gael disconnected their phone conversation. Fliss sighed and replaced the receiver in its cradle. Then she picked it up again and dialled Colm Maguire.

'I was just checking that everything was still going ahead tomorrow?' Fliss asked, in an anxious whisper. They were listening.

'Of course, Fliss. If there was a problem, I would have let you know. In fact, I'm just doing some preparation work now. I and Father Gillespie will be there, with our team.'

Colm Maguire smiled down the telephone. She had a beautiful voice, he thought. It reminded him of honey.

'How many of you are coming?' Fliss looked up at the ceiling. The banging upstairs had started again. 'I thought it was just you and your colleague.'

Still smiling, Colm Maguire replied, 'Oh, I was thinking of bringing the army of the Lord, also.'

The banging got louder.

Fliss sighed. 'I'm beginning to think I need them.'

She put the phone down again. Realising she was sitting hunched over the small telephone table in the corner of the living room, she sat up straight and tried to relax her shoulders, but she found relaxation was impossible. She leant over the table again, afraid of she knew not what. The atmosphere in the cottage was restless, untethered, like the air before a storm.

When you know something is building and that there is going to be a release, an event, a happening and the anticipation builds into unbearable tension. Fliss put her head in her hands.

'Come on darling.' Cornelia's voice drifted through the thick, tar black churlishness that unravelled through the cottage; layers and layers of anger and regret choking the air, until Fliss found it difficult to breathe.

'Am I doing the right thing, Corny?' Fliss asked, looking up from her crouched position, trying to unlock her hands, which were balled up fists.

Again, Cornelia's voice was no more than a suggestion, fluttering through the tension.

'You are doing what you feel you must, and if that includes marrying Gavin, then take no notice of that odious Frenchman. Do what you feel you must.'

***

'I am doing what I feel I must.' Phillip Harmer declared, standing in front of Amelia's parents.

He, Lord Winterton, wasn't too much of a problem. He was probably grateful that, at last, someone wanted to take Amelia off his hands. Lady Winterton, she was more difficult. She looked at Phillip in such a way, he wanted to curl up into a tight ball.

'Your rent has not been paid, Sir.' Lady Winterton was saying now. 'Your bailiff tells me that your mills are falling into disrepair. You have not paid your quarterly contribution to the Consortium – a business arrangement which Sir Robert Peel entrusted capital to – and yet, Phillip Harmer, you wish to marry our daughter?'

Phillip quailed inwardly. He'd not known that Lady Winterton would have such a grasp of business arrangements, or that she would have investigated his financial standing rather more than he had investigated his brother's before taking on the estate and the guardianship of his two children. His resounding confirmation, 'Yes, your Ladyship, I do,' sounded, even to Phillip himself to be a lot more confident than he felt.

Leonora Winterton looked at her husband and saw the imperceptible nod.

'Very well, Sir. We agree in principle to a match between yourself and our youngest daughter, Amelia. In exchange, Sir, we shall repossess full title to all the properties within the Harmer Estate, including Harmer House. The land surrounding it reverts to the Mountbattens, as part of your brother's settlement on Isabella upon his marriage to her. In addition, the shares you hold within the Consortium shall revert equally to Sir Graydon Mountbatten and to my husband, who will settle your debt to the Consortium.'

'But Harmer House is my home!' Philip expostulated, in astonishment.

'Can you afford to pay the rent, Sir?' Lady Winterton's response was direct.

Phillip hung his head. He could not and he knew it, and so did she.

'And the Mill, my mill at Holcombe? Lady Winterton, I am perilously close to being unable to operate it – there are mounting debts and workers are being laid off as I cannot afford their wages.'

Lady Winterton took in the expensively cut clothes, and then cast her eyes outside to where Phillip's carriage stood, with a liveried footman waiting for his master's return so that he could open the door and assist Phillip inside. She thought of Georgina, being privately schooled, and William, at school in Winchester. She had never liked Thomas Hamer. She liked his brother even less.

'You can sell the mill to my husband and clear the debts from the proceeds. There should be ample money available to enable you to continue the children's education and, in the holidays, Georgina and William shall come here to Winterton Hall. We will be responsible for their upkeep as there will not be room for them in the cottage.'

Phillip gasped. 'The cottage on the hill? Harry's cottage, where my brother died?'

'I don't know why you sound so incredulous, Sir.' Leonora replied, 'You clearly cannot expect to remain in Harmer House once we have sought possession? How will you afford it? The cottage is empty; and you need somewhere to live with Amelia, who does not have any grand designs in life. She will be happy there, as she will be happy wherever her husband choses to take her. You may live there rent free. You will work as the Factory Manager in the Brooks Bottom Mill, as it is so close to your cottage. You will have a steady income from that, and you will be entitled to a share of the profits, dependent upon the performance of the mill under your ministration. I believe this arrangement to be an incredibly generous one, Sir, given your brother's inability to add up and take away. You may go.'

'My brother died in that cottage, Lady Winterton!' Phillip could not help but protest.

Leonora Winterton got up from her fireside sofa and walked over to where Phillip was standing. The combination of his lack of height, and her being tall for a woman meant that she was able to look him straight in the eye.

'Your brother died in that cottage, my Lord, whilst being in the process of shooting another man, so rumour has it. There is talk, from old servants who worked in Harmer House, that your brother had some sort of hand in your sister-in-law's death; so, do not plead to me about your emotional reservations of living in this cottage which our generosity bestows on you. The name Harmer means little to the inhabitants of this village at the moment. You would be as well to remember this as you are not in a position to do anything about it.'

She turned away from him, leaving him stunned, and open mouthed, but with a chance. It was one he had no option but to take.

***

Fliss stood at the door, stunned and open mouthed.

'Gael! What on earth are you doing here? Why are you not in France?'

Gael smiled unpleasantly. 'Come now, Felicity. I am not *en* France because I am here, on your doorstep and I have come to prove to you that you do not love this – Gavin, whom you say has asked you to marry him.'

Fliss folded her arms belligerently.

'Of course, I love Gavin, Gael. Just because you are incapable of loving anyone or anything does not mean that it is impossible for anyone else to fall in love.'

'I can prove it.'

'You'd better come in.' Fliss stood aside, but he shook his head.

'Go inside, Felicity. I must fetch something from my hire car.'

Fliss glared at him, enraged, and went inside, throwing herself onto the sofa. She did not need this sudden re-appearance of Gael in her life right now. What on earth was the man thinking of? That she was going to fall at his feet and declare undying love for him just because he'd got on a plane from Paris after her telling him she was thinking of getting married? Maybe once upon a time, last year, yes. She would have done just that, but she had grown up and grown away from Gael and had her own, new life here now.

The sound of footsteps distracted her from her thoughts and from the rapidly deteriorating atmosphere in the cottage.

Gael strode indoors and behind him, at a more sedate pace, was a small, blonde haired woman. She was immaculately dressed. Fliss looked from her back to Gael, questioningly.

'This is Claudia. I asked her to marry me yesterday.'

Fliss was glad she was sitting down, because if she hadn't been, she might have fallen down with the shock. Gael getting married!

The revelation brought stinging tears to her almond shaped brown eyes. Eyes that Gael had once adored; had once told her were like gazing into a melting pot of hot dark chocolate. Why were Claudia's immaculately made up, cornflower blue eyes the ones that Gael had asked to marry him? What was wrong with brown eyes? She looked away until she was composed enough to turn back to them both and mutter some form of congratulations.

Without being asked, Gael sat down on the sofa next to Fliss and gestured to Claudia to sit in the wing chair. She crossed stunningly shapely legs, revealing lace stocking tops and a little suspender clip. The woman tugged at the hem of her skirt and pulled it down, which made Gael smile. Fliss noticed both the smile and the stocking top and wanted to weep.

'This man you are going to marry, may I meet him?' Gael smiled at Fliss, who glared angrily at Gael.

'No, you may not. He's at work and then going home. We don't live together, not that it's any of your business.'

Gael reached out and swept a lock of Fliss's shiny dark hair back from her forehead tucking the loose strand behind her ear. The glare became angrier still.

'Such beautiful hair, *ma fille*. I always liked your hair.'

'It is very sheeny,' said Claudia.

'Shiny!' Both Gael and Fliss corrected Claudia's mistake at the same time and the three of them laughed.

'I always liked holding it when I fucked you.' Gael told Fliss, who looked uncomfortably at Claudia.

'It is okay,' Gael said, noticing the look, 'Claudia is far more – adaptable about sex than you, *ma bebe.*'

'You mean she doesn't object to sharing you, you mean?' Fliss's heart hurt. It felt like she had been punched in the chest and that she could not breathe in enough air.

Gael shrugged. 'We do not set boundaries, but whatever we do, we do together. I only strayed, Felicity, because you would not walk the path with me.'

'It wasn't a route that I enjoyed.'

'Ahh, but you set the boundary before you started the journey, Felicity. That was why it hurt.'

Before she could retort, Gael pulled her face to his, and he kissed her on the lips. Fliss was horrified about what Claudia would think. But then, Fliss noticed that the woman had slipped her hand up her skirt, spread her long, elegant thighs and was now rubbing a glistening, wet clitoris. Fliss groaned, and gave herself up to Gael's kiss, demanding and enticing; all the while, she was thinking of the woman sitting a few feet away from her masturbating in front of them.

'*Allez.*' He commanded when he broke away from Fliss's mouth.

Claudia moved over to the sofa and sat on the other side of Gael, so that she was on the left of him, and Fliss to the right. Gael started to kiss Claudia, and instead of being revulsed and jealous, as Fliss thought she might, she found herself being turned on at the thought that Gael's mouth, which had just explored hers, was now kissing another woman. She watched, enthralled, and felt her hand slip inside her blouse, and her fingers seek out her nipple. As she watched Gael's tongue encircle Claudia's pretty cupid's bow of a mouth, Fliss wondered what Claudia tasted like.

Gael saw the movement of Fliss's hand into her blouse, and he smiled, breaking away from Claudia. He stood up and pulled both women off the sofa. Without being told, Fliss guided them up to the bedroom. Gael lay on the bed, fully clothed and commanded both women to undress. She was fascinated by his control of Claudia, and of his own raging hard on, which she could clearly see pressing through his thin trousers.

Claudia had a beautiful body. Beneath her shift dress, she was naked except for those lace stockings and the suspenders. Fliss fumbled badly with her blouse buttons, and Claudia reached over to help her unfasten the blouse which fell, open and off her slim shoulders. It was Claudia who unclipped Fliss's bra and pulled it away from her luscious breasts.

'You have superb breasts.' Claudia told Fliss, as she bent her blonde head and put her mouth to Fliss's left nipple, which hardened in Claudia's warm and expert mouth.

Fliss was almost delirious with excitement when Claudia let her nipple fall that beautiful mouth, and she felt herself being pushed down onto her bed, where Gael's hands were waiting to grab hold of her wrists. Gael held Fliss's wrists together behind her back with one hand and then slipped his other hand over her breasts, which were heaving in anticipation and excitement.

Claudia pushed Fliss's legs apart, and bent towards Fliss's aching pussy, which reacted instantly to the gentle touch of Claudia's fingertips, moving in slow motion, circular waves of pleasure, making Fliss shake with excitement and need. Gael's fingers pinched her nipple and she moaned softly. The sensation between her legs was so maddeningly good, so absolutely pleasurable, that she could feel her orgasm building already. She could feel her clitoris tightening and growing hard. She desperately wanted Claudia to suck her clit, to make her shudder with the release of the pent-up desire she felt. Fliss's honey sweet juice poured out from her pussy, over Claudia's teasing fingers.

Fliss opened her eyes briefly to watch Claudia withdraw her fingers, then lick them clean before she shimmied down and Fliss felt her hot breath against her bare, exposed sex. She shivered and felt Gael's hand on her wrists tighten its grip. Another moan escaped her as Claudia's mouth enfolded Fliss's hot bud and with a practised and rhythmic movement, Claudia began to suck the delicate hardness until Fliss could bear it no more and simply let herself freefall into orgasm, the shuddering, shaking, hot, white pleasure which made her body ache with the sheer, superb climatic consummation of her desires.

As she came, Claudia moved to the side of her, and lay next to her on the bed. Gael released Fliss's wrists, and Claudia began to kiss her on the mouth so that Fliss could taste her own orgasm as Gael fucked her, then Claudia, then her again and again until he was able to spurt his juices all over both pairs of breasts.

Later, when Fliss was released from her sexual need, Gael and Claudia asked if they could shower and Fliss listened to them sharing each other in her power shower and she wondered why she had done it and what her actions proved. Did she want Gael more that Gavin? Had Gael wanted her more than, or at least as much as Claudia? In going to bed with both of them, should Fliss be worried that "normal" sex with Gavin would not be as exciting anymore?

They left, a while later, after tea and biscuits and a flurry of *merci's* and *au revoirs*; leaving Fliss not quite alone again in her crowded cottage thinking that it was not only the spirits which haunted her. It was her own self.

THIRTY

'Sometimes I worry that it is my own self causing these disturbances.'

Fliss confided in the two priests, as they all sat drinking coffee and munching cakes at the local garden centre. Father Maguire had cautioned against the briefing session being held at the cottage, knowing something of the atmosphere within it. He genuinely worried for Fliss's safety, both of body and mind, but he kept his worries to himself, because living at that cottage, she would have her own fair share of worry.

'Are you suggesting that it is yourself who requires the cleansing, and not the house, Miss Keating?' Father Gillespie asked, in between mouthfuls of Victoria sponge cake. 'For if that were the case, then you would need a psychological evaluation before this ritual could be performed.'

Fliss shook her head.

'I don't need a psychological evaluation, Father Gillespie,' she said, firmly. 'I merely wonder if the disturbances would be as prolific if I were not a psychic medium.'

The young priest looked sceptically at his older colleague.

'I am satisfied, Father Gillespie, that the cleansing of the cottage shall be sufficient. I do not believe Miss Keating requires cleansing. Well, only in so much as we need to rid her home of the spirits within it in order for her to attain peace within her own soul.'

Father Maguire looked at Fliss, who appeared withdrawn and haggard. He felt a tremendous compassion for the young woman and disliked his colleague for the mere suggestion that Fliss may somehow be mentally incompetent.

'Then let us proceed, Father Maguire,' said the other priest now, patting Fliss's hand in an attempt at reconciliation for his harsh judgement of her.

'I'm used to it, Father Gillespie, it's quite alright,' she smiled, sadly. A smile that Father Gillespie remembered all his life, and which equipped him to deal with similar situations with empathy and not suspicion.

***

'Life's a funny old thing,' Father Maguire announced, when he and his colleague crossed the threshold of the cottage, which was simmering in its own hatred and vitriol. 'It nearly always ends in death. That's where it is supposed to end, and that is why I am here today.'

The air seemed to hiss. Father Maguire noticed it but said nothing and if he felt any fear or any sort of emotion, he hid it well as he unpacked a small bag and put the contents on the table.

Father Gillespie walked slowly around the ground floor of the cottage, feeling its venom; he shivered involuntarily. He wondered how the woman, Felicity Keating, their client, he supposed, he wondered how she could have stayed in a place like this and kept her sanity.

He put his foot on the stairs which lead up to the bedrooms and suddenly there was an almighty crash from above the living room. Father Maguire raised his eyebrows as he busied himself in preparation for what was to come. Fliss was sitting, surprisingly, in the wing chair which she usually avoided because of the sightings of a man, a spirit who favoured the chair. She was clutching hold of the arms of the chair, her knuckles white as her fingers gripped the leather as though clinging on for dear life.

Noting her discomfiture, Father Maguire went over to the chair, and hunkered down on his haunches so that they were almost at eye level.

'It is not something which you need to be afraid of, my dear. It's rather like asking unwelcome guests to vacate the room.' He reached out and prized one of Fliss's hands off the chair. She felt cold.

'First of all, I use this,' he told her, indicating a large smelly stick, 'it's sage and sulphur. A cleansing mixture. I light the stick and we walk around the house and repeat what is known as a cleansing ritual, or prayer. Then, we will seek protection by making the sign of the cross on all doors. We use this oil to do that.'

He picked up a bottle from the coffee table and smiled at Fliss, who looked more and more ill at ease.

'Finally, we have our holy water and our salt. Holy water is blessed, and we sprinkle it in all corners of each room. It is a cleansing ritual and will rid any demons or spirits which lurk in the darkness. The salt is also sprinkled over thresholds and in corners. This is for protection. Finally, if the atmosphere has not returned to what is considered "normal", I will recite an exorcism prayer as I walk through the house.'

He smiled at Fliss's unease. 'Come now, Fliss.'

She heaved a sigh. 'I just want it to be over, Father. I want to be able to sleep of a night without seeing people hanging or hearing children screaming.'

'Then let us begin. Father Gillespie, are you there? Let us all be present in the living room, we will put on our robes and we will say, first, the Lord's Prayer and then the prayer of St Michael, which is a breastplate. They are both excellent protection against the unknown.'

The two priests dressed in their surpluses and full purple robes, and all three went into the living room. The two priests each held one of Fliss's hands and then joined hands with each other.

A loud hammering made all three of them jump, and then

Fliss realised it was the heavy metal door knocker.

'Fliss! What is going on?'

It was Gavin, looking worried and when Fliss let him into the living room, he stared in amazement at the two priests.

'What on earth? Fliss, the exorcism? You never told me it was happening today!'

Father Maguire seemed to be the only one who noticed that the banging had started again, upstairs.

'Join hands with us all,' he said to Gavin, before Fliss could speak. 'We have visitors.'

Gavin joined the circle. The tension in the room became unbearable, the air seemed to stand still.

The rich, strong sound of Father Maguire's voice filled the silence, cutting into the expectation with the Lord's Prayer. There came the sound of weeping. A child's heart rendering sobbing. Tears sprung to Fliss's eyes.

Next, the breastplate prayer. Father Maguire touched each of them as he asked for the Lord's protection in front of them, at the side of them and behind them.

Shadows encroached the room, filling the spaces with unease. The priest took the sage stick and walked through the house, amidst the noise of banging; the sound of a chair being overturned; the whiplash crack of gunfire; over and over again. Father Maguire raised his voice, repeating the cleansing rituals. Then, he told the spirits that he was protecting the house, and its inhabitants with the sign of the cross on all the doors, a litany of safety, the power of protection and the sanctity of the cross.

He walked through the house, a man safe and confident in his faith; with the knowledge before him, surrounding him, that his prayer would be enough to cleanse the cottage and deliver peace to those that sought it.

For the first time in his life, Gavin felt the power of prayer.

Fliss was crying. Her sobs mingled with those of the unseen child. The cottage grew darker; the colour of thunderstorms, the air filled with a growing electricity.

'Father Maguire!'

The other priest nodded towards Gavin and Fliss. Standing next to them were a man and a woman. The man carried a length of rope; the woman wore a peacock blue dress.

'Regna Terrae; cantata Deo; psallite cernunnuos.'

'Regna Terrae; cantata Dea psallite Aradia.'

Father Maguire's voice boomed above the noise, the wretchedness that filled the air. The house was wrapped in complete darkness as, with a feeble flicker, the lights went out. The terrified scream could have escaped from Fliss, who had flung herself into Gavin' arms and buried her head into his chest, or had it come from elsewhere, outside of the room?

The voice of the priest was getting louder now. Sorrow and anger filled every available nook and cranny, the banging and the crying competed with each other to be heard in the blackness of the moment. The air was rancid, congealed. There was a terrible smell. It was making everyone cough as the atmosphere thickened. There were voices, crying, angry shouts, the screams were loud enough to wake the dead, thought Gavin, or maybe they *were* the dead! He held Fliss tightly to him, afraid.

'I command you, in the name of Jesus Christ, Our Lord – spirits, demons, ghosts and unwelcome visitors not meant to be present here today – I command you by the power of Christ – BEGONE!'

Father Maguire's final word resounded into silence. An echo of faith had dispelled the clamour. The noise ceased. There were no bangs, no sobs; the feeling of wretched unhappiness had gone. The light trickled back, edging the darkness away. The air cleared; the smell of sage filled the room.

The two priests recited the Lord's Prayer in thanks, and Gavin and Fliss watched as two shadows, a man and a woman were finally reunited in death, as they should have been able to live whilst they were alive.

***

Much later, drinking some excellent whisky, and gathered around Fliss's wood burner, which she had lit and thrown some sage leaves into the flames for additional cleansing and protection, Fliss and Gavin listened to a story unfold. A reason, perhaps, why the cottage had such a troubled past.

'I'd researched the house, before I came the first day,' Father Maguire told them. 'Henry Winterton, or Hal, or Harry as he was known, built the cottage. It was a respite from his responsibilities towards the mills and the large estate he ran, but also, he and Isabella Harmer had fallen in love. This was their love nest.'

'Enchantment Cottage,' murmured Fliss, taking a sip of *Glen Rothes*. The warm, amber liquid was soothing and pleasantly numbing.

Father Maguire shook his head. 'For them, maybe. Not so for Isabella's poor husband, Thomas. I think their marriage was a business transaction – Isabella in exchange for money and land – Thomas was already in debt and running his mill badly when they first married. I think the Mountbattens, Isabella's parents, were very clever. They even got the better of the Wintertons, so far as the land surrounding Thomas's home was concerned. However, Thomas made the silly mistake of falling in love with Isabella once they were married. He was twenty years her senior, they had nothing in common and Isabella was enthralled with Harry Winterton. Thomas never stood a chance.'

'You think his is – was – the angry spirit – the one responsible for all the problems the cottage has experienced?' asked Gavin.

'Yes and no,' Father Maguire replied. 'For all her love of Harry Winterton, Isabella wasn't a particularly nice woman, she was very capable of causing problems here. If anyone killed Phoebe Cooper – Clarke, I suspect it was Isabella's spirit that had a hand in it, as retribution, maybe, for the loss of her own daughter, Belle. Anyway, back to Isabella, she was rumoured to have had an affair with a George Avery. He was a schoolteacher, just up the hill there, and whether or not there were other lovers, I'm not sure. After Avery, it seems that she and Harry Winterton rekindled their affair. I think the child who inherited the Winterton Estate – Jasper – was his. He was a cripple. As a child, it appears Jasper fell out of the window at the back of the house here. It's not clear why he was here, or how he survived, but he did.'

'So, far from being enchanted, the cottage was a den of iniquity?' Fliss sighed, wishing the story had a more romantic ending.

Father Maguire smiled. 'It appears that way. I believe Isabella entertained George Avery here, and possibly others. Harry had numerous liaisons after Isabella, who died shortly after giving birth to Jasper. Harry seems to have committed suicide – he hanged himself here. It seems he was the good guy in all this, despite having an affair with a married woman. He did genuinely love Isabella, and that was why he took his own life; he couldn't live without her. At that point, the cottage seems to have been bought by Thomas Harmer – what for and why, or even how, as he was so short of money, nobody knows. What is known is he and George Avery had an exchange here and that shots were fired and they both ended up dead, because the gun Thomas was found holding misfired and released two bullets instead of one. One for George, and the other seemed to have released out of the chamber backwards, killing Thomas.'

'What a terrible tale the cottage tells.' Fliss got up to replenish everyone's drinks.

'That's not all.' Father Maguire happily accepted a second

whisky and continued the tale.

'When Thomas died, his son William inherited the estate, but he was only a child, so it was Philip, Thomas's brother who took up the responsibility. He looked after Georgina and William, who were supposedly Isabella's and Thomas's other surviving children. By the time Philip took guardianship of the estate, the debts were out of control, and it appears that he had the bright idea of marrying Amelia Winterton, Harry's sister. I think he was hoping she would arrive with a suitable dowry to help him get the estate out of debt. But history tells us that the Harmer estate and this cottage, which was part of it at the time of Thomas's death, passed to the Winterton's. Philip came to the village expecting to live a life of luxury at Harmer House and ended up living in this cottage with Amelia and working in the mill for Peveril Winterton – Harry's father. Whether Philip thought that he and Amelia might inherit it all eventually, I don't know – there were no other male relatives of Peveril who would have got it. Except that unfortunately for Philip, Jasper Winterton survived. He got the lot.'

There was a silence.

'Poor Thomas.'

Everyone looked incredulously at Fliss.

'Well, think about it. He was cuckold by Isabella. She had these children, none of them his, yet there he was, bringing them up as his own, giving them his name. Isabella and Harry, as nice as he may have been, behaved abominably.'

Father Maguire smiled. 'You could be right, Fliss. The sad tale goes on to tell us that Isabella never told Thomas she was pregnant with Jasper. For whatever reasons, I do not know but there are records which point to her having gone to Scotland around the time Jasper would have been born. But there is no record of her returning from her sister with a child. It's believed she left the child, Jasper, with foster parents in Scotland, and it was Leonora, Harry's mother, who found him and brought him back here. Secondly, and more interestingly, medical records show that Thomas was infertile. Sterile. So, he couldn't have fathered any of the children Isabella claimed were his. Whether or not Isabella knew this or not, is something the records don't tell us, but I suspect she didn't and when she got pregnant by one of her lovers, she passed the child off as a child of their marriage, not knowing that Thomas fathering a child was impossible.'

'In that case, I think if I'd been Thomas, I'd have haunted this cottage too.' Father Gillespie declared, mildly merry after a second dram of whisky.

Fliss sighed again.

'Have you ever traced your family tree, Miss Keating?' Father Maguire asked. 'We know Gavin here is a descendant of the Winterton family – I suspect Jasper would have been your great, great, great grandfather, Gavin. However, I also have reason to believe, Felicity, that somewhere in your ancestry, you are related to Isabella, who was a Mountbatten by birth.'

'My grandmother's maiden name.' Fliss said, quietly.

'How many children did Isabella have, then, that she tried to pass off as Thomas's?' Gavin asked.

'Four,' replied Father Maguire, 'Arabella, who died aged four; Georgina, who ended up a governess for Jasper's family; William, who joined the army and went to France. He married a French woman, and strangely, he took her name upon the marriage. He didn't want to be a Harmer, he didn't want to associate with the debt and the bad name of his "father", so he became a Leclerc and of course, there was Jasper, who undoubtedly came up trumps, despite falling out of the window.'

Fliss had gone quite pale. Gavin asked her what was wrong.

'My ex-boyfriend, the French one – his name is Gael Leclerc.'

There was another silence.

'My buying this cottage was no accident, really, was it?' Fliss whispered.

'I put it down to my excellent estate agency skills!' Gavin declared, lightening the mood somewhat.

'Plus, the fact that you're a Winterton.' Fliss smiled at her boyfriend and, forgetting the presence of the two priests, she kissed him hard and deep on the lips.

'And this is where we bid you goodbye, Miss Keating!' Father Maguire laughed, stretching, and standing up, pulling his slightly intoxicated colleague with him.

'Thank you for everything.' Fliss shook his hand and then, on reflection, she stood on tip toe and kissed him on the cheek.

Father Maguire put his hand to his face, as if he wanted to grasp hold of the imprint of her lips.

'All part of the service as Deliverance Driver!'

With a final laugh, the two priests departed and with a wave at their receding backs, as they walked up the hill, she closed the door of the cottage.

EPILOGUE

Dust bunnies skittered across the floor, as the gentle breeze caused by the front door being opened dislodged them from their hiding places in the quiet, dark corner of the empty cottage.

The estate agent apologised to the young woman he was showing around as he stood aside and let her walk into the living room ahead of him. Memories assailed him as he stood on the threshold.

'I'm sorry it's a bit of a mess,' he said, 'my wife and I have neglected it lately. We've been incredibly lazy about putting it on the market.'

'It's gorgeous, despite the dust bunnies,' smiled the young woman, her eyes drinking in the wall of exposed stone, the wood-burner, and the beamed ceilings. The floor was wooden, with age old planks, scarred with time. In the corner by the fireplace stood an old leather wing chair. In the silence of the surroundings, she could hear the sound of the river at the back of the house.

'Why on earth did you want to leave?'

'It's simply too small now, with three children. We've stayed in the village, though. It's a delightful place to live, and we were here for several years, in the cottage, very happily.'

The woman smiled again and said, 'I think I'm going to like it. I really do. It has a lovely atmosphere. I'm Amelia, by the way, Amelia Harmer. I think some long-ago relatives of mine used to live here.'

There was a small, chill breeze. A frisson. In the dark corner of the living room, by the fireplace, there was a slight movement in the shadows.

It had begun again.

"It's going to begin again, Gavin, mark my words.'

Felicity Keating-Winterton stared at her husband in disbelief at his nonchalance, which she found somewhat annoying. Granted, many years had passed since the small family had left Enchantment Cottage and bought their rather grand five bedroomed detached house which stood proudly on the border of Winterton village and its neighbour.

She hadn't been surprised when it transpired that the house which she and her husband had purchased off a harassed looking builder, worried about rising costs and slumping sales in the wake of Brexit and Covid-19, had actually been previously reserved for one Madison Cooper-Clarke. Fliss knew that this was no co-incidence, although Gavin had poo-pooed her idea. He'd pointed out to her that they lived in an area of astronomically rising house prices where demand for larger properties, such as the one they lived in since moving out of the cottage, was significantly lower because wages simply hadn't risen commensurately with the housing market. It had nothing to do with the fact that Madison Cooper-Clarke had been the previous occupant of Fliss's cottage, or that she was dead, like so many previous occupants were.

'Fliss, you need to get a grip on that imagination of yours. It's over, done. Whatever happened in that cottage before we were married, it never continued. We lived there quite happily until Harry was born. We only moved because it was too small.' He spoke with a certainty Fliss did not share.

She watched him shrug, indifferent to her distress and she sighed. Once Gavin had an opinion, that was that; there was no convincing him otherwise, so she had stopped trying. There had been numerous things over the years that they had not agreed over and at the start when she was younger, crass, and stupid, she used to argue with him until she learnt not to. Wandering into the family room, which adjoined the dining kitchen at the back of the house and was, for once, devoid of family, she peered restlessly out of the patio windows. Above the backdrop of the village far below the steep incline upon which Riverbank, their house, stood; a brooding guardian for the meandering river on the other side of which, Fliss knew, was Enchantment Cottage.

Suddenly, the memories of what had happened there trickled through her crowded mind, causing the involuntary fear to make her shiver despite the warmth of the room and the bright sunshine streaming through the windows. It was as if a dark menacing cloud had settled around her. Was it her psychic abilities, awakening because of the portent of danger she knew was about to disrupt their if not equable, then at least, not temperamental life? Until now.

***

Amelia Harmer sighed with contentment and looked around her new living room. Her own furniture was mostly antique, picked up from jumble sales and second-hand shops but fitting perfectly into their surroundings. The velvet chaise longue sat in front of the huge stone fireplace and the little wood burner stove, which she had lit. A cheery fire burnt the applewood logs happily and a delicious aroma stole through the house. Her sideboard, with the oval mirror back stood against the wall opposite the tiny window. Upon it she had placed lots of photographs of her long, gone relatives, encased forever in silver and wooden frames. Inside the sideboard, a cupboard held her best china and silver cutlery in a wooden tray.

The kitchen, she had moved upstairs to the room which had once been a dining room and previously an office. She was not going to clatter up and down those perilously steep stairs every time she wanted a cup of tea. The newly installed units were of an antique design with a small aga and hanging from the ceiling was a wind up, wind down drying rack which she had spotted in the same antique shop Vera had bought her tea service. Vera was another reason why Amelia decided to turn to basement kitchen into a laundry and storage room. She didn't want to have to see Vera laid at the foot of the stairs every time she went down there. Once a week to do the washing and put out the bins was enough.

Letting out another sigh, she wandered into the kitchen and stood by the window whilst she waited for the kettle to boil. She glanced upwards, away from the sight of the child, laid crumpled and still in the rockery flower beds. The Euonymus had broken the child's fall, so he had spoilt things by surviving. Focussing on the middle distance, Amelia's eyes settled upon the outline of a housing estate, built on the other side of the river, and beyond the viaduct where the steam trains chugged by periodically. *She* was there, Amelia knew. Felicity.

The kettle let out a frustrated whistle, breaking Amelia's chain of thought. Busying herself with her tea, which she was sure Vera would have appreciated, a nice Oolong Gingersnap chai. Taking the tea with her, Amelia strode back into the living room, her mind full of the past, which was after all, the reason why she had decided to buy the cottage in the first place.

She briefly wondered what Thomas was going to do with it, when he bought it off Harry Winterton's parents. There was a story there, she was sure. The gun backfiring was typical Thomas, he never did take enough care, and in the end, it wasn't Isabella's infidelity which killed him, it was his own carelessness. Stupid man.

As for his brother, Philip! He actually believed that the Winterton's would leave their entire estate to him, on the premise of marrying their youngest daughter. What a fool Philip had been. He deserved all he got, in the end.

Amelia sipped her tea and smiled as she felt the sudden

charge in the air, that feeling of anticipation and fear. No, not fear, she thought, that was silly. They were only ghosts. She put down her teacup and waited as they gathered around her. The temperature in the room dropped slightly, and a strange atmosphere settled around her. She knew they were here.

She waited, watching the daylight darken into the eerie, early evening inkiness, spilling across the blue, cloud patched sky. The air in the cottage grew thick, the darkness invading the pretty picture Amelia made, reclined on the velvet sofa, hands crossed on her lap, the remains of the tea cooling in the dainty patterned cup.

An unnaturalness settled around her, whispers of the past, the long dead, the forgotten. Those who had lived and died breathed again; their frozen breath exhaled into the warm, cosy glow, creating cold spots in the room which would make people shiver, and rub their arms, looking around for where the draught was coming from.

The aged, scarred floor creaked as though someone were walking across it, although no-one was there. Hinges on the interconnecting door groaned and made a squeaking sound as if the door were being opened and closed by an impatient child, although no child could be seen. Unexplained noises could be heard coming from upstairs, the scraping of a chair, the scratching of an indignant window catch, a giggle, a bang.

As the darkness enveloped the room, and Amelia's outline became blurred and fuzzy, shapes shifted and shadows drifted across the floor, forming, disappearing, reforming and finally settling into the dark corners and the nooks and crannies. There was nothing really there.

Amelia smiled, and stood up, crossing the room to the corner by the old leather wing chair to light the floor lamp she had placed behind it. Clicking the switch, she swathed the room in a soft, peachy blush. She turned to close the curtains against the encroaching night.

'Hello, Thomas,' she addressed the handsome man in the bloodstained riding coat who was now sitting in the wing chair. 'I wondered when you would get here.'

***

Across the river, in the big, comfortable detached house where the newest generation of Winterton's lived, Fliss excused herself from the dinner table, pleading a headache and leaving Gavin to clear away and supervise the children's bedtimes, she headed upstairs to her little study. She could hear Bella and Jasper begin coaxing their father to let them stay up beyond the strict nine o'clock upon which she insisted. A small smile played on her lips. Gavin would give in, of course, he always did. And she would then have two tired, querulous children to home school tomorrow. Harry, by contrast, would go to bed at eight, as usual and whilst his brother and sister were struggling with their lessons, Harry would have his finished and be allowed extra time watching television, which would be the next thing Bella and Jasper would argue and complain about.

Reaching the study, Fliss felt a little uncomfortable lying about her headache. She had simply wanted to look out of her study window and watch what was happening at the little cottage across the river.

She knew she did not like the young woman whose offer had secured the purchase of Fliss's former home and she knew without a doubt that since Amelia Harmer's arrival in the village, Fliss had felt something she could only explain as her hackles rising. Her psychic abilities, dormant for so long, were awakening and that could only mean one thing.

***

It had begun again.

ABOUT THE AUTHOR

D.C. Cummings is a writer of supernatural, erotic novels which take us back in time and cleverly weave together the past and the present in a haunting climax.

The Cottage was her debut novel, first published in 2019. Since then, D.C. has also published *The Hotel* which takes us to the untamed Scottish Highlands and her third novel, *The Castle*, set in medieval Wales, is due for release in 2021. Is *The Cottage* going be revisited? Follow D.C's writing progress on Twitter @AuthorCummings and @WeAreProvoco.

D.C. is 'electively single', after a couple of brief but disastrous, forays into the marital state, and is determined to stay that way!

When writing *The Cottage,* she lived in North-West England, deep in the spectacular and rugged Lancashire countryside, in a cottage reputed to be haunted. She has since moved to another countryside location, with her ever-faithful dog, Max, and now lives in another cottage which, thankfully, isn't occupied by anyone except herself.

AFTERWORD

Was Enchantment Cottage haunted? I really couldn't say. I know strange things happened there while I lived there. Lights would switch themselves on and off; things would be where they were not supposed to be; the dog would refuse to sit in a particular corner of the living room.

But are all these things signals that there is an afterlife, and that there are "ghosts", or "spirits" as Vera liked to be known? I think the existence of anything not of this life is down to our interpretation of it, what we think and what we feel.

I have a strange affinity for Thomas. He was cruel, and stupid, yes, but in the end, he was wronged. Whilst two wrongs don't make things right, Isabella was the catalyst in all this. Capricious, selfish, arrogant, she cast aside Thomas's love and picked someone else's instead.

And speaking of love, does it survive? Does it carry forward to the next world when it has been denied in this? Who knows?

I do know I was sad to leave The Cottage, which is perhaps why I've decided to pick up the story where Fliss left it. She was encouraged by Gavin to abandon her psychic abilities when they married, and they subsequently bought the house Madison Cooper-Clarke had once reserved.

Gavin thought it was a co-incidence. I've never believed in that mindset. I think everything happens for a reason, and sometimes you have to believe in the unexplained to find it.

We are all ghosts, eventually.

D.C. Cummings

Printed in Great Britain
by Amazon

76695714R00142